PRAISE FO[R]

DARKNESS ON THE ED[GE]

'It's exquisite writing. Graceful, revealing, pitch perfect. Cole is an author who pays sharp attention to the world around her. And she deserves to have the world pay her some attention in return.'
Ed Wright, *Weekend Australian*

'Jessie Cole writes with the most deceptively simple language. She pulls you into the story and along its threads until bam! She hits you right between the eyes. This is great storytelling.'
Meredith Jaffé, *Hoopla*

'Cole captures the joys and menace of small-town life and human relationships that are never black and white but always grey.'
MX

'Jessie Cole's writing has the clarity of good modern novels, words that aren't fancy and full of complex sentences, just a measured quietness that makes the story sing.'
Brittany Vonow, Brisbane *Courier-Mail*

'This work operates at deeply engaging and emotional levels while excellent story-telling drives it.'
Nigel Krauth, *Westerly*

'*Darkness on the Edge of Town* proves difficult to put down as it hurtles towards its confronting conclusion.'
Who Weekly

'… it's an accomplished portrayal of how seemingly random events can trigger life-changing outcomes.'
Sunday *Canberra Times*

Jessie Cole

DEEPER WATER

FOURTH ESTATE
An Imprint of HarperCollins*Publishers*

Australian Government

This project has been assisted by the Australian
Government through the Australia Council, its arts
funding and advisory body.

Fourth Estate
An imprint of HarperCollins*Publishers*

First published in Australia in 2014
by HarperCollins*Publishers* Australia Pty Limited
ABN 36 009 913 517
harpercollins.com.au

HarperCollins*Publishers*
Level 13, 201 Elizabeth Street, Sydney NSW 2000, Australia
Unit D1, 63 Apollo Drive, Rosedale, Auckland 0632, New Zealand
A 53, Sector 57, Noida, UP, India
77–85 Fulham Palace Road, London, W6 8JB, United Kingdom
2 Bloor Street East, 20th floor, Toronto, Ontario M4W 1A8, Canada
195 Broadway, New York, NY 10007, USA

National Library of Australia Cataloguing-in-Publication data:

Cole, Jessie, author.
  Deeper water / Jessie Cole.
  978 0 7322 9858 6 (paperback)
  978 1 4607 0200 0 (ebook)
  Families – Fiction.
  Healing – Fiction.
A823.4

Cover design by HarperCollins Design Studio
Cover images by Lilli Waters
Typeset in 12/18.5pt Bembo by Kirby Jones
Printed and bound in Australia by Griffin Press
The papers used by HarperCollins in the manufacture of this book are a natural, recyclable
product made from wood grown in sustainable plantation forests. The fibre source and
manufacturing processes meet recognised international environmental standards, and carry
certification.

For my mother

1.

They say every hero has to leave home, but what those first steps are like I'm yet to know. Where I live you'd think there was no world to discover, all hemmed in by such endless green. Cow paddocks gone bushy, forest trees taking back the rolling hills. You've got to cross six creeks just to get to my house, and if the sky lets loose and the water rises, there's nothing to do but sit and wait. Some days, time seems to stand still. The weather might be wild, but the minutes tick by as though they're weighed down by an invisible load. And then some days the whole world changes, and when that movement finally comes, it's fast, like a raging river, nearly knocking your legs out from under you.

That afternoon Bessie was birthing and I followed her about in the rain, scared she'd do herself some kind of harm. Cows are silly that way sometimes. There can be only two trees in a paddock, close together like lovers, and a cow will get herself wedged between them. If there's one space in the whole world a cow won't fit, that's where she has to be. Bessie was a big cow, and I don't suppose I could have stopped her from doing things her way, but I figured she'd probably want some company, and I like watching things being born, even in the pouring rain.

When she headed down towards the creek, I was worried. Flooding water is unpredictable. New rivers spring up out of nowhere, charging across the sodden ground like runaway trains. They can look harmless enough from afar, but usually it's best to stay on high ground. We stood in the lowlands, and Bessie gave a long sad bellow. She looked at me and the rain streamed across her thick eyelashes and down her brown face. The water was rising around us. I needed to get her moving.

I don't know what made me look downstream towards the bridge. Sometimes there's a change in the air, some small shift in pressure maybe, or the hint of a sound. But in the distance a car was trying to cross, the mounting water pushing it against the railing of the bidge. Even from where I stood I could hear the splintering of timber, and then the car just floated off the side.

I was running along the edge of the water towards the bridge before I knew it, but all I was thinking about was Bessie. What if the calf was born and it washed away? By the time I got close to the car I was angry. Who crosses a raging river in flood?

The creek was racing but the car bobbed along, incongruous with the wild torrent. 'Hey!' I screamed through the rain. 'You've got to get out!' There was no way I was going in, but I didn't want to stand there and watch the car just disappear.

'Hey!' My voice seemed lost in the roar of the creek and

the drumming of the rain. I looked around for a strong enough branch. 'Open the window!'

Even though it was a car, all steel and glass, it didn't make a sound in the water. Sometimes we get floods so big you can hear giant boulders rolling down the river, crashing against the rocks, but we weren't nearly there yet. I grabbed a big branch from the ground and moved along the creek dragging it behind me and yelling. There was no sign of a person inside and I was starting to get scared.

Suddenly the car stopped, like it was stuck against something. The water built up around it. My breath stilled. It was going to go under. Then the window opened a crack. I could see fingers poking out.

'Smash it!' My voice was hoarse. 'You've got to smash it!'

The branch I'd picked up was heavy, too big for me really, but it needed to be long to reach the car. I lifted it, my arms shaking, water running down inside the sleeve of my dad's old raincoat. The window of the car was still above the water and I knew I only had one chance to hit the spot. Swinging the branch down, I closed my eyes and heard it clunk on the glass. There was a cracking sound and I opened my eyes and the window smashed, caving outwards. He'd done it himself. I shoved the branch forward so it was caught in against the window frame. I didn't want it to get swept up by the water before he'd grabbed it. The fingers reaching out the window became an arm and then a body.

'The branch!' I yelled. 'Grab the branch!'

It was a man. I didn't know if I'd be able to hold him.

He pushed his top half from the window, staring through the rain from me to the branch. I nodded, willing him to understand. There was a sapling near me and I grabbed it, hoping it would give me a hold. My end of the branch was knobbly. I hooked my fingers around the stubs to try to get a better grip. The man leaned forward, grasping the branch hard. I stepped backwards, tugging it free from where it was jammed, and the pull of the water seemed to suck him from the car. It disappeared behind him, bubbling as it went down.

Once I had him it was easier than I thought. I held tight and he held tight, and eventually the water pushed him to the side, out of the rapids. He staggered from the current towards me, but I was already peering around for Bessie.

'Fuck, you're just a girl,' he said, shaking and choking back tears.

I was glad my mother wasn't there to hear that. I couldn't think of a better way to provoke her loathing, but I chose not to see the comment as a slur on womankind. The truth is, I'm not a kid anymore, but I guess in this oversized raincoat it was hard to tell. He put his arms out like he was going to collapse into a heap around me, but I didn't want that.

'We've got to find her,' I shouted over the sound of the rain. 'She's having a baby.'

'What?'

The water was running so hard down my face, it was worse than tears.

'Bessie!'

'Who?'

'Come on.' I started to run back along the waterline. I could only see a little way in front of me, but I heard her bellowing not far away. 'She's up here!' I yelled as he stumbled along behind me.

She was standing right at the edge of the river bend, water lapping around her silly cloven feet. Suddenly my heart was in my mouth.

'A cow?'

'We got to get her to move away from the water.'

I scrambled up beside her, putting my face against her wet flank. Even through the rain I could see the calf was on its way out. The birth sac was like a water balloon, almost transparent. Up close there were two hoofs inside the bubble, sticking out beneath her tail.

'Come on!' I shouted over the rain, but he just stood there gawking at me. 'Help me! We got to move her.'

He came and stood beside me and together we pushed, but she didn't budge. I closed my eyes, rain flowing over me like there was no air left. When I opened them his face was right there beside mine, eyes open and bright, the lightest blue, raindrops welling in his lashes.

'Maybe we've got to shock her,' he said. 'Give her a whack?'

I shook my head. 'She might bolt the wrong way. I'll go see if I can pull her from the front. You keep pushing.'

She didn't move, even though I tugged with all I had.

'It's coming,' he yelled from behind. 'Fuck! It's coming out.'

And it was, wrapped in that translucent sac. We stood there then, waiting, the rain still belting down, water coming up around our ankles. It felt like the land was falling away, like it must have in the Great Flood. Just me and him, Bessie the cow, and the yet to be born.

Finally the calf slithered out, a crumpled mess in the water at our feet. I tried to pick it up but it was too heavy.

'Get it!' I shouted up at him. 'It's going to drown.'

He hesitated a second, and then scooped it up, birth sac and all.

'Is it breathing?' I tore a hole in the yellowy film to see.

He clutched at the baby a minute, feeling for its breath. 'Yep.'

I pulled the sticky sac away from the calf's face. It looked dazed, but at least its eyes were open. It blinked against the rain.

'Okay. Let's go. She'll follow us now we've got the baby.'

He nodded and I pointed up the hill.

It doesn't take long to get to my house from the creek, but when it's flooding and you're carrying a calf, it's a bit of a trek. I had to go real slow so the man could keep up. Bessie trailed along behind us. When we got to the top paddock, I wasn't sure she would stay put.

'I'm going to grab a rope,' I called to him and headed for Mum's shed. We had all sorts of bits and pieces in there and I knew I'd find something to tie her up with. There was no power and it was pretty dim, so I had to feel around with my hands. It was a bit creepy, especially knowing there were always snakes about, but eventually I found some old rope.

Back in the paddock, the man looked pretty strange, standing there in the rain still holding the calf. Slick with water and trembling, he could have just been born.

'Let's tie her under a tree, out of the rain.' I rushed past him, pointing to the edge of the field. He followed more slowly. Luckily there was an old fence post I could tie the rope to. Bessie didn't seem impressed about being tethered but I wasn't taking any chances.

'Can I put it down now?' He tried to shake the water from his face.

'Yeah.' I could see him better under the tree, without all the confusion of the rain. He looked almost as dazed as the calf. 'Bessie should do the rest.'

He knelt down with the calf and put it on the mushy ground. It staggered about in the remains of the birth sac for a few seconds, trying to get to its feet. Crouching beside it, I pulled at the filmy sac till the calf was upright, then stepped back and waited. The man slid backwards on his knees in the mud. Bessie put her head down and nibbled a few stray blades of grass.

'Come on, Bessie,' I groaned, 'that's your baby.'

After all that work I couldn't believe Bessie was going to ignore it.

'What do we do now?' The man tried to flick some of the birth gunk from the sleeves of his jumper.

I glanced at him but I was still thinking of Bessie.

'Just wait, I think. She'll come good.'

The calf stumbled around for a bit, every now and then knocking against Bessie's legs. Eventually she gave it a lick and then it was all on. She was a mother. I didn't realise I'd been holding my breath until it came out in a rush.

The man clambered up from where he'd been kneeling. He was a mess—drenched and covered in mud and fluid and bloody bits from the birth.

'You're not going to be able to save that one.' I pointed to his jumper. 'It's done.'

'Everything's in the car. Fuck. My laptop. Fuck.' He pressed his dripping palms against his eyes. 'It's got everything on it. *Everything.*'

We didn't have a working computer, so I guess I didn't know what that was like.

'I'll find you some fresh clothes, come on.'

He patted his pockets. 'I don't even have my fucking phone.'

He looked about ready to freak out.

'There's no reception out here anyway.' I shook my head, watching him. 'You may as well come inside.'

2.

I opened the door gingerly. Mum hates it when I come in wet and leave footprints all over the floor. It's hard enough keeping the house dry in the rainy season without all my coming and going. There's always a towel hanging on the back of the door knob and I'm supposed to strip off and dry myself there, but I didn't want to do that with the man waiting in the shadows behind me, so I just stood there dripping onto the floor.

The power was out and the kitchen was lit up with candles. The floods mess with our electricity—as soon as something gets wet, the whole system blows. Mum glanced back at me from where she was crouched in front of my sister, but she didn't see the man. He stayed out of the glow of candlelight, waiting for me to call him in.

My sister lives in a cabin a kilometre or so from us, but she often comes to stay when it's flooding. Walks across the paddocks—there's no creek between us. I looked her over in the candlelight and she didn't seem good. She sat dully in a chair at the table, not meeting my eyes. Her forehead was all bruised, like she'd been banging her head against the wall. The baby sucked at her breast and swiped with wobbly fists at her damp hair, but she didn't respond. Just looking at her lately hurt my eyes. 'What happened?' I asked softly.

'You know,' my mother answered, still squatting there, tending her.

'Not that. What happened to her head?'

Mum looked around at me.

'The cupboards, you know. He closed all the cupboards. She'd open them, he'd close them. You don't notice stuff like that till someone's gone. She keeps banging her head on all the open doors.'

I didn't know what to say. Sophie's bloke left a week or so ago. Just drove away. I guess she didn't see it coming, though he never seemed like the surest bet to me. She's got two babies on her own now. This little one and Rory.

'Rory's asleep in your bed,' Mum said, stroking Sophie's arm. I nodded, not knowing how to bring the man inside. I was used to my family, the odd way we hung together—the shape of us— but it was strange to see us from an outside view.

'You got something there, love? That wet dog from next door trying to come in again? We've already got our own wet dog and I've shut her out the back. You're not bringing in another.'

My mum didn't miss much.

'A guy washed off the bridge in his car and I got him out,' I said and waited for Mum to react. She was distracted by Sophie, but I saw the moment my words sank in.

'Alive?' Mum always thought the worst.

'Yeah, I didn't mean that. I've got him here.'

The man stepped up behind me and I moved to the side so my mum could see him.

'Not from around here?' she asked him, frowning. She had a thing about stupidity. Dying for nothing. 'You're lucky to be alive.'

'She saved my life.' His voice was shaky, but he looked straight at Mum's face.

'Yes, she's good at that, this one.' Mum smiled across at me, just a flash and then it was gone. 'How'd Bessie go?'

'I've tied her up outside. Thought she might wander off.'

'The calf?'

'Looks good. Bit wonky at first.'

'They all are.'

Mum didn't get up from the floor, but she turned around properly to look at us. I took off my raincoat and hung it on a hook on the back of the door. I was still pretty wet underneath. 'He's covered in birth gunk,' I offered up. 'It was all a bit grubby.'

'I had to pick it up. She said it would drown.'

Mum was quiet a second, thinking. 'There's no power, so the shower's not working.' We needed electricity to power the pump. 'Grab a bar of soap,' she pointed to the sink, 'and then strip down out there and soap up. Wash off in the rain. I'll bring you both towels.'

It was warm enough outside, even in the rain, but there was no way I was stripping anywhere near him. There was a time in my childhood when nudity was the norm, any excuse for a spontaneous strip-down, but nowadays I wasn't buying it. There'd be enough water in the pipes to wash my hands in the bathroom while he was outside. I pulled the towel off the hook on the door. 'It's alright. I'm not that wet. I'll go find us some clothes.'

The sound of the rain was muted indoors, and after I cleaned myself up I found my way to the bedroom in the dark. That hush of little-fellow-sleeping filled the room. I stood there and breathed it in. I loved Rory, loved having him in my bed. Sometimes I imagined crossing the paddocks between us by moonlight and slipping into my sister's bed. She'd be caught in between her babies, breathing in their sweet smell, and I'd snuggle in close and steal some of their easy sleep. I never actually did it, though there was nothing to stop me. I guess I knew I'd be there in the morning. Rory's two and a bit, and when he's awake he can be trouble.

I changed out of my wet stuff, grabbing some clothes by touch. I didn't know what to get the man, what he'd fit into. Slipping into Mum's room, I had a feel around and came back out with an old pair of cargo shorts and a giant-sized jumper. She's a big woman, my mum. He'd have to make do.

Mum passed me in the hallway, the baby on her hip. She pulled Sophie gently along behind her. My sister gave me a crumpled-looking smile. I could see she'd been crying.

'I'm just going to lie down with them,' Mum whispered as she went by. 'Try to get them both off to sleep. You'll get him sorted out, won't you? The flood guy? He'll be feeling shaken up,' Mum said, glancing towards at the kitchen. 'It's too much tonight. I just can't deal with it.'

I nodded. There wasn't anything to say.

He was standing in the doorway, wrapped in his towel. Except for the blue of his eyes up close, I hadn't really taken in what he looked like. He was older than me, not sure how much. Maybe in his early thirties. He had an invisible quality, like if he stood still enough he'd camouflage in against the walls. I thought perhaps in the daylight he'd be handsome. I was careful of beautiful people. There was something untrustworthy about them. They'd always been the ruin of us.

'I hung my stuff over the railing,' he said. 'Left the soap out there.'

I nodded, holding out Mum's clothes. 'This is all I could find.'

'Thanks.' He looked around for somewhere to change.

The rain on the roof was steady, a constant thrum.

'Get dressed in the bathroom if you like. Take a candle, though.'

I pointed down the hallway, and he crept away, the quiver of his hands making the candlelight jump.

We had a gas stove, so that was useful in a blackout. Mum had made dinner—rice and some kind of curry. I spooned out two servings and got us both a drink. He was back out in a few minutes, holding the towel awkwardly, like he wished he knew where it should go. I took it and chucked it into the corner. No point doing anything else till the rain stopped and the power came back on.

'Eat.' It had taken a good part of the day for Bessie to birth her calf. I hadn't eaten since breakfast, and as I sat down at the table, my stomach growled.

He stood there, gripping his forearms, as if his body was locked and he was trying to force it open. I pushed his bowl along the table towards him.

'It's good. You'll feel better.'

He trembled a little as he spooned food into his mouth, so I didn't look at him for a bit—let him get his bearings. The curry was good, and the quiet in the kitchen made me think of when I was little and we hadn't got electricity yet. There was always a lull in the evening around dusk. A turning. It didn't matter what action had gone on before, there was this long moment of quiet when the day changed into night. Now we just switched the lights on and kept moving with the rhythm of day, but back then it was as if everything slowed. Sometimes we'd all sit in the kitchen together and wait for it to come. Maybe at first there'd be chatter, but after a few minutes the quiet would engulf us. Eventually Mum would rise and start lighting the candles, and it would be like waking from a very deep sleep. The hassles we might have had falling away in those long moments of waiting. They were special, the days before the lights.

'Thanks for this food.' He broke into the quiet. The neckline of the jumper I'd found him was wide and it kept slipping down his shoulder. His exposed skin was pale in the candlelight, like he didn't see much sun. He pulled the material up and even in the flickering light I saw him redden, as though he'd been caught naked. Blushes always made me giggle but I tried not to smile. Figured he was having a tough enough time already.

'Do you think I could use your phone after this?' he said. 'See if I can work some stuff out?'

'Sure.' I pointed to the wall behind him. 'It's just up there.'

He glanced around and then back at me.

'That the only phone you've got?'

It was one of those old-style ones with the twisty cords. No point having a cordless up here when the power went out every time it rained.

'Yep. That's it. Works fine, don't worry.'

He looked doubtful but didn't say anything, just kept eating his food. So far, he wasn't much of a talker. When he was finished I stood up and took the bowls to the sink.

'You're hurt,' he said, noticing my limp.

'Nah, I'm fine.' It was always a thorny moment, explaining about my foot.

'You're limping. You need some ice or something?' He looked around helplessly, as though he'd like to take charge but didn't know where to start.

'I have a club foot. It's the way I was born.' There was no easy way to tell him.

'Oh, right.' The rain on the roof seemed suddenly loud. I could see he was making himself hold my eye, like it mattered to him to be a certain sort of man. 'I didn't notice out there in the rain.'

It pained me that such a small thing like my foot could make people so uncomfortable.

'We were both lurching around, don't worry about it.'

I don't think about my foot when I'm in the midst of things. I forget I even have it. Why wouldn't I when it's always been this way?

'What's your name?' he asked. Introductions. We were doing everything backwards.

'Mema.'

My real name is Artemesia, but there was no way I was telling him that. 'Yours?'

'Hamish.'

'Nice to meet you,' I said, laughing and reaching out a hand for him to shake. I felt like I was in a play. A silly stage production. Formality makes me nervous. It's hard to carry off. He hesitated a second, looking down at my hand as though it was a foreign object, but then he shook it, gently.

'I thought you were a kid.'

'Yes, I'm kid-sized. A biggish kid!'

'Yeah.' He nodded, looking uneasy.

'But I'm twenty-two, twenty-three in June.'

There was still some water left in the pipes and I turned around to fill up the kettle for some tea.

'I thought I could cross,' Hamish said from behind me. 'Thought the car was high enough. But the water started coming up out of nowhere.'

'It's flooding.' I shrugged, sitting back down. 'That's what happens.'

He looked at the table, deflated.

'You're not from around here, how would you know?' It was always newcomers who got washed away in the floods.

'I know about floods. I just thought I could cross.' He glanced up at me and I could see he was mortified. 'Stupid bloody tourist, hey?'

I didn't know how to respond. Sometimes the most dangerous mistakes are the simplest. Smiling, I tried to change the subject. 'Bessie was so stubborn. I can't believe she gave birth right into the water.'

'You saved my life, Mema.'

This made me feel a little queasy. Who wants someone's life on their hands?

'No, I—'

'The window was jammed. I couldn't open it.'

'You smashed it in the end.' But I knew he'd been close, close to going under.

'I had to use my fucking laptop,' his voice was strained. 'It's the only thing I had in the front. My suitcase was in the boot.'

I hadn't thought of how he'd broken it.

'See, you saved yourself.'

'No, it was you. You had the branch.'

'You could have swum out by yourself.' I didn't know that for sure, but I preferred to believe it.

'That water sucked my shoes off. And my socks,' he said quietly. 'I don't think I would have gotten out without something to cling onto.'

I looked away, tapping my fingertips against the table, thinking of Bessie's big dark eyes. It was disconcerting that she'd give birth into an overflowing creek. Instincts gone awry. Sometimes I wondered whether humans made animals that way—domesticated them to the point of idiocy. But most days Bessie didn't seem stupid. She had a mysterious way about her, and I trusted her more than a lot of humans I knew. She wasn't going anywhere fast.

'Well, you saved the calf's life, so let's call it even,' I said finally, glancing across at the water on the stove to see if it was boiling.

'A man for a calf?'

'Yes. It's a fair trade.' It seemed like a joke, but really, I meant it.

I got up and poured the hot water into some mugs, scanning the jars of tea in the candlelight. We didn't have much black tea left. Thought I'd better save the real stuff for the morning.

'Peppermint or camomile?'

He looked mildly perplexed.

'Camomile's supposed to be relaxing.' I was dubious myself.

'Okay, I'll give that a go.'

I handed him the steaming mug and he put it on the table.

'You want to use the phone?' I was beginning to feel tired.

'Yeah.' He stood up patting his thighs, searching his pockets.

'What you looking for?' I asked, sipping my tea.

'It's just …' he rubbed his hand across his collarbone restlessly, '… without my phone I don't think I know any of my numbers.'

I didn't have a mobile. Wasn't any point without reception. Round here we all had the same first five digits, so you just had to remember the last three. I knew all of them from childhood. Nothing ever changed.

'What about your home number? You could call that maybe and get some others that you need.'

'I don't know it. Not off the top of my head.'

'Oh.' I was nonplussed. 'Okay.'

'I mean, I know my old home number from when I was a kid, but no one lives there anymore. I know my mate Dave's number from way back, but he's living in Scandinavia. I don't know, I just don't need to remember numbers anymore.'

This seemed peculiar but I was distracted thinking about whether to scrounge him up a doona.

'When the power comes on I'll do it via email.'

I sipped my tea and felt my nose crinkle. 'We don't have a computer.'

'What?'

He looked as though he actually thought he'd heard me wrong.

'Well, we used to have one, but it hasn't worked for ages. You can only get dial-up out here and it's not really worth the hassle.'

He smoothed his hand across his shorn hair.

'I'll just have to go into town then. Tomorrow.'

There were some crocheted blankets in a basket in the corner. They'd have to do. It was summer so it wasn't exactly cold. I walked over and pulled one out, laying it over the couch.

'Look, when it's raining like this you can't get out. You just have to wait for it to stop and the water to go down.' Even in the candlelight I could see him go pale. 'It's okay. It happens a lot this time of year. We've got plenty of food and stuff. You'll be right.'

'I won't be able to get out tomorrow? I could be here for days?'

I knew he didn't understand flooding, what it was like, but I was tired. I felt Rory's warm little sleeping body calling me.

'You're lucky you didn't get stranded between bridges. Sometimes that happens. You get stuck between two creeks where there isn't even a house to shelter in. That's if you're silly enough to be driving around.'

He patted his pockets again and then crossed his arms over his chest. Even though he was a man, he looked suddenly like a little lost boy. I hadn't meant to be unkind.

'Alright,' he said, gaze on the floor.

I patted the rug basket. 'There are more blankets in here if you need them. You'll have to snuggle up on the couch.' I walked around the house blowing out candles until there was only the one left flickering on the low table by his makeshift bed.

He stood in the centre of the room staring at me.

''Night, Hamish.'

'Goodnight.'

3.

Being an insomniac meant I had plenty of time to think. The rain was still pounding on the roof and I lay awake in the early morning hours imagining my brothers and what they might be doing now. I'm the youngest of six, the last one off the assembly line, and when I was little, puberty hit the boys one by one, morphing them into unrecognisable beasts. Their shoulders grew wide and strong, their knees large like bowling balls. Fluff grew on their faces, the only softness left. The house could no longer contain them and they'd bang their heads together like giant clumsy antelopes, knocking into furniture and damaging the walls. My mother's angry voice was drowned out by their constant bickering, and oftentimes they shoved past her when she tried to peace-make between them.

I don't know what is meant to happen to turn wild boys into men, but my brothers seemed overtaken by a force so completely out of their control that instead of growing up they just grew wilder. There was a closeness in the house once, but when the wave of adolescence came it seemed to wash the boys out to sea, and the distance between them and us became vast. At first my mother fought hard to hold them. Tying down their sails, penning them into corners, but in no time at all they got bigger than she could manage and simply broke through the fences and ran. Every now and again Jonah or Sunny will come back, just for a day or so, but we haven't seen Max or Caleb for years. They don't even ring to let us know they're alright.

The dawn light was seeping into my bedroom and I knew Rory would wake up soon. It was still raining outside, but not quite as heavily. Thinking of my brothers made me sad. How completely they'd shaken us off and disappeared into the world. I watched Rory sleep for a bit to soothe myself. He was peaceful, mouth slightly open, dark hair wisping around his face. Rory's dad was one of those crazy mixtures. Part Scottish, part Maltese, with an Italian grandmother and Dutch grandfather on the other side. Not a local boy—he'd blown in from some other place. He used to say he was a mongrel, and considering recent events it was hard to disagree. So Rory had come out dark, and the new baby had come out fair, and neither of them looked much like Sophie. I guess you never really know what you'll get.

Soon as it got light enough I went to check on Bessie and the calf. Crept out before Rory woke up and hounded me for breakfast. You'd think Rory was starved the way he'd carry on. We called him 'the Ibis' 'cause he constantly scabbed for food. If you didn't watch him he'd steal the dog's breakfast from right beneath her nose. Poor old thing, having to fight for every morsel with a two-year-old. She'd just sit back and watch him, looking at us with her big sad eyes, hoping we'd intervene.

The rain was drizzly and light, but I slipped on my dad's raincoat anyway. Dawn is my favourite time of day, the sky so light and pale and clean you can almost forget how dirty the world is. When it's not raining I like to go out early and watch it turn a proper blue, but what I could see through the spitting clouds was grey and shapeless.

The ground was sloshy underfoot and I wished I had gumboots. When I got to the tree near where we'd tethered Bessie, I could see that the calf was feeding and Bessie was munching on grass, as though nothing had changed. I walked over and held out my palm. The farmer who owned Bessie before us used to feed her treats now and again, so she was always curious about what I might have. Sometimes she'd charge at me from across the paddock like a dog welcoming home its master. Bessie at full trot could be intimidating, even for me, but I was used to her now. I didn't have any treats that morning so I just let her nuzzle my palm, searching. It was a nice feeling, wet and warm in the gentle rain.

The calf still had that trembly look about it, all big eyes and ears, sucking away at Bessie's teat. It was remarkable that an animal as large as that could have been tucked up inside her yesterday. The step between being in the world, or yet to be, seemed suddenly inconsequential. The calf had been there all yesterday too, just taking up a different piece of space. I thought about this for a little bit, but I didn't come any closer to understanding it.

The chickens had woken up too and I could hear them doing their morning clucks, ready to face the world. Chooks are funny like that, up at first light as though it's the most exciting thing. No matter the weather, they bolt out of their coop soon as you open the gate, all muscular legs and eager beaks, charging out to see what the day might bring. A few worms, some insects, lots of scratching around. They were the most enthusiastic creatures I'd ever known. When I got to the chicken coop they were waiting for me, slick with rain and bright-eyed. I opened the gate and they pushed out past my legs. Ready to forage—rain, hail or shine. The flood had made a mess of the coop. It was time to lay down some fresh straw. I didn't much feel like stepping into the muck to look for eggs, but if I left them there the chooks might go clucky. Start thinking they could hatch them.

The mud squished up between my toes, but once I got to their undercover hutch it was dry. When you think about it, eggs are miraculous things. I mean, whole, perfect creatures hatch out of them. When I was little it was my job to gather them up, and it always seemed somehow magical. Every day there would be fresh eggs, warm and perfectly oval. Just the right size to hold in my palm. Sometimes I'd sneak one into my pocket, sure if I kept it warm all day it would hatch. I didn't understand that you needed a rooster for them to be fertilised. For the first few hours I'd guard my egg, diligent and careful, but eventually I'd get distracted. Eggs are fragile, and by the end of the day it'd always be cracked and I'd be heartbroken. Mum started boiling me one in the mornings and then I'd carry it round like a talisman. It was safer that way, I guess.

After I let the chickens out, I figured I better go back in, see if Rory had woken the house. I trudged across the mud, pulling my raincoat off at the door and wiping my feet as best as I could. Keeping quiet in case everyone was still sleeping, I popped the eggs into their basket. In the lounge room Rory had the flood guy all bailed up in a staring competition. He looked like one of those territorial cats. Giving Hamish the evil eye—coming closer and closer, while keeping an unblinking gaze on his face. Hamish was lying flat, wrapped up in the blanket, like he thought burrowing was his best defence against the toddler.

'Rory, this is Hamish.' I stepped into the room, reaching out to my nephew for a hug.

'Hi, Rory. Nice to meet you.' Hamish looked relieved that I'd come in.

Rory didn't answer but bounded over to me instead. I picked him up, sniffing his babyish head.

'Who's he?' Rory asked me accusingly.

I realised I didn't have much of an answer.

'Hamish. I told you,' I said. 'He's stuck here while it's flooding.'

'He is *not* my friend.'

I looked over at Hamish and smiled. Rory was the rudest of the lot of us. 'Not yet.' I could only agree.

It felt odd being all cooped up in the house with a complete stranger. Everything that happened seemed magnified. Rory's tantrums, my mother's pronouncements, Sophie's silent, stilted sorrow, Old Dog's constant scratching on the door to come in. The ratbag cat was playing up with the rain, knocking things off the shelves, chewing up boxes, making himself out to be a lunatic. Even the new baby's bird-like cawing sounded unnatural under the stranger's gaze.

Forced by the rain into eavesdropping, we listened as Hamish made phone calls. He called the hire company and the SES about his car, and tracked down his work number through information. Nothing could be done to get him out until the creek water receded. As I predicted. We tried to ask him a few questions— about family, about work—but his answers were so non-specific it hardly seemed worth it. Family—broken up and scattered all around. Work—'consulting' for some big company I'd never heard of. It was pretty much gobbledygook to me. He didn't ask us anything. I don't think he knew where to start. Mum's not big on company these days and so after a bit she headed off to the storeroom, searching out fabric to make Rory some new clothes. Sophie crashed out with Rory and the baby around lunchtime.

At some point Hamish and I started playing flood games. Canasta, Monopoly, Euchre and finally Scrabble, and it was fun for a while but by the afternoon, time was starting to drag. I'd already snuck out a few times to check on the calf, and I was about ready to do a runner down to the creek to see how high the water was when Anja poked her head around the kitchen door.

Anja is my oldest friend. She's tall and gangly and strong like a horse and always wears the most revealing clothes she can muster.

Mum says she's a sight for sore eyes, but I can never tell if she's being ironic. As a kid Anja was wild, not in a naughty-type way, but like an animal. She's always lived with her dad up on the hill behind our place and they never got electricity. When she was real small she used to sleep in a hollowed-out tree trunk in the forest, right on the edge of a big drop. It was as if walls couldn't hold her. Somewhere along the way she got obsessed with Marilyn Monroe and everything changed. She dyed her hair bombshell-blonde and started wearing bright red lipstick all the time, even when there was no one around to see. I love her but I'm a little scared of her too. There's no predicting what she'll do next.

'Mema!' She stepped inside, shaking off the raindrops like a dog. 'I'm going crazy up there. Let's do something.'

She was wearing the shortest cut-off jeans you could possibly imagine, with a tiny halter-neck top. I glanced around to see Hamish visibly jolt.

'Fuck, who's that?' Anja said to me, blushing the brightest pink. She was a practising sex bomb but she didn't actually have much practice.

Hamish stood up and opened his mouth to speak but Mum got in first, shouting out from the storeroom, 'Mema rescued him from the creek, Anja! Like a kitten!' She chuckled loudly. 'A half-drowned cat.'

'I'm Hamish,' he said, the colour rising ever so faintly on his neck.

'Yeah? Hi.' Anja's voice was squeaky and she tossed her blonde locks.

It was a pleasure to see her, dripping water on the floor. I stood up too, and Anja came round the table and hugged me sideways, not taking her eyes from Hamish. Well, he was exotic in these parts. A fully grown, clean-cut man.

'So …' Anja was trying to make conversation. 'How long you been here?'

'Just since last night.'

Hamish leaned his back against the kitchen bench. He looked casual but I could see he felt awkward. Looking down, he turned a Scrabble tile in his fingers.

'You like Scrabble?' Anja asked.

'Yeah, it's okay.'

'I hate Scrabble, don't have the patience. I mean there are so many things you could be doing, right? Why would you spend hours staring at square letters till your eyes go foggy? Mema always wins anyway.' Anja was rambling now, but it was true—I always beat her. Scrabble was her least favourite game.

'Not against Hamish. He's a strategist.' I didn't really mind losing. I just liked the shape of words.

Hamish scratched the back of his neck. 'It is a game. You play to win.'

'It's all about winning and losing, Mema,' Mum called out. 'You remember that.'

I was pretty sure that was aimed at Hamish. Mum had a way of finding everyone's weak spot. It was a gift. I know it made some people nervous but I appreciated it. Weaknesses were far more potent when they stayed hidden. Your own and other people's. Rising up to ambush you in unexpected moments.

Hamish looked at the floor. I didn't know what he was thinking.

'I mean,' Anja was standing close beside me, her elbow clunking against my upper arm, 'I know it's still raining, but I thought maybe we could go do something.' She bent her head towards me. 'You know? Pick some passionfruit or something?' As far as I knew, there were no passionfruit to pick, but Anja was twitching at the edges, just a little, on the verge of some big emotion. Oftentimes her dad got to drinking and things at home unravelled. It had been like that from the beginning. She's spent half her life at my house.

'Let's go then,' I said, grabbing my dad's old raincoat. 'You want an umbrella?'

I knew she wouldn't. 'Nah. I'm soaked already.'

At least in summer it was so warm it didn't really matter how wet you got. I didn't want Hamish to come 'cause I knew Anja probably needed to get things off her chest, but he was glancing anxiously at the storeroom. Evidently, he didn't want to get stuck with Mum.

'You want an umbrella?' I asked him.

He looked down at the clothes he was wearing. Mum's oversized jumper, still hanging down low at the neck. Feminine on his broad shoulders. They were the only clothes he had.

'I guess so.'

Outside on the veranda I hunted for the umbrella. It was black and a bit buckled. I shook it out for spiders and then handed it to him.

'Thanks, Mema,' he said, really looking me in the eye. Hamish had a steeliness that mostly stayed beneath, but every now and then you'd catch a whiff of it. I nodded back at him, but I was thinking about my mum hiding herself in the storeroom.

Anja grabbed my hand, squeezing it hard, and then we all stepped out into the rain.

4.

When I brought the stranger home, I knew it would unsettle Mum. More than the flooding rain and more than Sophie's tears. More than the thousand and one irritations of our quiet life—no electricity, leaking roofs, crazy animals and dirty, wet footprints all over the wooden floors.

There were some things no one knew about my mum, some things no one knew but me. That's how it is when you live with someone forever—you become accustomed to their every move. Every sigh is full of nuance and even the tread of their feet on the floor has its own temperament. No doubt Mum felt the same about me. Secret habits emerge from the darkness and even the most hidden thoughts find an open space. This familiarity was among the things we never spoke about, and lately the list was getting longer. Privacy was a deep thing for my mum, though the town had always watched her. She didn't shrink away from the stolen glances at her big, overripe body, but she liked more and more to be alone.

There were things that everyone knew about my mum. That she made huge earthen pots out in the shed, curved and dark and heavy. That the sale of a single pot could make good money at the fancy city galleries, but that she didn't make too many sales. That her tongue was as sharp as a razor's edge, but her touch was gentle and sure. That for a bit of wood-chopping, or roof cleaning, or grass slashing, or even a basket of fresh bread and vegies, she was good for a roll in the hay. Even at her age, even now.

And so it was that sometimes I would happen upon her, pressed up against a fence post, skirt riding high, while some lonesome neighbouring farmer breathed in the smell of her. And though it wasn't a secret, I caught my breath every time.

The secret things I knew about my mum, and the things that everyone knew, had played on my mind for some time, since I was real little, I guess. Sophie and my brothers had such trouble at school, juggling all those knowns and unknowns, that by the time it came to be my turn, Mum didn't send me.

'What's the world got to offer you, Mema?' she asked. 'I'm not playing that game anymore.'

You don't even need a reason to home-school. You don't have to be a conscientious objector. You just have to prove you do it. And Mum had no trouble proving that. Those home-school inspectors had one peek inside, one look around those piled-high bookshelves, and they knew I was learning. Books are for learning, after all, so I was learning, and that was that.

I didn't fight it. School seemed pointless anyway. All the rules and regulations, made to be flouted. I'd watched Anja and my siblings become parched and sad with the stupidity of it all, and I figured I wasn't missing much.

What *did* the world have to offer me?

When I was small, all around me flowed, gentle and sweet like the quiet edge of the creek. Then my brothers grew too big to be hemmed in, and Sophie met a bloke, moved out and had babies, and things became harder. The older I got, the louder those secret things inside me became, all those knowns and unknowns, until—apart from Anja—I'd rather talk to animals than people. Chat with Old Dog, muck around with the crazy cat, or follow the wandering Bessie. Make friends with the magpies and whip birds. Listen for the squeaking of baby mice and leave out crumbs to help them on their way. Sit with my legs dangling in the creek and let the guppies nip at my toes. And it was the same for Mum, 'cause she stopped talking quite so much to me.

Outside, with Hamish in tow, Anja and I headed off to check the creeks. The rain was falling hard again, not torrential like yesterday, but steady, as though it would never end. Our house is up on a hill and the paddocks curve gently downwards to the closest creek. From above, you can see the creek stretched out across the land like a giant serpent, winding off into the distance. Sometimes the view gets lost in clouds, or mist, or simply the rain, but when it's clear, it's magic. Those green hills stretching out forever, like they were sculpted purposefully to please the eye. When it stops raining you can hear the rush of the floodwater and it seems as though the creek is quite close, but actually it's a series of small hills and plateaus away. Big grassy paddocks. Easier on the way down than the way up. Used to be mostly dairy farms and bananas, but nowadays it's just the occasional small crop and a scattering of cattle. And then out on the flats, on the other side of town, there are the cane fields.

Anja started off walking, as sedately as she could, but soon she picked up speed and I knew it wouldn't be long before she broke into a jog. Running in the rain is quite a pleasure, especially if there isn't really anywhere you have to be. Anja and I discovered long ago that it could be twice as much fun in company, most specifically with each other.

Still holding my hand, she pulled me forward, testing my gait.

'How's the foot holding up today, Mema?' she asked, tugging on my fingers.

'Good-o,' I replied, smiling across at Hamish. I wasn't sure how to explain, and he looked puzzled under his umbrella, walking fast to keep up.

'How about a race down to the old footbridge spot?' Anja seemed to have decided ignoring Hamish was her best defence against awkwardness. 'I'll run in circles and you can go straight.'

She took off then, in a wide arc around us, like a puppy that was finally unleashed. I glanced at Hamish and shrugged.

'What does she want us to do?' Hamish asked, swapping the umbrella from hand to hand.

'Race. Down that way.' I pointed down towards a big tree at a curve in the creek.

'Why?'

It was hard to explain our rain-running, or the ways we'd invented to even out our discrepancies in pace.

'It's raining,' I said, hoping it was enough.

'Why's she running in circles?'

I looked down at my foot. 'To make it fair, I guess.'

Anja stopped in front of us then, oblivious to the raindrops bouncing off her face.

'Come on, Mema!' Her eyes were bright.

She finally spoke to Hamish, 'Come on, flood guy!'

'It's better if we do,' I said to him. 'Everything is better.'

Hamish looked from me to Anja, uncertain. A few seconds ticked by, like he was weighing things up, and then he tucked the umbrella down low over his head and took off jogging in the direction I'd pointed.

'He thinks we're crazy,' I whispered to Anja.

'Flick your hood back,' Anja said. 'You know it works better when you get totally wet!'

She reached over and pushed my hood away and the raindrops started pelting my head. Pretty soon my hair would be soaked and the drips would slide down my face, down the back of my neck.

'I need it today, Mema. I need it. Dad's been real bad,' she blurted out, looking down at the ground. 'I don't care about the flood guy. I don't care what he thinks.'

'Alright.' I knew the deal and I wrapped my arms around her, giving her a squeeze. She was wet and cold and jumpy. 'Let's run.'

I took off over the mushy grass and Anja circled wide around me. I guess with my foot it was more lope than run, but it always got me to where I was going. If we pushed it too hard my hips would ache and I'd be all creaky the next day. I'd been rain-running since I was real small so I guess I was used to it. Somehow or other, even with the bung foot, my body had taken up the slack.

It wasn't long before we caught up to Hamish, warding off the rain with the umbrella.

'Where exactly are we headed?' he called out to me.

There were all different places we liked to go along the creek, but when we raced it was always to the same spot. 'See that big tree down there where the creek curves? On the last flat?' I shouted back, beginning to pant. 'There used to be a footbridge there. That's the spot. You got to run!'

He picked up his pace.

'Go on, Anja! Stop circling me. Give him a run for his money!' I yelled to her as she raced out in front of me.

'You reckon?' She was starting to puff.

'Yep!'

And she took off like a rocket. Outstripped him in no time. I liked our rain-running, but partly I just enjoyed watching Anja. No doubt there were better runners in the world, but Anja put everything she had into it. Arms, legs, everything whirled. It wasn't graceful but it was energy in motion.

When I got to the old footbridge spot under the tree, Anja was bright red. Her face held colour for ages after she'd run, like she'd been scalded. Hamish and her were both still faintly panting.

'That was … funny,' Hamish said, glancing from Anja to me. He was trying not to smile.

'It's alright to have a giggle.' I was still puffed. 'Giggling is part of it. That or having a good cry.'

Hamish laughed then, an unfamiliar sound.

'Fuck,' Anja said, and then her eyes welled up and spilled over.

'Do another lap,' I said. 'It'll all come out if you do another lap.'

And she took off again, out into the open paddock.

'You do this a lot?' Hamish asked me. Anja was just a speck, moving in the distance.

I shrugged. 'Only when it's raining.'

'What about you, Mema?' He was watching me closely. 'Laugh or cry today?'

'I don't know.' My breathing was slowing. 'Usually it's only the two of us and I guess we bleed into each other. Usually we do the same. Together. But with you here I'm stuck in the middle.'

'Between laughing and crying?'

'Yep.'

'That's life, I guess.'

I didn't know what to say to that.

'How long have you known Anja?'

'Forever.'

'Only forever?'

He was trying to tease me.

'Yep.'

'She's …'

'She's pretty quirky, but I love her,' I interrupted, not really wanting to hear his verdict.

'She's very beautiful.'

This took me by surprise. Anja was one thousand things besides beautiful. It bothered me that it was the only thing worth remarking on.

'She runs pretty fast,' I replied.

'She's built like a thoroughbred. It's no wonder.'

Anja ran about in the distance, galloping at high speed. From the way she was slowing I could see she'd cried it out. After a bit she stopped in the centre of the flat and let the rain wash over her. Hamish stood watching her, and I watched him.

'I've never seen anything like this place,' Hamish said, his blue eyes back on me. 'It's different.'

'I guess.'

'You're different, Mema.'

I suppose deep down I knew that was true.

'In a good way,' he added softly.

I don't know what it was about those words but they got inside me. When I looked back at Hamish I saw something new. Something inside me opened, just a tiny crack. When eggs hatch, cracks are how the chicks are born. The smallest of fractures and the world seeps in. So maybe it was only a glimpse of me I was seeing, a part of myself I liked that I'd kept hidden. After that I watched Hamish in a way I hadn't done before. Keenly, as though he was the first man I'd seen. And just like that, everything changed, and it was fast, like rushing water, nearly knocking me off my feet.

5.

That evening it stopped raining and after it had been dry a while the power came back on. It was always like that. Some part of the wiring had got wet and we just waited for it to dry out. Once the weather cleared, it never took long. Anja had run home before it got dark. She was scared of her dad when he hit the booze, but she worried about him too, so she was always up and down, checking he was okay. I don't know if I'd be able to love someone who treated me so mean, but Anja was used to it, I suppose.

It's always a relief to get electricity back on, even though it's nice without it. The electronic clock on the fridge starts beaming the wrong time, someone sets it, and life gets back on track. There's a bunch of things that need power to get done—clothes in the washing machine, toast in the toaster. That low hum of machines at work slides so quickly into the background you forget how loud they sounded when they first blinked back into operation.

When the lights came back on, Sophie stumbled out of the bedroom mumbling, 'I'm going to have a bath.' They were the first coherent words I'd heard her say in a while.

'You want me to help you deal with your hair?'

Sophie has curly hair, a light brown, and it gets tangled real easy. Since she'd been out of action it had turned into one big knot.

She looked at me then, like she hadn't in days. Her forehead was still bruised and the skin around her eyes was puffy and red, more lined than before the mongrel left, but her eyes were clear. Clear and sad. I could see my sister was back.

'Mema, that would be grand.'

The truth is, I've always had a thing about my sister's hair. Something about the way the curls snake their way around my fingers makes it seem alive. When I was little she'd sit there all still and thoughtful while I tugged and played and plaited. Her hair bounces and springs when she moves—it's impossible to pass her by without tweaking one of her curls and watching it spring back into place. My hair is the opposite, dark and heavy like a horse's tail. I usually wear it in big fat plait down my back. There's nothing dancing about it, but when Sophie's feeling bright she tells me it shimmers like a waterfall in the night, and I should love what I've been given. Sophie says my dad had hair just like me. Her dad had curly hair and mine had straight, and she says I should be thankful 'cause that was his gift to me. That and the old raincoat. But I'm not sure it's much to celebrate, though the raincoat does come in handy.

'You go in and soak for a bit. I'll come in soon.'

The baby was sleeping in the bedroom but Rory was awake. Hamish was tucked up on the couch, trying to read one of Mum's books, ignoring Rory's advances as best as he could. Old Dog had snuck inside. We usually tried to keep her out on the veranda when she was wet, and even when it stops raining she takes a while to dry. I could see her tail poking out from under the couch, giving her away. I started packing up some of Rory's toys, clearing up floor space, but I was watching the two of them. Even though he was only little, Rory talked quite a bit. He usually gave a running commentary on whatever he was doing. Sometimes it made perfect sense and other times it didn't. Probably you had to know him pretty well to get the drift of his talk-stories. I liked his funny, croaky voice, even when I didn't quite know what it was he was saying, but every now and then, when the day was especially long, the buzz of his endless words could get inside my brain and I'd wish he'd stop.

'Come and give me a snuggle, Rory,' I said, feeling bad for wishing he'd be quiet. Rory was finely tuned to the frequency of feelings. He'd know about yours before you were even aware of them yourself. You had to be on the ball.

He stopped talking and looked at me with his big dark eyes. 'No!' He lifted his chin. 'No snuggles!'

I held out my arms but he just shook his head. He could turn in an instant. Happy to sad, gentle to angry—mercurial. I wanted him to stay calm 'cause if he got frustrated he'd harass Sophie in the bath.

'What's Nanny cooking for dinner?' I asked him. Any mention of food would usually do the trick.

'Dinner?' Rory repeated and then he was off to the kitchen, quick as a flash.

I laughed and Hamish glanced up at me from his book. The Ibis would always respond to the lure of food.

'He's a talker,' Hamish said, like he was fishing around for something to say.

'He talks it through,' I replied. 'Everyone does.'

'Not everyone.'

It was true. He didn't. 'You're quiet. No one knows what you're thinking.'

'Nothing worth reporting, that's why.'

I wondered about that. Other people's thoughts. All those knowns and unknowns.

Hamish turned a page of his book and then sat up and stretched. Watching him, something in my belly dropped. He had a stillness about him most of the time, so when he broke into motion it seemed like a revelation. I wanted to look away but I couldn't. Men had never been of much interest to me. I guess I saw them as just passing through, and I'd always been more immersed in the familiar, the enduring. Hamish was probably the most just-passing-through man I'd encountered, so it was strange that he should capture my attention.

There was only really the couch to sit on in our lounge room. Usually we all squashed on together, but I was hardly going to do that with Hamish, so I kept standing there, wishing there were more toys to clean up.

'Do you want to sit down?' Hamish said, shifting over a little.

I glanced at the space beside him—his arm stretched out along the back of the couch. Moving towards him would be like stepping into his embrace. 'What's the book?' I asked instead.

'Just something I picked up off your shelf—an old mythology book.' He held up the cover. 'I've never read much mythology.'

'Yeah? Mum was crazy about it at one stage.'

I hoped she wasn't listening from the kitchen 'cause I knew she'd yell out and tell Hamish about my name. It was one of her favourite stories.

'She the reader?' Hamish tilted his head towards the bookshelves.

'Well, the books are hers, but we all read them.'

I looked at the books, higgledy-piggledy, sagging on the shelves. The damp made everything warped. Some of the books had absorbed the water like sponges and sat bloated on the top of the rows, unable anymore to fit. When she was my age, Mum had done some kind of degree, travelled around a bit, then headed up here with Sophie's dad to start planning the revolution. There was a bunch of them, all buoyed by hope, thinking they would find a better way to live. Sophie says back then there were always parties. They'd pack mattresses into the back of their station wagons and all the kids would crash in the car when things got too much. But there was none of that now, the books were the main things left.

'How many of you are there?'

'In my family?' I paused. 'There's four boys between me and Sophie.'

He seemed surprised. 'Four brothers?'

'Yep.'

There was an old school photo of the boys on top of the bookshelf, obscured by a pile of books. I reached up and pulled it down, dusting off the spider webs. It was a shock to see their faces, still kids in primary school. Freckles and scruffy hair. Familiar and foreign all at once. I handed the picture to Hamish.

'Max is the oldest.' I pointed him out. 'He's probably the quietest of the lot.' Max had the same dad as Sophie. 'Then Caleb. He's the one with white hair. Everyone called him Snowy.' I didn't know how to explain who had which dad— who was more related to who. 'Then there's Sunny, he's a ratbag.' I touched a finger to his cheek in the photo. Out of all the boys, Sunny had played with me most. He was already seven by the time I was born, so he'd always seemed grown-up, but looking at his childish face, I saw how small he'd once been.

'Snowy and Sunny?' Hamish asked, smiling a little.

'Yep.' I knew it sounded funny.

'And who's the littlest?'

'Jonah.' In the photo he looked babyish, missing front teeth, the collar of his school shirt frayed and worn, handed down so many times before it got to him. 'They're all big now, though.'

'Four brothers, that's almost half a footy team.' He handed the picture back to me and looked around, and I guessed he was taking in the size of our house. 'They moved out of home?'

'Yeah, ages ago. Boys take up so much space.'

His blue eyes flashed up at me for split second, like he'd taken offence.

'Not you, though,' I added.

'Thanks … I think.'

Part of me wanted to stay there near him but part of me wanted to run. It was an uncomfortable feeling. I wasn't used to it. So I put the photo back where I'd found it and went into the bathroom to check on Sophie.

One of the dads remade the bathroom before I was born, and he did a good job too. It was a longish space, and the bath was set into the floor, right at the far end, so it dropped down next to the low window and all you saw from inside it was the bush outside. Sophie looked peaceful, but I knew that it might not be long before the baby woke.

'You ready?' I asked.

She turned her head real slow. 'Yep. Work your magic, Baby-girl.'

My sister always called me that. Even now I was grown up. I guess I'd been a baby to her for so long. It sounded especially strange when there was an actual baby girl in the house.

I came and sat on the edge of the bath and my sister moved forward so I could get to her hair. Picking up the jug we used for the babies, I dipped it in the bath. Sophie leaned her head back and I poured the water over her. I loved the way, even when it was wet, my sister's hair resisted straightening. I wondered about the structure of curls, what made them so unwilling to take another form. There was probably an explanation and if I searched hard enough I'd find it, but sometimes not knowing was almost as nice.

Sophie bent forward, resting her cheek against her upright knees, turning her face away from me, towards the window. I squeezed the shampoo in and massaged it through her hair. Rinsing out the soap, I added the conditioner. Sophie turned towards me, eyes still closed, her mouth upturned at the corners in a half-smile.

'You and your hair obsession,' she murmured. I reached out for the wide-toothed comb. 'You should let me wash your hair one day, Mema.' Sophie opened her eyes and looked up at me. 'I know you won't.'

'I don't like people touching my hair.'

'I know. You've been like that since you were born. You wouldn't let any of us touch your head at all. Mum let you run around like a scrappy-looking puppy until you finally started brushing it yourself. You were a sight to behold.'

'I know. There are photos.'

'Yeah, I took them, silly.'

Once I'd got the knots out, Sophie went right under the water and shook her head from side to side. Her eyes were squeezed shut, small bubbles of air hanging about her nostrils. I wanted to see if her spirals would stay curled under water, but it was hard to tell. Watching her through the screen of the water was like peering into another realm. She resurfaced and lay there a minute, resting her head on the bath rim. I had always watched Sophie like a hawk, but I wouldn't like it if she examined me that way. When you're the youngest in a big family, you can get away with being unseen. It was what I liked best about being Baby-girl. Luckily, Sophie never seemed to mind me staring at her.

Mum burst in then, the baby on her hip and a wooden spoon in her other hand.

'Rory's helping me cook,' she said, pushing her hair off her forehead with the back of her hand. 'You'll need to take bubs.'

I reached out and she handed me the baby. Lila was the baby's name, but none of us called her that. She wasn't really a person yet, I guess, and the name just sounded odd. She was wriggly on my lap, and I knew she'd start bellowing soon.

'Shall we put her in the bath? She's a bit sticky.'

I leaned down and sniffed her head. Little babies have that smell. It builds up fast. A kind of cheesy, clammy smell, especially in summer.

'Yeah, strip her off and hand her over.'

I untangled Lila from her clothes and pulled her nappy off. The closer to naked she got, the stiffer her body—like the clothes had given her something to relax into. I was used to the way babies worked, after Rory. I wasn't worried I would hurt her. Even though Lila was delicate, she didn't seem otherworldly. She seemed hardy, like an animal, I guess.

Sophie sat up and I passed Lila over. Instantly the baby snuffled around for Sophie's breast, making little grunting sounds. Sophie squeezed her nipple between her fingers, guiding it towards the baby's mouth. When Lila finally got it, the sound of her gulping milk echoed around the bathroom.

'You'd think she was starving,' Sophie said. 'Funny little gutso.'

'Yeah, Rory was a more refined eater at that age, remember?' It was true. Rory had breastfed quietly, like it was a dainty, private matter.

'I know and look at him now.'

She was quiet a minute, then she looked up at me. 'Poor little buggers, Mema. Like the rest of us. No dad.'

Sophie had never spoken much about her fella. Before or after he left. Like it was a terrain not fit for words.

'It's not so bad. We're alright, aren't we?'

'Speak for yourself.'

The baby was pointing her little toes and then flexing them again. Sophie held them together lightly between her legs, and then it looked like the baby was nudging to get back in. Nudging with her toes to go back where she came from.

'I still can't believe she came out of there,' I said.

'You always say that.'

'Well, it's not self-explanatory.'

Yesterday I'd watched Bessie's calf being born, but the whole thing still seemed like a mystery.

'Mema, ever since you were little you've wanted to know everything about babies. You're never going to know if you never have sex.'

It had become a bit of a joke in my family that I'd never get around to doing it. 'So you keep saying.'

'You should give Billy a go.'

Billy was a young bloke in town who'd asked me out once a couple of months back. An old friend of Sunny's. He did odd jobs and maintenance stuff for the council and he was often working on the road. We'd always known each other, just from living in the same place, but I'd never paid him much heed. Then I happened upon him on one of my walks and he called out to me—'Hey, Mema!' He was working on someone's land, chopping down a tree, all sweaty and covered in wood dust. 'What's three foot long and fucks a chook?' This question startled me. It came out of nowhere. I just looked at him and shrugged.

'An axe,' he answered, and then he asked me out to dinner.

Sophie said he was just nervous and that's why he told the joke, but I said no anyway, though I liked him well enough before that.

'Billy is …' I was thinking of the way Hamish rubbed the place just at the base of his neck, that it was the only sign he ever gave of feeling stuff.

'Alright, for your first time round.'

'I hardly ever see him anymore. He avoids me.'

'Hell hath no fury …'

My sister was sounding more like her old self with every passing minute. She reached down and broke the suction of the baby's lips on her breast with her little finger, lifting Lila upright so she could burp. The baby looked disorientated, and I guess it would feel strange to be always moving unpredictably through space.

'I hope she doesn't poo. Bath and baby poo right now is not my idea of fun.'

We'd seen this before, a few times. It basically meant starting the whole bath process again.

'Do you want me to take her and get her dressed?'

'Just let me wipe her quickly with a washer,' Sophie answered.

I handed my sister the wash cloth, and she smoothed it across her baby's skin, swiping it over all the creases, gently prising up her arms and neck to clean all her delicate baby crevices.

'She's wonderful, Soph,' I said.

'I know.' Sophie's voice was soft, like she was mesmerised. 'She's perfect.'

When she finished cleaning Lila, I bundled her up in a towel and took her out to find her some clothes.

6.

Half of my mother's pottery shed was filled with unglazed, unfired pots. They were majestic things, large and curved and white. She didn't make just pots, but huge plates and platters too. When they were fired they'd come out deep, dark colours, but I liked them just as much this fragile white. It was the same with most things in flux—I liked the caterpillar just as much as the butterfly.

Mum would disappear for days at a time, throwing pots almost bigger than her arms could span. Watching her at the wheel was like glimpsing the world at creation, like she held a whole universe in her arms. She taught me to use the wheel when I was small, and I can throw a pot as well as the next person, but throwing pots like Mum requires a strength and stamina that most people don't have. It's a gift, or that's what the gallery man says when he comes on his buying trips.

When the next day came out sunny, Mum headed to her shed straight after breakfast. Sophie bundled the babies up and took them back to her own cabin, so it was only me and Hamish left in the house. I'd been up early to check on the calf and let the chooks out. The water over the bridge was still too high to cross, but it wouldn't be long now. We'd be able to get out tomorrow.

With the sunshine out, Hamish was restless. I sat at the kitchen table, the old dog at my feet, but Hamish paced around, patting his empty pockets. Endlessly checking the time.

'I can't believe you don't have internet.'

It was the second time he'd said it that morning. I wasn't sure how to respond. I guess I didn't know what I was missing.

'Why's it so important?'

'You know, emails and stuff.'

'Not really.'

'You don't know what an email is?'

'Yeah—I mean, it's a message sent on a computer.' I knew that much. 'But I've never sent one.'

'You've never sent an email?'

'No.'

Hamish stopped moving and stared at me.

'Come on, you must have sent one once … somewhere along the line?' He sounded disbelieving. 'What about at school?'

Because we didn't have a working computer, I'd done all my school correspondence via plain old mail, but I didn't want to tell him that.

'Nup.' I leaned down and gave the dog a scratch behind her ears. She was a scraggly old thing, smelly but familiar. These days she didn't ask for much—a pat here and there and a bowl of food. She hardly left the house. I couldn't remember a time when her big brown body wasn't sleeping somewhere in a corner—ears twitching, dog-snuffling through her dreams.

'That's amazing.' Hamish shook his head. 'I would have thought everyone under the age of fifty would have sent an email.'

I was trying not to feel affronted. 'What about all those people in remote areas?'

'Yeah, maybe. But, Mema, this isn't *that* remote.'

I shrugged. I had no answer to that. 'What do you like about it so much?'

He started moving around the kitchen, checking out all the things in jars. We always had everything sealed up to keep the insects out. The pantry door fell off a few years back and we hadn't got around to fixing it yet. There were a few shelves above the bench too, so most of our food was on display.

'I'm not one of those guys who's glued to a screen twenty-four-seven or anything,' he stated. 'I mean, I hardly even update Facebook.' He sounded frustrated to be talking about it, even though he'd brought it up. 'It's not … my life. I just need emails for work. It's how my whole job runs.'

I was thinking about how panicked Hamish had been on that first afternoon when he realised he'd lost his laptop. I knew he must have been in shock from being trapped in the car like that, but standing in the pouring rain, sodden and mucky after the cow birth, he looked like his whole world had washed down the drain. As though the computer was everything he had.

'And, you know, I work to a deadline. They sent me all the way out here, and when I get back into town I'll have to work out how to retrieve all my data. I'm not stupid, I back up really important things, but not everything. I had so much stuff stored on that laptop, stuff I'd collected for years. It's just … annoying.'

He was still looking at the pantry, distracted by a jar of flour with obvious signs of life. Must have had weevils or something. He peered at it but he didn't comment. 'Will I be able to buy a new laptop in town, Mema?' he asked over his shoulder.

'I don't know, maybe. You'll have to ask.'

I tried to imagine what it must feel like to have everything that was important to you inside a small machine. It was hard to get my head around.

'Email is just such an instantaneous form of communication,' he said, almost like he was talking to himself.

'More than a phone?'

He stopped perusing the jars for a second and turned back to look at me, thinking. 'No, I guess not. It's just you don't have the time to talk to everyone, and so you send people things and they can read them when they want, you know? When they have time.'

'So, it's not instantaneous then?' It didn't make that much sense to me. ''Cause they might not read it straight away?'

'But they probably will. They just might take a little while to get back to you,' he said. 'Usually, you can be pretty sure they've read it.'

I wasn't really seeing it.

'But if you called them, you'd get to speak to them, and then you'd know for sure. Right?'

'But you'd have to go through all the small-talk parts of having a conversation. It's time consuming when you only want to tell someone one thing.'

I didn't much like talking on the phone, so I wasn't going to argue with that. Hamish walked across to the window and looked out over the rolling hills. It was always beautiful after the rain and I waited for him to say so.

'I can't believe I lost my laptop *and* my phone,' he said instead, squinting out at the view. 'That's a first.'

The whole time Hamish had been stranded in our little farmhouse in the pouring rain he'd hardly complained at all. This was the most I'd heard him speak. He had a way of choosing his words carefully, like he was weighing things up in his head. Most of the people I knew just blurted out their thoughts, but Hamish was different.

I didn't know what to do with him there. Normally in the mornings I might help Mum in the shed, throw a few mugs for the markets, muddle about in the vegie garden, or just clean up a bit. With the sun out I wanted to get on with things, but I wasn't sure how, especially since he'd finally started talking.

'When I get out, I'll get back online and there'll be one thousand emails waiting for me. And it'll take me forever to sort through them.'

'To do with work or what?' I was trying to think of something we could do for the day.

'Yeah, mainly to do with work, but other stuff too.'

'And you can't be away from them for a few days otherwise they bank up?' I asked. 'That's why you're getting stressed out?'

He was pacing around the way Anja's dad did when he needed a drink. Our ratbag cat was perched on the back of the couch, and even from the kitchen I could see his tail flicking from side to side as though he was listening.

'It's just, I have a deadline and I'm already behind. But I'm not stressed.' He stopped pacing and sat down at the kitchen table. 'Well, maybe a little jittery. I can't believe it's sunny and I still can't get out.'

I didn't know what to say about that. It was just a fact of life. Rivers rose and then they fell. The timing was unpredictable. The old dog sighed at my feet.

'I guess it's also that I'm missing out on things I need to know about. News and information. That kind of stuff.'

I put on the kettle for tea. It seemed a logical step. 'What kind of information?'

'What's happening in the world. You know. How do you find out what's happening in the world, Mema?'

'Sometimes we listen to the radio, or someone buys a paper.'

He glanced around at me standing at the kitchen bench. 'Sometimes?'

'On occasion.'

'Right.' He sounded deeply disappointed, as though that was the worst response he could imagine.

The truth was, the world outside didn't hold much interest for me. Hearing about conflicts in faraway places seemed pointless if there wasn't anything I could do. I knew there were all sorts of things happening out there 'cause sometimes I heard the news, but if everything was always shifting, if the world was in a constant state of change, I didn't really know why keeping up to date mattered.

'Why do you need to know?'

'What do you mean?' He was starting to sound frustrated. 'I like to stay informed.'

I thought about this. Being informed. 'But does it change the way you live?'

'Sometimes.'

'In what way?'

'In the decisions that I make. In what I'm willing to support.'

I wasn't sure about this—if he was talking politics or just the painstaking choice between quinoa or spelt, biodynamic milk or soy—which products were the healthiest, least destructive buys. That stuff is part of old hippie lore, and we'd always been careful, but I wondered if that's what Hamish meant.

'Do you mean voting? Or what you buy?'

He shrugged. 'Both, I guess. Plus, I need to be informed for work. Informed about current issues that might affect my work.'

'Like what?'

'Environmental issues. Stuff like that is always changing. New scientific discoveries. I need to keep on top of it.'

'Okay.'

'It's what I do for work. It's part of my job.'

'I thought you said that you were some kind of consultant.' I had no idea what being a consultant meant.

'Yeah, an environmental consultant.'

Clearly, I had missed that part of his job description.

'Companies pay me to assess the environmental impacts of their proposals, that kind of thing.'

'So what are you assessing now?' It was a world so far out of my experience I wasn't sure what to ask. 'Something around here?'

Hamish rubbed the back of his neck. 'It's a bit hard to explain.'

It wasn't much of an answer. I waited for him to say more but he didn't. Hamish often left a silence where someone else would try to fill the gap. It was a bit unsettling.

'Try.' I guess I liked hearing him talk.

'You know how there's a sugar mill on the outskirts of town?'

I nodded. It was a gigantic construction, always blowing out smoke. Been there since before I was born. It was on the other side of town from us, so I rarely went past it, but I always marvelled at the preposterousness of it, industrial and smoke-coughing, right against the forest-covered mountains.

'Well, there's been this proposal to turn the sugar waste into power, green power.' He tapped his fingers on the table. 'You know how they burn the cane fields?'

'Yeah, if the wind is blowing our way, sometimes we get some ash.'

'Well, instead of burning the cane in the fields, they've converted the mill so they can burn it there, harvesting it for power. In theory it could power the whole town, maybe even the whole district.'

'That sounds good,' I said, and it seemed a neat enough solution.

'The company I'm working for wants me to check it out. They're thinking of investing. They want to know how much it will cost and all that stuff, but I'm more interested in if it will *work*. How much power will it use? How much will it create? Is it really green? I've got my own agenda, see.'

'Agenda?'

'You know, all these ideas. I've got a billion ideas.'

'Really?'

'Yeah, but you know how it is. Hard to get them off the ground. Ideas are like arseholes, everybody has them.'

That was a statement. But I wasn't sure I did know. I didn't really feel like I had ideas. We sat in the quiet, waiting for the kettle to boil. I probably put too much water in 'cause it seemed to take forever.

'So, your mum makes a living from pottery?'

'Yeah, I mean, we don't need much. We get by.'

It was a tricky subject, even for me.

'That must be pretty unusual,' he continued. 'She must sell a lot of pots. She must be good.'

'Her pots are amazing. She loves it, she always has.'

'Maybe I could check them out later.'

He was still tapping his fingers.

'I'll take you out there, if you like. I could show you how to throw a pot. Have you done it before?'

He shook his head. 'You make pots too?'

'We all know how to do it. I just make small things for the local markets. Cups and things like that. Simple stuff.'

'I'm terrible at making things. But I'd like to watch you do it.'

I don't know why but this comment made me blush. The kettle was boiling so I got up to make the teas. 'Later on. When Mum's finished.' I poured the steaming water into mugs. 'You should have a go, though. Shaping clay makes you feel kind of powerful. It doesn't matter so much about the outcome, what you end up with. It just feels good to do.'

'Maybe.' Hamish seemed unconvinced. He squeezed his fingers into a fist to stop them tapping.

Being cooped up in such a small space with Hamish reminded me again of my brothers. When I was small they used to sneak out when it stopped raining to ride the creeks on their body boards. Mum didn't like them doing it 'cause it was dangerous, but they weren't taking any notice of her by then. Sometimes when the water dropped a bit they'd take me and Anja too. And sometimes, when we could get away with it, Anja and I would still go. We had boards stashed in the branches of a tree beside the creek, upstream from the bridge, out of reach of even the highest flood. It was one of our secrets, even more precious than the rain-running. And then it dawned on me that it might be a good thing to do right now.

'We could ride the creeks,' I said, passing him the teacup. 'The creek's still high but it would probably be okay.'

I watched his hands as he held the cup. His fingers were pale, not sun-darkened like mine, but they were strong.

'What's that involve?'

'Going upstream a little way to a spot that's not running quite as fast, then jumping on a body board and riding the creek back down.'

'Is it—you know—safe?' He took a sip of tea. He didn't seem scared, but maybe he was remembering washing off the bridge.

'Mum doesn't like us doing it, but sometimes we do it anyway.' I picked up my teacup, not really wanting to drink it. 'She doesn't know.'

'Sounds fun.'

I couldn't tell if it was the idea of doing something Mum didn't like that had the most appeal for Hamish. But maybe that's why I suggested it in first place.

'If it looks too high we don't have to go in.'

He took one more agitated look around the room and then said, 'I'm in.'

7.

It took a while to get to the secret tree, the moist heat settling around us, and once we arrived we had to climb it to get the body boards down. Things like that were harder for me with my bung foot, so I stood there and gave Hamish directions. It was a big old camphor laurel, like most of the trees around. Someone brought them in from China years ago and now they'd run wild like rabbits, occupying all the hills the first settlers had cleared. I guess that's what happens—colonisation. They might grow like weeds but they were great for climbing. Big, with widespread branches, dark, waxy leaves. In spring all their new growth came out luminous light green, just around the edges, so from the distance it looked like they were glowing. Whole hillsides alight.

'What's that over there?' Hamish called out from up on a branch.

I knew what he'd be seeing. There was an abandoned shack a few paddocks away on Old Gordon's land. Probably the original farmhouse, people said. Been there as long as anyone remembered. Grey and disintegrating, faded walls all sagging to one side, a perpetual lean. We'd thought it was haunted when we were kids, but still snuck out and scavenged through its dusty rooms looking for treasures. Old Gordon had done his back in years ago, so he didn't get out on the farm much. In any case, he never tried to stop us rummaging. Last time I'd been there I was pretty little, but I remembered it—all ransacked, bits and pieces scattered around outside. It was where my brothers had stolen away to smoke their cigarettes and do whatever forbidden things boys their age did.

I still remembered the day Caleb told me I couldn't come. It was no place for a little girl, he said. No sisters allowed. I thought Sunny would argue but he didn't. He just hung his head and away they went. Maybe that was the beginning, the beginning of their leaving.

'An old farmhouse, no one lives there anymore,' I called back, trying to shake my brothers from my mind. 'It'll topple down some day.'

Hamish peered at the shack for a minute longer and then scuttled down with the boards.

'You reckon these things are going to hold us?' They were battered looking, washed down in some earlier flood, old with chunks out of them, but they worked alright. Hamish looked sceptical.

'Yep, they're unsinkable, I promise.' I couldn't help smiling. 'The problem will be staying on them. It's not as easy as you'd think.'

'So what's the plan?' He was staring at the creek but when he turned back, I could see he was worried.

'You don't have to go in,' I said, reaching out and squeezing his arm. 'Not if you don't want.'

When I touched him he went still. Almost like a camouflage mechanism.

He glanced down at my hand on his arm.

'I'm fine,' he said softly. 'I'm good.'

'Okay,' I said, taking my hand away. 'We get in here because the water's relatively calm and it's not too deep. Then we follow the current. There's a couple of bumpier places, but nothing too rough. We get out before the bridge 'cause it's dangerous to go that far down.' An image of his sunken car, on the other side of the bridge, resting somewhere out of sight, flashed in my mind. 'If you lose your board, it's no big deal, just swim to the side and wait for me. The only thing you have to look out for is debris that might be washing down. Big logs and stuff. That's the dodgiest part.'

The creek was still a brownish colour but in a few days it would be clear. I stepped closer to the water and pulled off my skirt, flicking it over one of the lower branches. I was wearing undies but Hamish didn't seem to know where to look. 'I can't swim in a skirt!'

Hamish nodded, not meeting my eyes, and after a few seconds he stepped up and took off Mum's big floppy top, hanging it over the branch. He was the whitest man I'd ever seen, tall and strong-looking, but the paleness of his skin gave him an odd kind of delicacy.

'Ready?' I asked, trying not to look at his shirtless chest.

He nodded and I stepped into the water. It lapped around my ankles, fresh and cool, but the day was warm and the walk had made me hot. In the shallows, I moved gingerly 'cause it was easy to get off balance, especially with my foot. The secret tree spot was the part of the creek farthest upstream from the bridge that was still on our property. The front of our land was bordered by the creek. It snaked around, each bend creating a different kind of waterhole. Some of them were more open— wider and deep. Other sections narrowed right down, became more like tinkling streams. Where the paddocks had been cleared for grazing, camphors had sprung up along the banks. In some places the trees were quite thick, almost forest, but even at the more open stretches there was usually a shady place to sit.

At the secret tree spot the current was relatively gentle, and I waded out deeper, holding onto my board.

'Come on, flood guy!'

Hamish laughed from the bank but he didn't get in. The water lapped around my belly, and the bottom of my singlet spread out around me. I dipped down until it was up to my neck.

'I'm going to go under. It's better if you're all wet,' I called out, and then I plunged deep, feeling the water rush at the skin on my face, feeling my scalp prickle with the coldness, feeling the current stream by. I loved that first plunge, and I stayed there a few seconds just to let the water soak right in. When I broke back through the surface, Hamish had his feet in the shallows, watching me. I moved closer to him, holding onto my board.

'It'll be okay once you get in,' I said, aware of my shirt sucked against my skin. If I was with Anja we would have gone topless. Being naked was part of the thrill. 'You lie down on it like this.' I lay across the board to demonstrate. 'And you just hang on. The creek does the rest.'

It took some coaxing, but after a few minutes I had him in the water and lying across his board. He was a bit wobbly but alright.

'Ready?' I asked.

'Ready.'

'What are the rules?'

He thought for a minute and then he replied, 'Hold on tight. If you lose your board swim to the side. Make sure you're off before the bridge.'

'And watch out for giant logs!'

I kicked off with my feet. Hamish followed a beat behind me and we were away.

At first the water carried us along quite gently. Hamish stopped clutching the board and looking grim. He actually started to smile.

'Okay, there's a rough patch up here—keep your knees high,' I called back to him. The boulders beneath the water made it bumpy, and every so often you jammed one of your knees on a rock. Hamish was heavier than me—I could only assume he would come out a bit banged up.

The current started to quicken and the water bounced us around. We were pushed along so quickly it was hard to think about anything much. I heard Hamish grunt behind me and knew he'd scraped a rock. Riding the creek always made me feel a touch light-headed. It was kind of a thrill. I started giggling, and then I couldn't stop. We went round a few sharp bends, ducked beneath a couple of branches and then the bridge was in view, way off in the distance.

'Start swimming to the side!' I called over my shoulder.

We paddled against the current until we were out of the rushing water. Climbing up the bank we flopped onto the grass and sat there panting. A few days ago the flood was up over this stretch of paddock and now the grass was all flattened beneath us. Hamish lay on his back, staring at the sky.

'Mema, that was great. Creek-riding. Another notch on my belt.'

It was a foreign concept, this belt notching, but I was distracted by the way the hair on Hamish's chest formed whorls when it was wet. It wasn't dark, his chest hair, but it wasn't blond either. It was a light woody colour. I watched him while he watched the sky.

After a bit he sat up and stared back at me. Sitting there beneath his gaze my skin seemed to tighten.

'So, what else do you do around here, Mema?' His question came out slow, his voice soft.

I looked away from him, thinking about what Anja and I would do. Raising myself up, I wandered back to the creek to collect some rocks from the shallows. 'You've got to come close to the water,' I called.

Hamish got up and moved down the bank towards me.

'Painting-rocks,' I said and crouched in the shallows. I rubbed the ochre rock I'd found against a bigger, smoother rock until it started to make a paste. Once I had enough, I reached out my hand.

'Come on.' I motioned for him to come closer.

'Will it come off?'

'Yeah, silly, it washes off in the water.'

I reached out to his shoulder and drew a long line slowly down his arm.

'See?'

He looked down at my hand and then up at me.

'And then you do dots,' I said, my voice a bit raspy. I didn't know why I was whispering. Dipping my little finger in the paste, I pressed careful dots beside the brown line on his arm.

'There's even different colours.' Fishing around in the shallows, I handed him a dull-looking yellowish stone. 'I like the bright red ones best, though,' I said, holding up a darker one.

I rubbed my stone on the smooth rock till there was more paste and then reached up a hand to paint his face. Perched beside me in the shallows, he stayed motionless beneath my touch. Goosebumps broke out across his shoulders and he closed his eyes. Hamish had been clean-shaven when he washed up, but now the regrowth on his face was thick, and up close I could see every hair. I drew a line from the middle of his forehead straight down his nose and then dipped my finger in the paste again and painted a line horizontally across each cheek. Taking the yellow stone from him, I rubbed it into a paste and drew a yellow stripe beneath the red one on his cheeks, then dipped my little finger in again and pressed on a row of dots.

'There,' I said, and he opened his eyes. Against the rich ochre, his eyes seemed strangely bright. Intense and otherworldly.

'Now your turn,' he said, surprising me and dipping his finger into the paste.

I closed my eyes and he traced a line down my forehead, gently, as though I might break. Stopping to get more paste, he ran his finger down my nose, right under it till he touched my lip. He added dots and a few more stripes and then he said, 'Done.'

When I opened my eyes, his face was so close I was startled. He bent his head, searching for stones in the space between us. After a minute he glanced up and said, 'You look pretty, Mema. Like a warrior princess or something.'

A huntress, I thought, like my name. But I didn't say it out loud.

Mum didn't believe in mirrors, so there were none in the house. I always got a surprise when I was out somewhere and I stumbled on one. I was much darker than everyone else in my family. Dark skin, black hair. Seeing myself made me think about my dad. About how different he must have looked from the men that came before. Mum had told me he was a 'handsome beast', and that after him she stayed well away from beautiful men. He was gone by the time I was born, but Sophie told me

Mum didn't get out of bed for weeks. He was the last bloke she'd ever let stay the night, so I suppose in the scheme of things Hamish was getting an easy ride. I'd always felt I was pretty, and there was no one to tell me I wasn't, but I didn't know what to make of Hamish's words.

'Thanks,' I said, a little confused. 'You look pretty too.'

He looked at me but he didn't speak. The silence felt dense and odd. It hung there, building around us. I don't know why but I stood up and scrambled back to the grass.

'Shall we ride the creek again?' I asked him, feeling jittery. 'We have to go back to the tree to get our clothes either way.'

He watched me for a few seconds then nodded and slowly pulled himself up the bank.

We could have crossed the paddocks, it would have been quicker, but we wandered along the creek bank instead. There were trees and it was shady and cool. The sound of the water tinkled beside us, and we were quiet. I was thinking of Hamish, of how the air around him felt charged. I was wondering if it was him or me that made it that way.

Sometimes when I walk through the bush, I stop seeing where I am. I get so lost inside my head that I don't notice much around me. But it's not always like that. Sometimes it's the opposite and everything outside myself becomes heightened. Every tiny curled frond emerging, every raised root beneath my feet. The tiny beads of water gathering on leaves, gradually gaining weight until they fall. At those times, it is as though I can sense every drop of water hit the earth. Time slows, and instead of moving through the land, I am somehow just within it. The hum of the place starts up inside me. But that day with Hamish I was lost in thought and so I didn't see the snake until we were almost right upon it. I stopped mid-step and Hamish bumped into me from behind.

'What is it?' In the quiet his voice seemed to boom.

'Shhhh,' I whispered, holding a finger up to my lips. 'It's a snake.'

The python was curled neatly in a spiralled lump at my feet. We were virtually on top of it. I tried to step back but Hamish was right behind me.

'Where?' Hamish whispered, looking at the bank on the other side.

'Right here!' I pointed down at the ground in front of us. 'I didn't see it.'

'Shit!' he said, stepping back quickly. 'You nearly stood on it.'

'Yeah, but it's only a python.' I moved backwards too. 'And look, it's not moving. It hasn't even stirred.'

'You can still get an infection from a carpet-snake bite,' Hamish said, shuffling back another metre and staring at the python.

I knew a lot about snakes because Anja was obsessed by them. She'd been bitten plenty of times. 'I used to think pythons were completely harmless,' I said, studying the perfect spirals of the snake, 'until one tried to eat my cat.'

'I've heard stories about them eating full-grown pets,' Hamish said. 'Hard to tell if they are true.'

'I was sitting inside eating breakfast and I heard this terrible screaming sound. I thought the cat had caught a bird, even though I'd never heard a bird make a sound like that, and I ran outside to rescue it.' I paused, remembering. 'But when I got there I saw a python had my cat, had wrapped itself around her neck, and she was screaming, the air slowly squeezing out of her.'

'I don't really like cats,' he said from behind me. It seemed a cold thing to say, and I half-turned to look at his face. We hadn't washed the rock-paint off, and the ochre was drying, going pale in colour.

''Cause they kill the birds, right?'

'They're an environmental pest.' His eyes were still fixed on the snake. 'A menace.'

'Cats have instincts. They follow them. It's not their fault.'

Hamish's lips were pressed together, hard.

'When I was a girl, sometimes the farmers would drop strays off to me. Stray kittens, stray pups. Back when no one desexed their animals. I don't know how they knew I'd look after them. They'd just drive up in their utes and drop them out the window. Sometimes they didn't even say a word.'

'Bet your mum loved that.'

'Yeah, well, if we had too many we'd take them to the market and see if we could find someone who wanted them. Usually someone did.'

'Sounds like you ran your own animal shelter.'

'Not really, just sometimes.' I thought of Old Dog, of the muted slapping of her tail-wag, and wondering how much longer she would last. Crouching down to get a closer look at the snake, I tried to push the thought out of my mind. The snake was bright and shiny in the dappled light.

'Anja is crazy about snakes,' I said over my shoulder.

'Yeah?'

'She's always kept them as pets, all different sorts.'

Hamish stepped forward and out of the corner of my eye I could see him rub his collarbone the way he did when he was anxious.

'Her dad made her all these cages, but none of them were exactly tight, so they were always escaping. Sometimes when I was younger, I'd stay at her place and a snake would escape and I'd wake up in the middle of the night with it wrapped around my legs. It was a bit creepy.'

I never stayed up there anymore, but it wasn't because of the snakes. Anja's dad had gotten worse. You could never tell how he would be.

'That sounds … bizarre.'

'Yeah. I'd have to wake Anja up so she could unwind it.'

He looked sceptical, as if I was making up stories. Lots of things about Anja were hard to believe once you said them out loud. Like when she found a dead animal, she liked to skin it and dry the skins out in the sun. I guessed that was something it was best not to mention.

'Do you think this snake has just shed?' I asked, turning to look at Hamish. The orche paint was starting to crack.

'I'm not much of an expert on snakes.'

'You're an environmentalist, right?'

'I haven't done a lot of fieldwork.' He reached out and plucked a leaf from a tree, twisting it between his thumb and forefinger. 'I specialised in communication systems. You know, how they affect the dissemination of information? That type of thing. I don't come from a biological background.'

He looked so serious.

'Are you talking computers again, Hamish?'

I watched the leaf in his hand.

'No, not only computers. It's a bit complicated. What I studied back at uni was the way information spread, and which kinds of information are more likely to instigate change. It's not something I really use now I do the consulting.'

He tossed the leaf into the air and it fluttered to the ground. The snake stayed curled up tightly. There was no sign it even knew we were there.

'So, what did you do when the snake got your cat?' Hamish finally asked. 'Could you get it off?'

'It was awful really. I loved that cat—Isis—and knew she was dying, but all I could do was scream. I guess I went into shock. Mum was in town and there was no one around, and I couldn't make myself do anything. Anja must have heard me screaming from up on the mountain because she came tearing down.'

Even though it was a bad story I smiled when I thought of Anja bursting through the trees.

'It took her ages to unwrap the snake 'cause it was so tightly wound. It kept striking at her hand the whole time, sinking in its fangs. It was crazy. She got a lot of bites, but she got the snake off, put it in a pillow case. Isis was dead though.'

Hamish just looked at me, didn't say a word.

'Anja tried to resuscitate her. She'd done CPR at school.'

'She gave the cat CPR?'

'Yep, but it didn't work.'

I stood up from where I was crouched over the snake. 'Anja dug a hole and helped me bury Isis, and then we let the snake go out in the bush.'

Hamish raised his eyebrows, nodding. Behind all the pale ochre I couldn't really tell what he was thinking.

'Did she get an infection—from all the bites?'

'No, she was worried about me 'cause I'd screamed so much, so she came down the mountain and stayed with us. She looked after me, and I looked after her bites.' I moved away from the snake, closer to where he was standing. 'Kept them clean, put some cream on. She was fine.'

'She sounds like your knight in shining armour.'

'Yeah, I guess she is.' I hadn't thought about it that way. 'Anja is a lot of things.'

Pointing to a gap in the trees, he stepped towards it, back out into the sunshine of the paddocks.

'I vote we go around the snake,' he said, taking the lead.

I took one last look at the bright skin of the python and then I followed.

8.

When we got back to the secret tree neither of us felt like riding the creek again, so we grabbed our clothes and re-stashed the boards. The paddock walk was hot and Hamish had turned a little pink.

'I think you're sunburnt,' I said and touched his shoulder.

'Probably.' He looked down at his body. 'It doesn't take much.'

'We should have smothered you in mud.'

'What?'

'Sun protection.' I grinned. 'You'll probably get stripy suntan marks around the face-paint.'

'Sunburn marks, you mean.' He touched his fingers to his face. 'I hope not.'

'You could jump in the creek and wash it off,' I said, tilting my head towards the water.

Hamish looked at the creek for a few seconds. 'Maybe I'd rather have a shower, if that's okay. But you jump in if you want.'

I waded back into the creek, the water inching up my thighs. It was wider here, and the flow was gentle where I was. More like a lazy river than a tumbling creek. Facing the current, I closed my eyes and let my hands drop so they were hanging in the flow. There were all different ways I liked getting into the water. Sometimes fast, diving straight under, so my whole body tingled in shock, and sometimes slow, so that by the time I was immersed my body could hardly tell itself from the water. I waded out real slow and let the water flow up around me. When it was deep and it hardly felt cold, I ducked under and pushed against the current. My hair flowed out behind me, the water tugging at my plait. I resurfaced and pulled the elastic off the end, unravelling my hair and going back under. Staying under as long as my breath would hold, I didn't burst up for air, but drifted to the surface. I liked to imagine I could breathe under water.

I went under again and this time my breath held longer. When I came up I could hear someone calling my name from the other side of the bank. I looked up, brushing the water from my eyes. It was Billy.

'Hey, Mema,' he said, lifting up his council shirt and wiping the sweat from his face.

'Hey.'

Billy looked from me to Hamish, staring hard, and Hamish lifted his arm in acknowledgement.

'What you doing?' Billy called out, though I guess it must have been obvious.

He was a good few metres away, so it was hard for me to hear. I didn't want to swim closer to him 'cause the current in the middle was stronger.

'Just having a swim.'

'Who's the guy?' He motioned to Hamish with his head.

'That's Hamish.'

'I never seen him before.'

From what I knew of him, Billy was alright, but he wasn't the type to beat around the bush.

'He's not from around here.' I shrugged. It was hard to explain about Hamish.

Billy looked hot, and I wondered if he wanted a swim. I didn't know if I should ask him.

'What you doing here?' I asked instead, thinking he must be working somewhere nearby.

'Tree came down in the rain. Blocked off Old Gordon's driveway.' He kept looking across at Hamish while he talked. 'He can't get out. Asked me to chop it up.'

'The creek's still over the bridge here.' I squeezed the water from my hair. 'Did many trees come down?'

'A few about the place.'

'Any damage?'

'Nah, not really.' He peered at me intently. 'What you got on your face?'

I realised I hadn't rubbed the paint off yet.

'It's just some ochre, you know?' I splashed water up to my face, trying to rub it off. 'Painting-rocks.'

Billy didn't say anything, just watched me. It was making me feel funny, the way he stared. My nipples tightened beneath my shirt and I hoped he didn't notice. I crossed my arms over my chest.

'Well,' he looked at Hamish one more time, 'I guess I'd better get back.'

Turning around, Billy headed off across the paddock. He must have seen us from a mile away and come to check us out. My cheeks were hot and I dipped down one more time, scrubbing my face underwater. Since Billy had asked me out, seeing him got under my skin. I didn't know quite what it was, but something about him made me feel more alert, sensitised. I guess I was conscious of being watched in a way I wasn't used to.

I swam back to the bank and stepped up on the grass.

'Billy,' I said, though Hamish hadn't asked.

He didn't reply but looked across the paddock to where Billy had disappeared.

'You think if I swam across now, he'd give me a lift into town?'

I knew Hamish didn't like being stuck with us but I suppose I'd expected him to wait for the water to go down, 'cause when he said that my stomach dropped.

'Probably,' I said, looking at the ground.

He was silent a minute, weighing up his options. 'But if I stay one more night you'll drive me in tomorrow?'

'Yep, we'd be going in anyway to get supplies.'

'Your mum doesn't mind, does she? She doesn't seem to like me much.'

I didn't know what to say about Mum. 'She's okay. You know, she's just … like that.'

He thought for a minute longer, still deliberating.

'Okay.' He finally nodded at me. 'One more night.'

I smiled and pulled my skirt off the tree, swinging it over my arm. I didn't want him to disappear just like that.

'Come on, flood guy, let's head back.' It was hard to hide my happiness, though something told me I should. He stood up beside me and we wandered back towards the house. The grass was springy beneath my feet. I marvelled at how flattened it got in a flood but how quickly it righted itself. Everything stretching out towards the sun.

'That guy Billy likes you, Mema.' Hamish nudged his arm against my shoulder. 'He thinks you're hot.'

I felt myself go red. No one I knew used that word. *Hot.* It sounded odd, hanging in the air between us. I thought of how he'd described Anja yesterday—*built like a thoroughbred*— appraising her like horseflesh at a market. There was something about it that wasn't quite right.

'Mema?'

'He asked me out a little while back.' I couldn't tell him about the chook joke.

'Where would you go around here on a date?' He gazed across the open paddocks with their smattering of trees.

'You haven't been into town yet,' I said. 'There's a pub and stuff. Couple of shops. Or—I don't know—you could go further afield, go out to the movies.'

'Did you go out with him?'

It sounded offhand but I could feel him waiting for my answer.

I looked at the ground. 'Nah.' I wasn't sure how to express it. 'He isn't my type.'

'What's your type, Mema?'

Up until that point I'd had no type. Hamish was glancing at me sideways and I wondered if he was teasing me.

'I don't really …' I could feel my face getting hotter, '… do boys.'

He looked startled. 'Girls?'

I shook my head. 'No, just not anyone really.'

'Oh.' He glanced away from my face.

We walked for a bit in silence.

'You've never done it? Not even once?'

I shook my head. I guessed it might seem odd—I wasn't a child, after all.

'How many times have you?'

'I don't know, Mema. Too many to count. I'm a guy.'

'How many different girls?'

Hamish shrugged. 'I don't know. I don't remember, exactly.'

My mind flashed with visions of unknown women, all different but somehow the same. Unmemorable. 'How could you not remember them?'

'Lots of guys wouldn't remember everyone they've slept with. Ask young Billy next time, he'll tell you.'

This was hard to comprehend, but with all the things I'd

been told about men, I suppose I shouldn't have been surprised.
I stored that information deep within me, best brought out and
examined at another time.

'But you're still pretty young, Mema,' Hamish mused,
looking at me again. 'I forget, 'cause you're a bit …'

My whole body seemed to lean towards him, listening for the
next word.

'Unusual,' he said finally.

'You think I'm weird?' I guess I was insulted.

'No, not weird, a bit different from other women your age,
maybe.'

'Right.' I wasn't sure where to put that sentence. He'd said it
once before, but this time I didn't know where to store it.

'I really like you, Mema, don't get me wrong.' He leaned
towards me, nudging me again with his shoulder. 'You saved
my life, remember. You're *my* knight in shining armour.'

I had to smile. 'We already worked that out. A man for a calf.
We're even.'

'If you say so.'

My house appeared in the distance, shimmering in the sun. It
was always peculiar seeing it from a distance when usually you
were inside. I wondered if Mum had finished in the shed, if
she'd be pottering around making lunch. This far away the house
looked gracious, like a homestead, but when you got up close
you could see the wear and tear. I had always loved it, filled with
the familiar, but it was different imagining it through Hamish's
eyes. So many things were. I felt suddenly self-conscious, and

even though I was still damp I stopped a minute to put on my skirt. Hamish kept walking.

'Your foot doesn't stop you,' he called back. 'It's pretty amazing.'

'I guess.' I flicked my wet hair back over my shoulder. 'I've got special boots and everything, you know, for walking in town, but I never seem to need them around here.'

Maybe it was because I'd been walking this land for so long, but I always felt it accommodated me. That there was a way to walk through it without being off balance, that the land somehow came to my aid—shored up all my weak points. In town I became clumsy, as though all the straight lines and pavements tripped me up. The world became even, no undulations, and I became off centre.

Mum was still in the shed when we went inside and I gave Hamish a towel for the shower. The clothes he arrived in were so covered in birth gunk they'd gone mouldy in the rain. In any case, the jumper was a write-off from the beginning. He was looking pretty scrappy, and I figured I should try to find him something better to wear, now the lights were back on and I could have a proper look. Having four brothers, you'd think we'd have a few old things lying around, but the truth was, I don't think they ever had much.

I was kneeling on the floor of the storeroom, peering into some of the bottom drawers, searching, when I heard steps behind me.

'Mema?' It was Hamish.

I turned around. He'd had the quickest shower on earth.

'I think I need your help.'

I grabbed an old pair of board shorts and a shirt and scrambled up, looking for clues on his face.

'With what?'

'Can you come and see?'

I followed him into the bathroom and he pointed at the shower recess. There were a couple of cane toads in the corner.

'Yeah, those guys are always there.'

'What do you mean?'

'They like it. The wetness.' I hadn't tied up my hair yet, and as I moved it kept flopping forward across my shoulders. It was slippery, my hair, that's why I liked to keep it plaited. 'I don't even know how they get in here. They're not supposed to be able to, but I think they jump up the stairs.'

'What should I do with them?' he asked me. 'Have you got something to kill them with?'

Even though I knew everyone hates cane toads, I still felt myself suck in a breath.

'We don't ever kill them,' I said. 'But I'll get the broom and move them if they bother you.'

He shifted on his feet and I could tell he was disturbed.

'Mema, they're cane toads. You have to kill them.' In the closeness of the bathroom I could see his jaw clenching. 'Don't you have a plastic bag? I'll put them in the freezer. They won't feel a thing.'

'No.'

I'd been showering with those toads for years. They weren't going in the freezer.

'Cats are bad, Mema, but cane toads are the worst.' I could feel his frustration. 'Anyway, you can't just leave them in the shower.'

'They'll keep out of your way.'

We stood there locked in an awful silence, staring into the shower. The cane toads seemed to know they were under scrutiny, 'cause they pressed further into the corner, flattening themselves on the tiles.

'Look,' I broke the silence, 'I know cane toads are bad and everyone kills them. It's a sport around here—cane-toad hockey, cane-toad golf, cane-toad musters—but they're still animals, Hamish. It's not like they introduced themselves.'

'You can't argue for a cane toad's life,' Hamish said. 'They eat everything, and then the things that eat them die from their poison. They are wiping out whole species at an incredible rate.'

I knew all that. There was no way you could grow up around here and not know all about the history of cane toads, home-schooled or not.

'You're not putting them in the freezer.'

Anja's dad kept a piece of old pipe handy at all times especially for eradicating toads. They were exceptionally hard to kill. I'd seen him bludgeon them for ten minutes at a time and then watched them try to hop away. Something about the violence of it always made me feel ill.

When I was small Anja and I used to catch tadpoles in the creek and watch them grow their legs and drop their tails. Sometimes they turned into little brown frogs, and other times they turned into little brown toads, but the thing was—you couldn't tell the difference when they were tadpoles. We'd spend weeks tending them and watching them grow only to find we'd raised the enemy. And then we'd be left with the sticky question of what to do with our babies once they'd grown. We couldn't toss them onto the road to get squashed, or put them in the freezer to die slowly. We'd grown attached. So in the end we'd sneak off quietly and let them go. Before anyone could stop us.

Looking at Hamish I could tell none of that was going to make sense to him. His face was closed, stern. The bathroom felt small, like there wasn't room for both of us.

'I came across a woman standing on the bridge once, leaning over the rail,' I said, feeling that sudden helplessness of misunderstanding rising up inside me. 'She was weeping. She used to live in a caravan under one of the big trees. I stopped and asked her what was wrong, and she pointed down at the water.'

Hamish didn't speak.

'She'd found a rat's nest filled with little pink babies and she'd thrown them into the water. But she couldn't leave. She just stood there crying. You could see their little bodies in the shallows, drowned and still.'

Staring at the cane toads, Hamish lifted his arm and ran his hand across the top of his head. His elbow bumped against my arm, and he stepped a little away from me.

'She was probably just having a shit day.'

'Maybe,' I answered, but I didn't really think so.

Hamish pressed his hand against the back of his neck and then ran it forward, over his head and down across his eyes. He wouldn't look at me. I watched his hands, admiring their shape. If you looked too long at something it was hard not to ponder its uses. I started thinking about what it might feel like if he swept his hands across my head and down against my eyes. I'd never imagined that before, not with anybody's hands. He pressed his fingers against his eyes and made a low sound. Not a word, more a hiss.

'Alright.' He turned and looked at me finally. 'No cane-toad killing today. But I'm not showering with the buggers. You've got to get them out.'

I handed him the clothes I'd been clutching and went to get the broom. It was a pretty inelegant business, sweeping toads. They rolled right over onto their backs, legs dangling in the air, soft pale bellies exposed. After a bit of jiggling around they'd right themselves and then try to jump away into the corners, but I was used to that. A couple of brushes and they were gone. Swept out onto the grass. But I knew they'd be back.

'It's not much of a victory, Mema,' Hamish said quietly, looking down at the floor.

I leaned on the broom a second, watching his shuttered face.

'I'm not playing to win,' I said finally, thinking of all the squashed toads on the road. I didn't think I was playing at all.

9.

While Hamish was in the shower I had a scramble around in the fridge to see if there was enough stuff to make us all sandwiches. The stand-off about the cane toads had left me uneasy. I guess I was looking for a distraction.

When Mum got working in the shed, sometimes she forgot to eat, so I usually tried to take her out something. The bread was a bit stale. I popped it in the toaster to freshen it up. Found some tomatoes, some cheese, picked a few lettuce leaves from the garden. That'd have to do. I wondered about what we could make for dinner. We'd been trapped in for a few days now and our supplies were getting low. I'd have to investigate what was at the back of the pantry. No one in my house was too good at cleaning things out, so sticking your hand into the depths of the cupboard was a bit of a lucky dip. Sometimes you might come out with something—a laksa paste and some rice stick noodles or a nice-looking tomato pasta sauce that wasn't out of date. Anything was possible. Shopping was a haphazard activity for us, not a regular one, so it was a bit hard to keep track.

Out at the shed Mum was spanning the whirling pot in her arms, its final shape solidifying. I stood on the threshold with the sandwich, watching her, appreciating how she knew the precise moment when it was ready. When I threw pots I was always unsure. Could they use a little more? Should they be a little thinner? Thicker perhaps? It was all indecision, but for Mum there was a precise moment. I watched her hands waiting for the moment. It wasn't anything she could describe in words, though I'd asked her many times. Maybe it was the simple knowledge of when something was done that made her the master and me the novice.

When the pot was finished she glanced up at me, smiling at the sandwich.

'Thanks, Mema.' She always emerged from throwing pots softer than when she went in, like it offered her some private solace. 'You're such a good girl.'

'There's not much left in the fridge,' I said. 'So don't get too excited.'

She took one last look at her giant creation and then moved across to wash her hands in the sink.

'You go down to the creek and do some ochre painting?'

I could see her checking out my face. I'd tried to wash it off in the water, but I guess it needed a good scrub with soap.

'Yeah, Hamish was getting stir-crazy. He started talking about *computers*.' I didn't want her to know we'd gone creek-riding.

'He'll be gone tomorrow.' She reached out and took the plate. 'Back into the world. He'll be happy.'

'He thinks you don't like him.'

I didn't mean to say it, but suddenly it was out of my mouth. My mum studied me a moment and then took a bite of the sandwich, chewing it slowly.

'He's alright,' she said finally. 'Just one of those guys, Mema.'

I wondered what exactly she meant but I didn't feel like asking. She took another bite of her sandwich and looked across the paddocks. In the photos from when I was little, there was only the faintest hint of the furrows that now lined my mother's face. I studied them, wondering how she could have got so lined in such a short time. Maybe that's how time worked—left you alone for years and then hit you with a big bang. It didn't seem to bother her. I'd never even caught her glancing at her reflection in the glass. She only seemed to see herself in terms of her function. Always in the midst of some action. She never sat still.

'You didn't make me kill the tadpoles, even when they turned out to be toads.' I said. 'I know you could have.'

She put the last bite of the sandwich in her mouth, chewing for a bit.

'You played with those things for hours. You loved them.' Mum always knew exactly what I was talking about. I never had to explain. 'You did the same with snails and slugs. You and Anja. How could I tell you which things were okay to love?'

I smiled, thinking of the snails. How their eyes would tentatively glide out on the ends of those strange tentacles. How slow and gentle they always seemed. The trail of silver they left in their wake.

'We're all weeds here, Mema.' She handed me back the plate. 'We're all just weeds.'

When I got back inside, Hamish was on the phone. I thought I'd better give him some privacy so I went into my room. One of the dads used to go to the auctions and buy up old furniture. It meant that all the rooms in the house had these giant old beds, dark and wooden. Mine was really pretty, with carvings on the corners, but it wasn't the most comfortable. It was missing some slats, and the mattress didn't seem to hold its shape anymore. I'd slept in it ever since I could remember, but it was only starting to bother me now. Even though I hadn't grown an inch since I was twelve, the bed seemed suddenly too slack and small. Lately my insomnia had got so bad that when I lay down on it my heart started to race, like it was preparing for the stress of not sleeping.

I had a funny bunch of things in my room—collections of sticks, odd shapes, pieces of wood that I'd picked out as having a pleasing form, stones of all varieties, mainly from the creek. They were all so familiar, but with Hamish here it made me look at them anew. It would be hard to explain what it was about the stones that Anja and I prized. They had to feel a specific way in the hand. They had to be a certain weight, have a certain texture. We didn't speak about it, we just knew. Then there was my nest collection. Nests were my favourite things. I didn't steal them from the birds. These were ones that had fallen out of the trees. I would come across them, perfectly formed, made from all manner of things—grass, sticks, leaves, moss. Sometimes their outsides would be made of long strips of grass, precisely worked into a hollowed-out circle, and the inside would be lined with moss. Such acts of devotion, such tenderness. I liked to bring them inside and sit them on my desk. They would start out immaculate, not a strand out of place, but eventually over time they would disintegrate. I liked that too. Liked to watch them decay. It was the world in motion.

I had a few old toys. Things I'd been given and didn't know how to throw away. A pile of books beside my bed, stories I was part way through. And a big rack of clothes. Mum sewed, and I wasn't too bad with the Singer either. We'd always made our own clothes. Well, we didn't make our own undies or anything. Still went to the shops for those. Mum had a whole storeroom of fabrics inherited from her grandma, plus lots of other pieces she'd picked up along the way. It was hard to give away clothes you'd made with your own hands, so I had a stack of them hanging on my rack. I didn't have a wardrobe. They just hung on a piece of dowel, against one of the walls. It was kind of nice looking at them, seeing how many outfits we'd made, how bright and pretty they all were, although there were plenty of things I never wore.

I wondered what Hamish would think of my nests. I wondered if he'd ever come into my room and see them. Tomorrow he'd be gone. Back into the world. I started thinking about what it might be like out there. What *did* the world have to offer?

* * *

I made old-fashioned French toast for dinner, which was funny 'cause it was usually a breakfast thing, but we didn't have much else. Around Mum, Hamish was quiet again. Between the two of them I was beginning to feel stifled. While we ate, I half wished Anja or Sophie would arrive and bring back a bit of chaos. Throw Rory into the mix.

The ratbag cat always seemed to sense when things were about to go awry, and he would start acting up. His name was Thor, on account of his tough exterior. He was very handsome, in the way some cats are—symmetrical markings and giant soulful eyes—but he couldn't abide much affection. Sometimes he let me touch him, but only if I stayed an arm's length away, reaching out with the tips of my fingers. He'd always been odd, but since Isis was strangled by the snake he'd got worse. Jumpy and highly strung, but attention-seeking too. Sometimes if we were all busy he'd sit behind the stereo and knock the CDs from the sideboard to the ground, one by one. Eyeing us off to see what we'd do. It drove Mum crazy 'cause the music was precious to her. Privately, I wondered if that was why he did it.

He was stalking around in the background, tail swinging from side to side. Mischief on his mind. While I was washing the dishes he jumped up onto the table, catching Mum and Hamish by surprise. My hands were all soapy, otherwise I would have reached over and given him a stroke. He walked towards Hamish, looking purposeful.

'What's he up to?' Mum asked no one in particular, narrowing her eyes.

Hamish tapped his fingers on the table and Thor came closer. The cat—my unfriendly, temperamental cat—leaned his head down and smooched it across Hamish's fingers.

'No way.' I wiped my hands on the tea towel.

'What?' Hamish scratched Thor behind the ears.

The cat started sliding the length of its body against the back of Hamish's hand. I'd never seen him behave like that, except occasionally with the dog. Those two were great pals. Hamish moved his hand away, like patting the cat wasn't his idea of fun.

'He's never affectionate with anyone. I've been trying for years to get a cuddle out of him.'

'He's a ratbag,' Mum said, on the verge of a smile.

'He's really trying to mess with my head.' I moved towards the table.

'I don't even like cats.' Hamish held his hands up out of reach.

'He's probably trying to mess with your head too, then,' Mum said, chuckling a little. 'What a rascal.'

Then Hamish leaned back away from the table and we watched the cat reach out a paw and place it on his chest. Mum laughed then, almost snorted. 'All the years Mema's been loving you, and now you throw yourself at a stranger,' she said to the cat, shaking her head.

Thor put his other paw up and started doing that pawing thing they do—claw in, claw out—right on the top of Hamish's chest. I couldn't believe it. I just stood there and stared.

'Where's your dignity, Thor?' I finally asked, laughter creeping into my voice. Thor looked ridiculous, but Hamish was so still and stiff and shocked, his response seemed comical too.

'Okay, that's enough,' Hamish said, pushing his chair back further out of Thor's reach.

I laughed aloud then, but I stretched out and smoothed my hand across the cat's head. He sat there looking insulted. You see something new every day, I guess.

'Mema, you reckon you could show me how you make a pot?' Hamish asked and I knew he wanted to get out of the kitchen.

The shed was set back a little way from the house, off to the side. It used to be a garage but we'd never used it for that. Nowadays, it was just three rickety wooden walls and a tin roof, the front wide open to the elements. The walls slanted at slightly strange angles, making the whole thing seem like it might fall over, but even though it looked precarious, it was never going to tumble down. It was so overgrown with vines, thick, wooded things, they'd become its structure. Mum said it would outlast the lot of us.

It was evening by then, but it stayed light for so long in summer you could still see when you were inside. The shed was neater than you'd expect, all Mum's pottery stacked on shelves in varying states of completion.

'Wow.' Hamish looked around. 'This is cool.'

'Yeah.'

The house could be in complete disarray, but Mum kept the shed well organised. She needed things to be ordered to be able to work.

Hamish put his hands in his pockets, as though he was afraid he might knock something over. 'These are amazing.'

'Specially when you consider what they began as.'

'What?'

'Lumps of dirt, you know?'

I pointed out my little shelf, the place I stored the cups and things I'd made for the market.

'You did these ones?' He gingerly picked up a mug. It was a deep-blue colour, the firing leaving some darker flecks.

'They're fairly hardy,' I said, 'cause he was handling it so delicately. 'You'd have to drop it on the ground for it to break.'

He turned the mug around and inspected its speckled surface.

'They're really pretty, Mema,' he said, placing the mug carefully back on the shelf. 'If I had any cash I'd buy some.'

'Yeah?'

I didn't see that was much of a compliment, but I knew what he meant. He had lost everything in the flood. Not a cent on him.

'Maybe you'll come to the market one day.'

'Maybe. I'll be around for a bit. Week or so, at least.'

I didn't realise he'd be staying longer. Something inside me surged. Excitement maybe. It was disconcerting. I turned to switch the lamp on.

'Maybe we can hang out.' He smiled sideways, just outside the rim of light. 'I don't know … do whatever you do around here?'

He said these words easily, as though they cost him nothing, but I couldn't help feeling that there was some kind of invitation in them. My heartbeat clattered around inside my chest. I wasn't sure if I could reply. I just nodded and started setting up the wheel.

The lamp was one of those old metal things, on a big stand but plugged in at the wall. It created a circle of light around the pottery wheel and made me feel like I was in a spotlight, up on stage. Hamish was watching me so carefully my heart wouldn't slow. At least the process of throwing a pot was routine enough that I could do it with my mind distracted. I leaned down and sawed off a chunk of clay with the string then I got the wheel turning.

The wheel was old-style, the top plate attached to a heavy flywheel down the bottom that I kicked with my feet. I built up momentum and then it would go on its own for a bit. The whole thing was a stop–start process. Kick-work, kick-work. It had its own tempo. The flywheel made a soft, rhythmic clunking sound that, under the circumstances, I found quite soothing.

'So it spins just by you pushing that bottom wheel?' Hamish asked, squatting down to see how the motion worked. 'You don't use any other energy?'

'Nope. It's the momentum. Centrifugal force … whatever that is.' Mum had described it all many times, but sometimes it felt like the explanations got in the way of the pleasure.

'What a great machine,' he said, staring up at me from where he crouched. 'So simple.'

I wasn't usually worried about my wonky foot, but it felt like Hamish was peeping beneath my skirt, checking out the workings of my legs.

'Yeah, I guess.'

I banged the clay down onto the plate, giving it a couple of thumps to make sure it was solid.

'You have to centre it,' I said, looking across at Hamish, just out of the rim of light. 'You feel with your thumb until you find the exact place where there's no friction. That's the centre.'

It was interesting to think about what exactly the sensation of discovering the centre was. That lack of push or pull. I was seeking that small nub around which everything turned, measuring it with the waxy pad of my thumb. When I had the centre, I pressed down quickly, almost to the bottom, and that was the inside of the pot.

'It doesn't look too hard.'

I could sense him shift as though adjusting his view. 'You can have a go in a sec.' I wanted to get out of the light, but I kept on dipping my hands into the water bowl and wetting the clay as it turned, the wheel still bumping along gently beneath me.

After all the pots I'd made, it still felt a little magical how quickly the forms emerged. I held my hands like a clamp around the spinning lump, fingers on the inside, heels of my palms against the outer surface—moving them only the tiniest bit— and it all turned beneath my touch, taking shape. I didn't try anything fancy, just a simple round pot.

'That was ... fast,' Hamish said, standing back up.

I smiled and ran the string beneath the clay, so it wouldn't stick to the base, then stood and lifted it onto the drying shelf. All the unwanted clattering that had been going on inside me had settled with the making of the pot. It had ironed out my creases and I remained there—in the centre of everything—calmed and peaceful.

'Okay, your go.' I turned and sliced off some clay for him from the slab on the shelf. He sat down on the stool, getting his bearings and I banged the clay down on the top plate, shaping it into a circle, ready for him to begin.

'So, I get it started with my foot, and then it should run by itself for a little bit?'

'That's right. And when it loses momentum you start it again.'

He looked uncertain but he gave it a go. The wheel began its gentle clanking, the clay spinning unevenly on the plate. Hamish put his hands down gently.

'Feel for the centre,' I told him, nodding my head.

'The place with no friction?'

'Feel with your thumb.'

'I don't feel anything. It all feels the same.'

'There's no rush, just keep searching.'

This time Hamish was inside the circle of light and I was on the perimeter. I liked it much better that way. I could watch him without him watching me. He touched the clay lightly with the tips of his fingers, moving his hands carefully out to the edge. Pottery is something you do with your hands, you can't think about it too much. Hamish was concentrating so hard I could see he was struggling.

'Close your eyes,' I said, and then I walked around to stand behind him. 'Feel the clay moving against your fingers. That's it.'

The wheel was slowing so I reached around him with my foot and pushed against it a few times, getting the momentum going again. He sat still on the stool, eyes closed, fingers poised on the top of the spinning mound, as though waiting for some inexplicable revelation. Leaning down, I put my hand over his. His skin felt warm against my fingertips.

'Okay, here on the outside you can feel the push-pull.'

He nodded slowly, his head tilted slightly to the side. I moved his hand across the clay towards the centre. 'And feel, it gets less and less?'

He shifted a little on the stool and my breasts swayed against his back.

'Yes, I feel that.' His voice was low.

'When you feel nothing, press in.' I was whispering, my mouth close to his ear, the feel of his back against me.

'Now?' He sounded confused.

'Go! Press!'

Hamish hesitated, so I pushed his thumb down with my own, and just like that the clay gave way. A bit wobbly, but okay for a first try. He froze then, like he didn't know what to do next, but if he didn't start working it he'd lose the momentum. I reached my other hand around to steer him, pushing on the top of his fingers. The clay spun beneath our hands, the mud pushing up between his fingers and through mine. We were only throwing a pot but in those few seconds it seemed like something larger. It was an odd feeling, like we were merging into one. The clay was taking shape and I felt strangely triumphant.

'Good, you've got it,' I whispered. 'You've just got to mould it into something more elegant.'

Slowly, I straightened up, moving my hands away.

'Better open your eyes now,' I said, and I don't know why but I laughed a little. He turned to me and under the bright light I could see the colour on his neck was high. I stood still, mud sticky between my fingers, pinned beneath his gaze.

'Mema,' he said softly, 'that was a little bit *Ghost*-esque.'

There was a fierceness about his gaze. I felt he was calling me on something but I didn't know quite what.

'Ghost-esque?' I looked at the clay. It was sagging slightly sideways, and I restrained myself from rescuing it. 'Don't stop now,' I said, 'you've almost got it.'

He turned back around, touching the sides of the half-made pot with careful fingers but the wheel was slowing again.

'Give the wheel another push.' He looked like he'd had enough but I didn't want him to give up yet. 'Come on, you may as well finish it.'

I moved to the side so I could see him properly, but whatever impetus he'd had with the pot was gone.

'Have you even seen the movie *Ghost*, Mema?' he asked, and the clay sagged and collapsed in his hands. 'Demi Moore? Patrick Swayze?'

'Nope.' I didn't have a clue what he was talking about. We've never really had a working TV.

He shook his head. 'I guess it figures.'

'Why?'

'It's got this opening scene. A sex scene. Involving clay.' He said this like an accusation.

'A sex scene?'

He was silent, watching me. I couldn't help remembering the feel of my breasts pressed up against his back, his fingers in mine. My skin tingled just thinking about it. I was in over my head.

'Were they ghosts—I mean—in the sex scene?' I spluttered out.

'No … that came later.' Hamish sighed then, turning away, his shoulders sagging a little. 'It doesn't matter. It's a shithouse movie.'

He'd stared at me so hard. I couldn't help wondering what he saw.

'I don't believe in ghosts.' My voice trembled.

'No, neither do I.'

Hamish sat on the stool for a second staring at the squashed pile of clay. 'Things are not always how they seem,' he said quietly, almost to himself.

I didn't need convincing. I watched Hamish under the spotlight in the shed, his face illuminated and stark, his body still. And in that moment he was more of a stranger than he had ever been.

10.

That night, after I'd turned off all the lights and gone to bed, I lay awake thinking about the clattering of my heartbeat in Hamish's presence, and as soon as I remembered it, it started up again. It was a sensation I was unfamiliar with. I could hear the throb of my pulse in my ears and felt sure if I wasn't holed up in the dark I'd have been able to see the rhythm of my heart's quick beat through the skin of my chest. I held my fingers between my breasts, pressing against that pounding place, but it didn't slow. A sort of tightness built around my heart that seemed to rise up and squeeze at my throat. The feeling was alarming and exhilarating at the same time.

I suppose I knew deep down that it was some kind of desire, but it was disconcerting that it should rise in me then. And how to ignore something that took such a physical hold? In bed, my fingers pressed hard against my racing heart, I wondered what could be done. If my body was wanting, I knew I could soothe it. I had touched myself that way since I was small. But I'd always concentrated on the swelling feel of it. My own body and how it responded. In my mind, I'd never needed the intrusion of another person. I didn't want to think of Hamish. I didn't want to feed that hungry thing inside me. I didn't want it to grow.

I thought of diving into the cool waters of the creek, of its icy softness engulfing me, of being enveloped in its velvet touch. I imagined the creek as endless, shimmering, the water stretching out before me like a silver ribbon. I could drift without air forever, sliding with the current. Beneath the surface, I was free.

Eventually my body softened and I got to thinking about my mum, and Sophie, and all that had happened before me. It was troubling to come at the end of a family. All the life and colour and drama that had gone before me could only be passed to me in stories, and what if no one was talking? I imagined them instead— the fathers before mine, how one replaced another. All the babies growing like weeds, wild and untended. My mum moving from man to man, like they were ice-cream flavours, and Sophie— older and wiser—tending us all as best as she could. Or that's how it sat in my head. From the snippets of things said, and unsaid, I had constructed a picture of my family before me and then I'd run with it, wherever the fancy took me.

Sometimes I liked to imagine my mum, crazy in love with babies, unable to stop having them. Lost in that world of gurgles and half-smiles, wind and burping, feeding from the breast. Freshly washed white nappies flapping on the line, luminous and clean. Caught in a cycle of renewal, as though every time she gave birth she could start over. As though every child was a clean slate, perfect and unsullied. And each time she was new too. I imagined her tucking us into the folds of her, keeping us close, until we were so big we toddled right off, and then she'd start again. And all the while, the community she'd helped to build dissolving around her, disenchantment seeping in. I wondered when she noticed almost everyone had gone.

But when I thought of the fathers, it was a whole different story. I imagined them washed up like survivors of a shipwreck, lost and beaten by the waves, my mother some kind of beacon, a lighthouse. And for a while they'd circle her, filled with wanting. And there was something she gave them, some indefinable need fulfilled in her embrace. It would be peaceful for a while. The lull of a pregnancy. But gradually the fathers healed and heard the calling of the world. That tantalising hum of possibility that there was something else out there, something they were missing. At first they ignored it, staring into their new baby's mysterious eyes, watching the infant breaths rise and fall, but eventually the hum got louder and louder until they could not shut it out, and before long, like the rest, they would be gone. I imagined them one by one—big bodied and strong—awkward in our small house surrounded by babies.

But I never knew if it was true.

And sometimes I'd think of Sophie, the only girl for so long. Pretty with her curls and pink cheeks, done up like a doll in Mum's wild homemade dresses, unaware that she was to be overrun by the rest of us, her childhood swallowed by a flood of brothers and then me. It was hard to imagine Sophie as a baby. I'd always known her as defiantly grown-up. But when I really tried, when I focused my mind, I could see her—gentle and open, tiny and beloved, the first one to suckle at my mother's breast.

My brothers were becoming like shadows. Figures that clung on the fringes of my mind—there, but always slightly out of view. I pictured Sunny's face, trying to recollect the details. The way his front teeth overlapped, just slightly, and how his eyes squeezed shut to almost nothing when he smiled. The last time he'd come home, he'd only stayed for a day, and most of that he'd spent out hunting for his friends. I thought, and not for the first time, about how my brothers so easily abandoned me. Took off without a thought. About how little they held me in their minds. And my heart tightened in a different way, sad and pained, and I pressed my fingers hard between my ribs, hard enough to hurt. There was a soft spot there, a hollow, ever so slight, and when I pushed it I could feel all my hurts rising. In a strange way, it soothed me. Lying there in the dark, pressing into my pain, I wondered about the hum of the world outside and why it didn't seem to call out to me.

I thought again of Mum and Sophie and how they'd stayed, and it struck me then that Sophie might have taken up with her fella as a kind of escape, and perhaps that's what all the different fathers were about too.

And maybe I was just like Mum and Sophie—looking for escape in a shipwrecked man, my body flinging me in its own clumsy way towards him. And secretly, right down in the depths of me, I wondered whether that would really be so bad.

* * *

I'd already let out the chickens, fed the cat and Old Dog, been out to check on Bessie and the calf, and had a quiet cup of tea before Hamish began to rouse himself on the couch. Mum had headed out to the shed early, before the heat set in.

He woke gradually, opening his eyes and gazing at the ceiling for a bit, unaware of me watching him from where I sat at the kitchen table. I stayed as still as possible, prolonging those undisturbed moments, wondering about his morning thoughts. The thoughts I had on waking were often the most peculiar I had all day. When Anja slept over, sometimes we'd lie in bed in the mornings and whisper our waking thoughts across the pillows. We were both early risers, and in the half-light this seemed a natural thing to do. And even if you shared the weirdest thought you could possibly imagine with Anja, she'd come up with something weirder. It was a comforting quality in a friend. Anja hadn't been back since the rain-running. I wondered if she was staying away on purpose.

Hamish turned towards me, still looking sleepy. There were crease marks from where the couch pressed into his face. He rubbed his hand across his eyes and mumbled, 'You're already up.'

He was right. I'd been up for ages.

'You want a tea?' I asked, tapping my fingers against my cup. I felt suddenly impatient but I wasn't sure why.

He looked around the room before answering me, as though it was taking him a while to remember where he was.

'Sure,' he said, and I could feel an awareness of his leaving, tumbling into the space around us.

'Where's your mum?'

'She went out to the shed to do some work before she takes you into town.'

I stood up and lit the stove for the kettle. There were only a couple of black teabags left, but I knew we'd get some more in town later so I didn't feel bad using them.

'You're not going to take me?'

'I don't drive,' I said, turning back to study his face. 'I never learned.'

He looked at me then, like he was finally taking in my whole form. 'It's not your foot?'

'What?' It was the furthest thing from my mind.

'Your foot doesn't stop you from driving?'

'No.' I reached out and grabbed some teacups. 'Just, there was no point, I guess. Nowhere I needed to go.'

Hamish shook his head at that, like he had some thought that he wasn't willing to share. He sat up on the couch. 'But you're going to come, right?' His voice was morning-rough. 'You'll come into town with me.'

I smiled then 'cause he looked forlorn. 'Sure,' I said, echoing him, waiting for the water to boil.

Usually I got up in the morning and made my way steadily through the day. Especially when it was sunny, not a rain cloud in sight. But that morning every second felt weighed down and ponderous. Even though I didn't want Hamish to leave, I was restless for things to begin.

'When do you think your mum will want to go?'

'I don't know. I guess it depends on how she does in the shed.'

'The artist at work.'

'Yep.'

The kettle finally boiled and I poured the water into the cups, leaning over them to get a whiff of the scent. The feel of the steam on my face was soothing—an instant warmth.

'I like your hair, Mema,' Hamish said, out of the blue. 'It's really ...' he lifted his hand up, smoothing it through the air, '... shiny.'

This took me by surprise and I tucked some loose strands behind my ears.

'It kind of ... flops,' he added.

'Thanks,' I said, peering intently into the depths of the brewing teas.

Hamish stood up and walked across to the fridge to get the milk. Mum and I were pretty good at being flooded in by now and we usually kept a few cartons of that UHT stuff stashed away in the cupboard. It didn't taste as nice as fresh milk, but after days of flooding rain no one complained. Hamish got it out and peered at the label.

'I wonder what they do to this stuff to make it keep.'

Obviously he wasn't feeling as uncomfortable as I was about the hair compliments.

'Mum probably knows. Ask her when she comes in.'

Hamish shook his head and handed me the carton. 'I'll be able to google it this afternoon.'

I wondered how easy it would be for Hamish to find a computer in town, but he looked so cheerful I didn't want to bring it up. I poured the milk into the teas and handed him a cup.

'It's a nice day today,' I said, glancing out the window. 'Pure sun, like yesterday.'

He sipped his tea, eyes focused on his cup, thoughts hidden.

'We could go for one last swim, get cool for the trip into town.'

Our car didn't have air-conditioning, and on summer days it was stinking hot. Made it feel like your blood might boil. I wasn't looking forward to it.

'Cool.' Hamish glanced at his reflection in the window. 'Maybe I can even out my weird-arse tan.'

It was true. In the morning light I could see the faint difference between where he'd had the ochre paint and where he hadn't. White stripes on his face where yesterday they'd been brown. I guess he looked pretty funny, standing there holding his steaming teacup—the beginnings of a beard, old tattered, mismatched clothes, odd markings on his face. He looked like he'd been *through* something. I wondered what they'd make of him in town, especially driving in with me and Mum. I'd be surprised if tongues didn't wag.

We went down to the creek for a swim but we didn't speak much. Hamish's leaving was a load inside me and I kept thinking of that shimmering ribbon of water from the night before. Things were always different in the daylight. There was less room for the fanciful, the wayward. The creek seemed ordinary in the brightness of the sun. The water level was still high, though it no longer covered the bridge. All the surrounding banks had been washed clear and clean, like there was no mystery in them at all. I felt exposed just looking at them.

'You going in?' Hamish asked, pulling off his shirt.

The sight of his chest unnerved me.

'You go,' I said, shaking my head. 'I'll come in a second.'

Hamish was different from the day before, more purposeful, less cautious. He strode forward, pushing through the flow and diving quickly beneath the water. My heartbeat started up its clattering, and I pushed that hollow place between my breasts, hoping against hope for it to stop. I watched him under the water, swimming like I had imagined myself, him the one who was free, not me. It made my eyes sting and I wondered suddenly if I might cry.

Hamish resurfaced, shaking his head like a puppy, droplets springing from him into the air, scattering onto the surface of the creek, a myriad of glassy spots.

'Come on, Mema,' he called out, smiling.

'Okay,' I said, my body loosening at the sound of his voice, hesitation slipping away.

Once in I felt better. Enlivened, less stuck. Even the bottom of the creek was clean, no sticks or leaves, no slippery moss, only flood-roughened rocks. It never stayed clean like that for long. Two or three days max. Sometimes the entire layout of the creek would change in a flood. Where it used to be deep it would be shallow. Stretches that were narrow would widen. Nothing as it used to be. I swam about, putting my feet down to test the different depths. Relearning the terrain, making it mine.

Hamish floated on his back, staring at the sky. I did my best to ignore him.

In a while he righted himself and swam towards me. I stood on my toes in a deep section, stretching out my neck to keep my head above the surface. If I moved forward an inch my mouth would go under. He hovered in front of me, treading water and watching my face. My submerged body quivered.

'You're quiet this morning, Mema,' he said. 'You alright?'

What could I possibly say? I stood there a minute, my heart pulsing. In my mind I could see the vibrations of it moving outwards from me like rings on top of water. I wondered if Hamish could feel it somewhere deep inside. In the end I just nodded my head, taking in a mouthful and spitting it back out slowly in a fountain. Anja and I were good at this trick, having practised it over the years. We could propel the water quite far with very little effort.

'Impressive,' Hamish said, taking in his own mouthful and giving it his best shot.

To my surprise he was actually pretty skilled. I must have looked piqued 'cause he seemed inordinately pleased.

'You don't have to live next to a creek to be good at spitting water, Mema.'

'I suppose not.'

I took in another mouthful and shot a small stream out between my two front teeth. This was my specialty. The gap in my teeth was the perfect size, not too big, not too small. The water flew in a wide arc over Hamish's head, the end of it landing in soft drops on his hair.

'Show off,' he murmured.

'That gap comes in handy.'

'They say a gap means you'll be rich.'

I smiled, feeling the space with my tongue.

'It's good fortune.' He thwacked lightly at the water with his hand, flinging some droplets my way.

'Who says?'

Actually, I'd been hearing this prophecy since I was a child. It was a part of hippie lore.

'I think it's Chinese. A Chinese thing.'

'It's not a very big gap.' When I was little I believed I'd been born lucky and the gap in my teeth was confirmation.

'Big enough.' Hamish clapped down on the water a bit harder and it splattered around my shoulders.

'That's cheating,' I said, opening my mouth to refill.

'Okay, okay,' he said, holding up his palms. 'You win.'

I guess it was pretty childish to try to beat him in a spitting game. My eyes started to sting again and I knew I could cry. Right then and there. I could feel it welling up, that uncontrollable urge to weep.

'Should we go back?' Hamish asked. 'Your mum might be ready to go.'

I dropped beneath the water, trying to wash away the crying feeling, and when I resurfaced Hamish was already across the creek, his expression unreadable, closed.

'Okay.' I wiped my face with my hands, and together we clambered out of the creek and back up the green hills.

At the house, Mum was waiting. I could see her in the distance pottering around in the garden, grey curls caught up in an elastic on the top of her head. When we got closer I noticed she'd tucked up her skirt exposing the largeness of her calves and her knobbly, damaged knees. Potters always have bad knees 'cause pushing the wheel is an awkward sideways movement. It was one of the drawbacks of the trade, but Mum never complained. I'd tried to get her to invest in an electric wheel but she wasn't ready to let go of the old one yet.

'Cooled off?' she called out and Hamish and I nodded.

I headed inside to get changed. Hamish didn't have anything else to wear so he just stayed out in the sun. He'd dry off in no time. In my room I looked at all my bright hanging skirts, considering which one I should wear. Usually I enjoyed the boldness of their colours, the bright, joyful lines of their prints, but today I wondered whether they might make me look strange. Stranger than I already looked. I pulled my boots from the cupboard, the ones specially made for my bung foot. They were black old-style lace-ups that rose well above my ankle. Nowadays, you could get most shoes made up for a foot like mine, but I didn't see much use in it. These had always been enough. Putting them on made me feel more of an invalid rather than less. But they were also a kind of armour, they helped me feel ready for all the straight lines of the world.

Back outside we all climbed into the car. It was an old Corolla station wagon, white and dingy with hideously scratchy seats. I let Hamish have the front, which didn't seem to please him, but I wanted to be able to watch him from the back, watch him try to make chitchat with my mum. Maybe, since he was leaving, this was my way of making it hard on him. I don't know, I'm not usually so mean.

I noticed straight away that something wasn't right. Hamish hesitated before opening the car door, and by the time he sat down there were huge balls of sweat standing out on his forehead. It was hot, but we'd just been swimming, and the car was parked in the shade of one of the big old camphors. Compared to outside, it was cool in the car. Mum glanced across at him and turned the engine on. I could tell she knew something was up too, but she didn't say a word. When Hamish pulled his seatbelt across, his hands were shaking real bad, his skin paler and paler by the second.

Scrambling into the middle of the back seat I leaned forward and put a hand on his shoulder, but he shrugged off my touch.

'Mum?' My voice came out like a croak.

Mum put the car into reverse and turned to look behind her.

'Try to breathe,' she said quietly to Hamish. 'I'll go slow.'

As Mum nudged the car slowly backwards, Hamish's breaths started coming in quick. He was almost panting, sweat pouring down his face in rivulets. Mum paused a second, watching him, and then she put the car in drive.

'You tell me to stop and I will,' she said gently. I don't know why, but something about my mother's softness with him made my eyes fill up again. I tried not to let them spill over.

Hamish kept looking straight ahead. He lifted his shirt with shaking hands and wiped his face.

'What's happening to me?' he choked out, his breath sounding strangled.

'Looks like a panic attack.' Mum moved the car forward at a snail's pace.

'A panic attack?' Hamish repeated. 'From getting into a car?'

Mum just shrugged, driving real slow. We bumped down the driveway, every rock seeming to punch into the tyres. It probably only took a minute or two but it felt like forever. Soon the bridge loomed up ahead and Hamish started grasping at his throat, and I knew then that he wouldn't go over. Mum must have known too 'cause she stopped the car and turned the engine off. Hamish grabbed at his seatbelt, trying to get it off. I opened the door and pushed myself out, pulling his door open too. He propelled himself out of the car with such force he nearly bowled me over. It took me a second to find my feet.

Squatting in the grass, he looked like he might retch. Mum didn't get out, but put the car into reverse and drove it back up the drive and into the shade. I watched her get out, close all the car doors and stand in the front yard, observing us. I wasn't sure what to do. How to get Hamish to come out of the sun. If he was one of the animals, I'd have known how to comfort him, but he didn't seem to want me anywhere near. He wouldn't look at me at all. Finally, I stepped up towards him and crouched down on the grass nearby.

'You alright?' I knew it wasn't much but it was all I could muster.

'Fuck, fuck, fuck …' He rubbed his hands across his shorn hair, hard.

'You nearly died trapped in a car. It's not surprising your body doesn't want to do it.'

I could remember the sound of his car sliding against the wooden railings of the bridge. The loud splintering crack of it breaking through. I glanced up and looked towards the bridge. From where we were crouching I could see the remains of the broken railing hanging loose. I hadn't really considered what it must have been like for him to be on the inside.

'This has never happened to me before.' Hamish's voice was so low and quiet I could barely hear him. I crept a little closer and he didn't move away. 'I can't believe I couldn't even get into a fucking car.' He pulled at the neck of his T-shirt, as though he still couldn't get enough air. 'How the fuck am I going to get out of here?'

'It's probably half a day's walk.' I knew he didn't really expect an answer, caught as he was, but I had to say something. 'We could do it.' I tilted my head sideways to try to see his face. 'Maybe we could even scrape together some bikes. There's a few old ones in the shed, might need to scrounge up some parts. It's not impossible.'

He was silent for a while, staring down at the grass. I didn't know much about men, but I knew they didn't like to seem weak. I could see him trying to gather his defences, dig a kind of moat between him and the world—between him and me—and it made me feel sad. Sad and suddenly weary.

'Come on out of the sun,' I whispered. I wanted to hold out my hand but I didn't. 'Come in and get a drink. Then I'll show you the bikes.'

He didn't move straight away, so we both crouched there in the midday heat, looking down, not at each other. I wondered what my mum was thinking. I wondered if she'd already heard the clattering of my heart whenever Hamish came near, if she'd seen me press my fingers against that hollow place. I knew there wasn't much she missed. Whatever the case, she was choosing to ignore it, and I couldn't help but be thankful for that.

11.

There were a couple of bikes in the shed, old ones of my brothers'. There was a stage they went through when they collected things. Not just bikes, but any wheeled contraption really. There was a patch behind the house that resembled a junk yard, so strewn was it with half-rusted pieces of machinery. Mum cleared it away once the boys had all gone, though every now and again I'd come across some stray nuts and bolts, or the occasional spanner buried in the dirt, like archaeological evidence of some tribe who'd gone before.

The two bikes in the shed were BMXs, a little too small for Hamish, but the perfect size for me. They didn't even need any new parts. We just gave the tyres a pump up and oiled the chains. When I saw how workable they were, I wondered why I'd never thought about riding them before. It had been so long since I'd ridden a bike I wasn't sure I still knew how.

Hamish was quiet while we worked. When he held the oilcan, his hands trembled, but whatever was happening on the inside, it didn't show on his face. Once we'd got both bikes in working order we wheeled them out into the front yard.

'You get on first,' I said. 'See if you can peddle without your knees hitting the handlebars.'

He settled onto the bike, peddling it slowly around on the grass. His knees came up high, but if he stuck them out to the sides, they didn't hit the bars up front. It looked clumsy but not impossible.

'Lots of the way into town is downhill, we'll be able to sail down.'

Hamish stopped peddling. 'You don't have to come, Mema.' It was like he'd been silent all that time, building up strength to tell me that. 'I'll be alright.' He kept watching the ground as I tucked up my long skirt and stepped gingerly onto the bike.

'I know that.' I put one foot on the pedal. 'But Mum will come in later to get some supplies. She'll pick me up. I won't have to ride back again.'

He didn't like to feel indebted but I knew he wanted me to come.

'I've never ridden into town,' I said. 'Be something new.'

He took a deep breath and sat up a touch straighter. 'Alright,' was all he said, but the breath rushed from him in a sigh.

Mum came out then, with a drink bottle and a small backpack, and a couple of sandwiches in crumpled brown paper bags. She looked at Hamish on the bike, knees up, all askew.

'That's going to be hard-going,' she said to him, handing me the backpack. I opened the zipper and she popped the stuff inside.

'Here, I'll take it,' Hamish said, holding out his arm for the pack. I handed it over and he slipped it on his back. Quiet hung about us and I could tell Hamish was struggling to know how to say goodbye.

'Well ...' he said at last, 'thanks for having me.'

My mother just laughed. What were we going to do? Make him sleep in the shed?

I looked at Hamish, gauging his response. He was doing okay. He held out his hand for my mother to shake and she grasped it like a man.

'I'll see you in there later, about four,' she said to me. 'You two got helmets?'

'There weren't any in the shed,' I replied. Mum had a thing about physical safety. I'd been hoping she wouldn't notice.

'What if you fall off?'

'We'll be fine.' It always baffled me that Mum could be so untroubled by most things but stressed out about creek–riding or helmets.

'We'll be going pretty slow,' Hamish said, tilting his head down towards his knees. 'And I doubt there'll be much traffic.'

She stood there towering over us, shaking her head. 'I don't like it,' she said finally. 'Wait a second.' She turned around and went back inside. I was seriously hoping she wasn't going to try to wrap our heads up in towels, or something equally as ridiculous.

Hamish looked at me and I could see he was ready to go. I shrugged but didn't move.

Mum reappeared holding a big straw hat in each hand. 'I know these won't save your skulls but they'll keep the sun off.'

Considering what I'd imagined Mum might insist on, a hat was an easy compromise. She leaned over and plonked one on each of our heads. I adjusted it till it was comfy.

'Thanks, Mum,' I said and turned the bike around so it was facing the driveway. 'See you this afternoon.'

'Be careful,' she said. 'Watch out on that corner before the Smiths' place.'

'Okay, Mum.' It was amazing how quickly I could feel like a little kid around her.

'Go on,' I said to Hamish. 'You take the lead.'

I didn't much like the idea of him riding behind me, studying my rickety take-off. It was unsettling even thinking about his gaze on the back of my legs. He bumped the bike forward, still pushing it with his feet on the ground. The hat came down low over his face, half covering his eyes. For the first time in ages I wished that my mum wasn't standing there watching.

Hamish waved to her and then he pushed off towards the driveway. I followed, wobbly, in his wake.

There was a thrill in it—the leaving—as though the whole world was starting fresh from that point. I didn't turn back to look at my mother, standing in the front yard. I didn't look back to see the shadow of the old dog, or the silhouette of the cat through the window, or the pecking of the chickens in the grass. I didn't scour the landscape for the shape of Bessie and her calf. I didn't even glance around. I watched the wheel of Hamish's bike turning in front of me until we got close to the sloping driveway, and in the rush of a downhill ride we were off.

Riding into town was different from driving. In the car, the trees whipped past, and after a while it looked like one green blur, but on the bike everything became singular. *That* crooked leafy tree, *that* stick across the road, *that* fallen twig. And the road itself—how subtly it undulated. On the bike you could feel every ridge in the bitumen, every slight dip. It was like mapping the world with a different tool. Feeling the shape of it beneath the tyres. It made me think of blindness and reading with Braille. There were six bridges between home and town, and the two we'd already crossed had felt so different—our one was bumpy, the other smooth.

We hadn't been passed by a car yet, so Hamish and I rode side by side. We didn't speak. I wanted to ask him if he felt that riding was like Braille, but I didn't know how to bring it up. It was peaceful—the quiet between us—and it seemed a shame to break it. Our pace was leisurely, faintly downhill, there was not much need to peddle. There'd be a few steeper stretches before we got close to town, but so far it was all pretty easy. I wondered how long the trip would take.

On both sides of us the hills rose up covered in forest. One of the old farmers had told Mum that when he was a boy everything around was bare, even the mountain tops. The trees had gone to make way for the farms, but no one used the hills for anything nowadays, so slowly the trees had taken them back. It was hard to distinguish the different types from where we were down on the road. Up on the distant hills it looked like one green mass, thick and glowing in the sun. Mainly camphors. Right next to the road it was mostly flat paddocks, grazing for the occasional fat cow.

All along the fence lines the camphors flourished, large and graceful with their luminous leaves, grown from seeds in the droppings birds scattered while they rested on the fences. Randomly placed by nature, the camphors always seemed perfectly positioned. Boundaries still standing when all the fences were gone. It was interesting the way nature worked, throwing up these neat lines, adapting to what was at hand.

Hamish peddled along, taking in the landscape from under his hat. He seemed calm and soothed, and even though we were on bikes I felt like drawing closer to him. It was a practical impossibility. I wasn't a skilful enough rider, and his poking-out-knees would surely knock me off, but that didn't stop me from feeling the urge.

I ignored it as best as I could.

The grasses in summer grew long and thick on the roadside. All different types with minute feathery flowers. Even though there was nothing spectacular about them from afar, up close the flowers were delicately pretty. Often with the smallest hint of purple—soft and downy. When I was little I was always picking bunches of grass flowers to bring back to my mum, and she would dutifully put them in a vase, but I could tell she wasn't that impressed. Something about them spoke to me—the fineness of their beauty, the ordinariness. They were in full flower along the roadside and I put out a hand to touch their softness as we rode. In winter they would turn a deep purple and then brown and rustle in the wind, but on that day they were blooming. The only sound besides the brush of our tyres on the road was the crickets chirping, and even that seemed far off in the distance.

Hamish turned then and smiled at me, the slightest flicker of his lips, but it was enough to make my heartbeat quicken. I tried to smile back.

'Cat got your tongue?'

Sometimes my mum would say that, but it sounded different coming out of Hamish's mouth. I shook my head. 'You're quiet too.'

'Just thinking.'

I rode along, waiting for him to tell me what he was thinking about, but he didn't. While the going was downhill it was effortless, but eventually we hit an uphill slope. I stood up on the peddles, using my weight to turn the wheels, and Hamish tried that too, but it was harder with him being so tall. Once we slowed, the heat of the day began to bear down. The sting of the sun was sharp on my forearms, my hands moist and sticky on the bars.

'You could get off and walk it,' I called across to him. 'Just for the uphill bits.'

I knew Hamish didn't like to be beaten, but he stopped struggling and stepped off the bike, still holding onto the handlebars. He was about to say something when we heard the humming of a car in the distance. Hamish steered across to the side of the road and I slowed right down to a stop. It took a good few seconds for the driver to come into sight. I recognised him straight away—it was Frank Brown in his truck. Frank owned a lot of the land around us. He was a gentleman farmer, kind and softly spoken. Probably a few years older than my mum. I liked him just fine. When the bananas or avocados were in season he often left a bag of them at the bottom of our driveway, under one of the big trees. He was different from the rest of those men. He never sniffed around, never even came inside.

When the truck got closer it slowed right down, pulling up beside us.

'Not too hot?' Frank called across from the driver's seat, through the open window. He always wore an old farmer's hat, even in the car. 'Want a lift?'

I glanced at Hamish, knowing that he couldn't get in the car.

'We're right,' I called back. 'It's a nice ride.'

He looked from me to Hamish and back again. It was obvious he was trying to place him.

'Could throw your bikes in the back.'

I guess it seemed bizarre to choose to ride undersized BMXs to town in the midday sun when a lift was on offer.

Stopped there on the side of the road it was baking hot. I could feel a line of sweat trickle down my back beneath my shirt. 'Thanks, Frank,' I said, watching Hamish. 'We're fine, though.'

'Frank Brown,' Frank said, unclicking his seatbelt and leaning across the car, holding out his hand for Hamish to shake. I wasn't good at manners. I'd forgotten to introduce them.

'Hamish.' He took Frank's outstretched hand and shook it firmly, but he didn't elaborate.

'You the fella who washed off the bridge?' Frank asked, his engine still humming.

There was so little traffic on the road into town that sometimes there'd be two trucks, going opposite ways, stopped in the middle of the road for a chat. It was kind of endearing, except when you got stuck behind them.

'Called the SES?'

'Yeah.' The sweat was building on Hamish's face. 'I got disorientated.'

'Must have given you one hell of a fright.' Frank had a slow way of talking, as though there wasn't any place he'd rather be. 'Heard the car sank right to the bottom. Have to wait for the water to go all the way down before they can retrieve it.' He still had one hand on the steering wheel. 'You were lucky to get out.'

Hamish tilted back his hat and wiped his forearm across his forehead. 'Mema got me out,' he said, glancing across at me.

I wasn't used to wearing my boots and I was starting to swelter. In the distance I could see the heat vapour rising from the bitumen. I felt myself nod.

'You didn't go in, did you?' Frank asked.

'I used a branch, you know.'

Frank nodded. 'Good girl. Could have lost the both of you. Wouldn't want that.'

He didn't seem in any hurry to get going, but I wasn't sure I could stand much longer in the sun. 'Well, better get moving,' I said, putting a foot on the peddle.

'You could clamber onto the tray,' Frank said. 'Get out of the heat. Throw the bikes up there too.'

Hamish peered at the back of the truck.

'What do you reckon?' Frank asked.

I could see Hamish was thinking about it. I guess maybe he wouldn't feel so trapped in the open back of a ute.

'You want to?' Hamish asked me softly, taking in my hot face.

I nodded, pretty sure he'd made up his mind.

'You'll have to hold onto your hats,' Frank said with a smile, 'but the wind'll cool you down real quick.'

'Okay,' I said, hopping off the bike.

Frank opened his car door and stepped down from his seat. 'You two jump up and I'll pass the bikes in.'

Standing, he was a big strong fellow. He picked up a bike in each hand.

Hamish popped into the back of the ute easy, but I didn't think I'd be able to. I clambered onto one of the wheels and then up over the side. It was pretty inelegant, but it didn't seem like either of the men noticed.

'Resourceful. That's what you are, Mema,' Frank said, surprising me. 'Just like that mother of yours.' I let that comment slide. 'Now get comfortable in there.' He kept talking, unhurried, easy. 'Best to sit with your backs against the cab.'

Hamish took the bag off and we shuffled backwards on our bums. Frank passed the bikes up as though they weighed nothing. We were pressed together, Hamish's shoulder against mine.

'Like two peas in a pod,' Frank said.

Hamish didn't speak. I was guessing that he couldn't. I wanted to urge him to breathe, but not while Frank was standing there watching us.

'Now, hold onto your hats!' Frank called out as he climbed back into the front.

Riding in the backs of utes was one of the things on my mother's list of 'far too dangerous activities', so even though I'd lived in this place all my life, surrounded by farmers and their trucks, I'd never actually travelled this way. I suspected that it would live up to my expectations. Part of me wanted to reach out and grab Hamish's hand, but I figured I shouldn't push it.

'Hamish?' I whispered as Frank's door slammed shut. 'You alright?'

He didn't say a word, just pressed the heel of his palm against his collarbone again. I couldn't see his face beneath the big hat.

'You got to breathe.' I bent forward a bit so I could see him. He was pale, pale as this morning in the car, his eyes wide and panicked. The truck started to move forward, slowly picking up speed.

'Look at me.'

'I'm alright,' Hamish muttered, looking away. 'Just give me a second.'

It's impossible to help someone who doesn't want helping, but in my mind I imagined climbing over and straddling his lap so all he could see was me. I didn't move an inch and the truck bumped along gently. Frank was a cautious driver, and I suppose he was thinking of the bikes bouncing around on top of us too.

He was right about one thing—as he gathered speed, we both reached up to grab hold of our hats. We were shaded by the cab of the truck, so once the wind started rushing I pulled my hat right off and held it between my legs. I liked the feeling of the wind in my hair, and if I hadn't been squashed in alongside Hamish I would have felt utterly free. His arm against mine, moist and hot, kept jolting me back to the thought of climbing astride his lap. I hadn't known how much unwanted thoughts could make you feel like a prisoner.

Reaching up, I pulled the elastic from my plait. If this was my one chance of riding in the tray, I wanted to feel all of it. My hair streamed out around me, the wind whipping it about. Hamish took his hat off too and leaned his head back against the cab, face tilted towards the sky. He closed his eyes, and the hand he pressed against the base of his throat relaxed and dropped slowly to his lap.

And that's the way we rode into town. Hamish breathing slow and steady, eyes closed, like he was praying to some unknown saviour. And me, half wild with the freedom of it, but all the while fighting thoughts of him trapped beneath my hungry touch.

12.

Wind-whipped and wild-looking, we pulled up in front of the bank. The whole town seemed different from the back of the truck. Less stale and ordinary. From that height I could look at it as though it was a place I'd never been before.

As soon as the truck stopped, Hamish was jumping over the side. He seemed a bit unsteady, like a sailor adjusting to solid ground. He looked up at me, his face bright. 'I did it, Mema!'

If he was another type of person he would have punched the air, or maybe put his hand up for a high-five. Frank climbed out and walked around to help us get the bikes out.

'You want a hand down?' he asked, and I let him help me. I wasn't used to people doing things for me.

'Sorry.' Hamish watched Frank. 'I should have done that.'

I shrugged. Frank seemed to have a way of making things feel natural. I didn't feel like a cripple around him, but like a lady from one of those old-fashioned books Mum had a bunch of— Jane Austen and those Bronte sisters. I'd never felt like a lady before. I liked it more than I expected. Re-plaiting my hair, I quickly twisted the elastic around the end.

'So where are you two headed?' Frank asked as he lifted down a bike.

'First step, the bank—try to get some money out.' Hamish fished around in the tray for the backpack. Handing it to me, he pulled the other bike down. 'Then, I guess I've got to try to find somewhere to stay.'

Our town was only really this one street, you could see all the shops in a sweep of the eye, but Hamish didn't know that yet.

'Well, there's either the pub just up there,' Frank pointed to the left. 'Or the motel out on the highway, near the petrol station.'

'I'll check them out,' Hamish said. 'Thanks, Frank. Thanks for the lift.'

Frank squared his shoulders. 'The pub's full of drunks and the motel's a sad old place.' He took off his hat, so worn and well loved, and I knew it meant he was going to say something important. 'If you don't find them to your liking, there's a spare room at my place.'

Frank's wife had died of cancer a few years back. She'd always been a quiet sort. Kept to herself, so I hardly remembered her. But I realised then that he must have been lonely with her gone. Truth be told, I hadn't really given Frank Brown a lot of thought. I watched his fingers inch slowly around the rim of his crooked old hat.

Hamish seemed surprised, but he took it in his stride. 'I think I'll need to be in town,' he said. 'For work.'

Frank nodded. 'Well, let me know if you do. Mema's got my number.'

That was true. I knew it off by heart. I always had to ring him when one of his cows strayed into our yard.

'Thanks, Frank.' Hamish held out a hand to shake and Frank grasped it. 'I'll certainly keep it in mind.'

Part of me wanted to stand up on my toes and give Frank's leathery cheek a kiss goodbye. Mainly because he was being so sweet, but partly—I guess—'cause he had made me feel like a lady. I didn't move though.

He put his hat back on and held up his hand in a wave.

'You take care now, Mema. Take care of that mother of yours too.'

I nodded and he turned and strode off towards the hardware store.

Hamish stared after him. 'He was nice.' He reached into the backpack and pulled out the drink bottle. 'He's not gay, is he?'

This was something I had never considered.

'My gaydar is usually pretty good, but out here everything's a little weird.'

'Gaydar?'

'You know? Gay radar?'

'No.' I'd never heard that term.

He shook his head like I was a lost cause. 'Do you think he's gay?' Hamish asked again, taking a swig of water and handing the bottle across to me.

'He's been married the whole time I've known him.' I took a sip of water and it was only when it hit my throat that I realised how thirsty I was. 'His wife died a few years back but I've never heard anything about him being gay.' I handed the bottle back to Hamish.

'Not that I care,' Hamish continued. 'I'm not funny about it.'

He drank from the bottle and I couldn't help thinking that his lips were exactly where mine had been only seconds before. It made the heat in my body rise.

'I'm just,' he wiped his mouth with the back of his hand, 'checking what kind of offer he's making.'

I reached out for the bottle and he handed it over. 'I think he was just being friendly.'

Hamish nodded. He seemed to have a whole new lease of life, now we were in town. 'Okay, well it's good to know I've got Frank Brown up my sleeve.'

Hamish surveyed the street like he was ready to roll, but I was feeling a little lost. Something about being in town with him was unsettling me.

'Let's stash the bikes somewhere. I'll pick them up later with Mum. I need some food, I think.'

We wheeled our bikes round the corner to the river bank. The town was built around a road that crossed the main river, the whole place perpendicular to the water. It was shady on the river bank, a few old trees and a couple of park benches speckled with mould. I leaned my bike against a tree and Hamish leaned his against mine. We sat down on the bench, one of us on each end.

I pulled out a brown paper bag and handed it across to him. 'Lucky dip.'

He must have been hungry too 'cause he barely had the paper off before he was biting in. It only felt like a few seconds and his sandwich was gone. I was going more slowly with mine—the whole thing tasted wrong in my mouth.

Hamish looked down at the river.

'So, tell me about your town, Mema.'

I was silent for a little bit, thinking what to say. 'It's only that strip of shops, that one street.'

Hamish scrunched up his paper bag and threw it in the air, catching it again like a ball. It was something one of my brothers would have done.

'There's not much to it.' I'd always felt a bit ambivalent about town, always a little on the outside.

'Where do you and your friends hang out?'

I didn't want to tell him that it was only me and Anja. That I didn't have any other friends. That we hardly ever came into town, and certainly not for fun.

'Not really here.'

'You go further afield? To the movies and things?'

I guess he was remembering what I'd said the other day about where to go on a date.

'Sometimes,' I said, looking at the brown flow of the river. 'The markets are pretty fun. We do them once a month.'

'But they're not in town?' he asked, throwing his paper bag up again.

'No, the markets are about an hour's drive from home, further than here. It's a nice spot. Everyone comes from all over.'

I was trying to imagine what would happen around here if you couldn't get into a car. There was no other way to get from place to place. I wondered how Hamish would go, where he needed to be for work.

'I'm going to have to get over the car thing.' He scrunched the paper bag up tighter, holding it in his palm. Evidently he was thinking the same thing I was.

'So, to the bank first?' I'd finished my sandwich and was itching again to get moving. We could leave the bikes here.

'Yep.' Hamish stood up and threw the ball of paper into a nearby bin. 'Then I'll be back in business.'

I stood up and put mine in the bin too, swinging the backpack over my shoulder.

'Let me take it.' Hamish held out his hand.

Handing the backpack over, I wiggled my toes inside my boots. They were making my feet feel stifled.

'You right?' he asked and I nodded.

I had nothing to say to that.

The bank was in the centre of town, an old building, all grey and red tiles, well maintained, with sloping supports below the windows outside that all the little kids in town liked to climb up and slide down. I did it when I was small too. Nothing ever changed.

There were a couple of toddlers climbing up the slope in their cheap plastic thongs, while a bunch of people chatted on a street bench, half watching. Even though the group looked vaguely my age, I didn't know any of them personally. My town seemed to specialise in young parents. Hanging out in clusters, dyed hair and piercings. There was a brittleness to them, pale skinned and dark under the eyes. Sophie always said it was drugs that made them look that way, but I didn't know anything much about that. Further along, a few blokes who'd gone to school with Jonah stood puffing on cigarettes. When my brothers were still around, they were always getting into fights with boys like that. Old school grievances hanging in the air, unexpectedly raw. Words would get said. Tempers flare. Walking past them nowadays, I was never quite sure what they might do.

Hamish strolled along, taking in the shops that lined the street, unperturbed by the crowd outside the bank. As we walked past I heard it, soft but clear.

'Slag.' One of the blokes coughed it under his breath. Softly, so it was half swallowed. The men around him tittered.

Looking at the ground I kept walking. At home words like that didn't mean much, but out on the streets of my town it was different, they came at me through the air like a slap. Time seemed to slow. I could feel Hamish glance across at me, but I didn't look up. These things didn't happen often, but enough to make me wary walking through town. To make me keep my head down.

A cough again. 'Slag.' And then someone else, 'Slut.'

This time Hamish stopped and turned, staring. I stopped too and everything went quiet. One of the men threw his cigarette on the pavement and ground it out with his shoe. The group on the street bench looked across at us. No one spoke. Hamish kept staring, and the men stared back. The air around us seemed to thicken. Everything felt clogged. I blinked a few times, as though hoping if I closed my eyes they all might disappear, but they didn't. We were caught there, ensnared somehow. Suddenly, the door of the bank swung open and someone stepped out. A toddler slid down the sloping wall, crying out as she hit the bottom. One of the mums jumped up to get her.

'You guys are such dickheads,' she muttered as she went past.

The men looked away, like the hadn't heard her. The moment that had held us in its power was over, and they all shifted back towards their business. Hamish took one last look at the blokes, then strode up the stairs and into the bank. The last thing I wanted to do was wait outside without him, so I followed.

We stood in the queue, waiting for the teller.

'What the fuck?' Hamish hissed sideways at me under his breath.

I didn't know where to begin.

'You heard it, right?'

It was far too complicated trying to explain about all the knowns and unknowns. How uneasily the town held our secrets.

'It's just,' I shrugged, 'people being nasty.' Mum always said words like that seemed big, but people only used them when they felt small.

'It's not okay, Mema.' He was whispering, though in the hush of the bank I wondered if everyone could hear. Two people stood in front of us, a woman and an old man, but neither of them looked our way. 'This is your town. You shouldn't get abused just walking down the street.'

The teller called the woman up and we stepped forward in the queue.

'Most of the time it's fine,' I said, wishing he would stop.

'But it's you.' He leaned closer to my ear. 'You don't even *do* boys.'

The old man in front of us didn't stir. He was probably as deaf as a post. I felt my cheeks go pink.

'Does that matter?' I asked, thinking of my mum. 'Would it be alright if I did?'

He rubbed the back of his neck in irritation. 'No, of course not. It's only … when it's you it's *really* not alright.'

The old man stepped up to the teller.

'It's not important, Hamish,' I said, wishing I was anywhere else. 'Just forget about it.'

Hamish shook his head like he wasn't finished and then it was his turn at the counter. I stood off to the side by the window. His banking had nothing to do with me. Every now and again I'd see a babyish face at the glass, one of the toddlers making it up the slope outside. Even in their pilled polyester clothes they seemed wholesome, open-faced with big toothy grins. I wondered what happened between then and adulthood. It was as though as they grew older something important shrivelled inside. It made me think about Rory, about whether that would happen to him. I looked around the bank—the drab carpeted

floor, the dull walls—there was nothing to attract the gaze but
a big white card behind glass displaying the date. Like the only
thing that mattered was keeping track of the time. Everything
looked so vacant and worn.

Hamish was having trouble with the teller. He leaned
forward, tapping his fingers on the counter, trying to make a
point. I moved closer. There wasn't anything I could do, but he
looked like he needed a hand.

'Look, I told you, I don't have any identifying documents,'
he said through the hole in the glass. 'I lost everything in the car
and I live two thousand kilometres from here.'

'Sir, we can't access your account without being sure it is
you.'

'I must be able to prove it's me without a document. Ask me
some security questions!'

The woman behind the glass looked pained. 'I'm sorry, sir, in
these circumstances that will not be enough.'

'What about my signature?' Hamish said, picking up a pen
from the counter. 'You must have that on record somewhere?'

'Maybe.' The woman moved back on her chair. 'Let me get
my supervisor.'

Hamish turned around to me. 'Fuck! They won't even let me
get money out.'

I looked at him—unshaven, strange tan marks, mismatched
clothes. It was quite possible they thought him half-mad. This was
a conundrum. Once someone decided you were crazy, how did
you convince them you weren't? Maybe every attempt to prove

sanity only made things worse. I suppose it didn't help to have me there—the lame girl with the handmade skirts. The supervisor came through from a door out the back and approached the glass. He pulled his glasses a little way down his nose, peering at Hamish over the top.

'So, you washed off a bridge further out? The whole car went under?'

'Yes.' Hamish was holding the side of the counter, fingers like a vice.

'Did the SES come?' the bank man asked, as though it was just an interesting story. 'They'd have a report.'

Hamish's eyes narrowed. 'They couldn't come because the water was too high. I've been stuck out at Mema's place for three days.' He gestured in my direction without looking. 'I rang them and they said they'd come when the water went down. That should be on record.'

The bank man nodded, taking it all in.

'This doesn't happen very often, but it's not without precedent.'

Hamish's fingers relaxed a fraction.

'Look, you'll need to get someone back home to send us through some documents, a copy of your passport would be ideal. Scan it in and send it by email. It wouldn't usually be enough without a JP's signature, but in these circumstances it might suffice.'

'Are you kidding?' Hamish leaned forward. 'I don't even have the change to make a phone call. How can I get that information through to you?'

The man looked from Hamish to me and back. 'Sir, if you'd like to step into our client room, you can use our phone to make the call.'

Hamish clenched his fists. 'Alright,' he nodded, and I stepped aside.

I glanced at the window as Hamish followed the bank man. The toddlers were gone. I didn't fancy staring at the date on the wall any longer than I already had, so wandered towards the exit, wanting some fresh air. Taking a breath I pushed the doors open, steadying myself a second on the threshold, but there was no one left outside. It was getting into afternoon. The sun going down on my town can be spectacular, all oranges and pinks. We don't get to see that at our place, so far into the hills. But it was summer and the sun wouldn't set for hours.

I looked down the rows of shops. None of them attracted me. I could think of nothing that I needed. Mum would be in soon, getting groceries, stocking up—moving from one shop to the next, checking for specials. Stretching our money as far as it could go. Sometimes it was a long wait between markets. At the end of the month it was all brown rice and potatoes. Anja would come down the mountain and we'd sprinkle the rice with soy sauce and fill our empty bellies, waiting for market day to roll around. Anja had a sweet tooth and she'd always have squirrelled away some chocolate then pull it from somewhere like a magic trick. Chocolate had a way of making us feel wayward. We'd both been banned from eating it when we were small and health food reigned. I wondered where

Anja had been. She didn't have a phone—it was impossible to ring her. If she didn't come down tomorrow I would trek up the mountain to find her. I moved towards Frank's truck, still parked where we left it, and leaned my back against the door. It was comforting to have something to gravitate towards, to not be stranded there alone.

In a few minutes the bank doors opened and Hamish stepped down onto the street. Even from where I was standing I could see the verve had gone out of him—all the vitality the ride in the back of Frank's truck had somehow restored. Deep in thought, he shook his head, as though in answer to a question no one was asking. He looked around and I waved to him, but he couldn't even smile.

'They won't give me any cash until they see a copy of my passport.'

The bank man had explained that while I was standing there, so I was hardly surprised.

'Can you believe it?'

'Could you get someone to email a copy?'

'I tracked down a friend but she couldn't do it till after work.' He looked forlorn, lost. 'The bank will be closed.'

I wanted to reach out and touch him. 'You can get it tomorrow.'

'Fuck, Mema, how can they leave me with no money?' he said. 'I mean it's mine and it's all sitting there. I just can't access it.'

'You'll be okay. It's only one night.'

I know I should have been thinking of his predicament but I wasn't. I was wondering about the girl. His friend. A new feeling opened up inside me, a savage kind of ache.

'They gave me the number for Salvation Army emergency relief.' He looked up and down the street and I knew he was seeing it with different eyes, seeing its failings. He dug a piece of paper from his pocket and handed it over. I unfolded it, glancing down at the details but I already knew them.

'That only operates once a week.' Anja sometimes had to ask them for help, when her dad drank all his disability payment. 'Not today.'

'What should I do?'

'You can come back to our place.'

'Mema, I don't think I can do that. I need to be in town for work tomorrow.' He sighed, stepping down beside me and leaning against the truck, pressing his fingers against his eyes. 'You guys won't be coming in again for a while.' He said this sideways, tilting his face towards me. It was true enough, though if he was desperate he could always ride.

'How often does Frank come in?' Hamish asked, dropping his hands. He stood up straighter and peered down the street, as though searching for Frank's form.

'He's out and about plenty. I don't know what he does.'

I always saw Frank's truck on the road. I'd never really thought about where he was going.

'I'll ask him.'

It was a neat solution.

'I've got to meet the head of the company tomorrow to discuss operations. I thought I'd have the cash to buy myself some new clothes.' He looked down at himself, standing there in the afternoon shade. 'Fuck. There's no way I can wear this.'

'They'll understand what's happened,' I said. 'You've already spoken to them on the phone.'

'I know,' he said. 'But it's more about how I'll feel.'

Hamish had never spoken a word about feelings.

'You need to make an impression?' I suppose even I knew what he meant.

'Not so much that. I just need to be able to hold my own.'

I thought of the way the bank manager looked down his nose at Hamish. I knew what that was like.

'I've got thirty bucks,' I said, feeling for the pocket in my skirt. 'We could go to Vinnies.'

Hamish looked down at my hand. 'But that's your money. I don't want to take your money, Mema.'

'Don't be silly. You'll have your cash tomorrow. You can pay me back.'

Mum and I always sewed secret pockets into our clothes. There was nothing more useful. I carefully undid the zipper and pulled out my money. One blue and one orange. 'Come on. We'll leave Frank a note so he knows where to find us.'

Hamish stared at me for a few seconds, weighing it up. It was a dilemma.

'You're serious,' he said at last. 'You'd lend me thirty bucks. How many mugs is that?'

Maybe I should have been insulted, but I wasn't.

'A few.'

'Okay. It's a deal.' He reached out and we shook hands. 'Thanks, Mema.'

'If we don't hurry up, Vinnies might shut. Sometimes it closes early.' The skin on my hands tingled where his fingers had been and I felt like laughing. 'You've got to go back into the bank and write Frank a note. Tell him we'll be at Vinnies or the Savoy.' I handed him the scrap of paper he had handed me. 'I don't have a pen.'

'Nothing else tucked away in those little pockets?'

I shook my head and he turned around and jogged up the bank steps. He was back in a few moments, paper in hand.

'The Savoy? Don't tell me. It can be a surprise.' Hamish's voice was lighter than I'd heard it. We popped the note under one of Frank's windscreen wipers and headed down the street.

13.

Second-hand clothes always harbour a smell. Something fusty and stale, even though I know they've all been cleaned. When Hamish and I walked in, the old woman at the counter looked up and smiled, then went back to what she was doing. The racks were all arranged according to size, men and women's clothes on opposite sides of the room. I could see from Hamish's face that he didn't know where to start. Everything looked unsightly and wrong, thrown in together, but I was confident we could find something passable. Sophie was always looking in Vinnies for things—it was one of her pleasures. Her little cabin was full of funny trinkets and treasures. Usually I didn't have the patience for op-shopping, but that day was different. We were on a mission.

The men's pants were jammed on one rack. I flicked through the obligatory pairs of brown old-man slacks and then I got to some jeans.

'What would you normally wear to work?' I asked Hamish, who was standing behind me, looking a bit at sea.

'Jeans would be okay, or some dark pants.' He pulled out a pair of jeans. 'Anything would be better than old ratty board shorts, I guess.'

'Pick a few and try them on,' I said, grabbing some that looked about right.

'You reckon?'

'Yep.' I handed the jeans over. 'I'll look at the shirts while you're in there.'

Hamish headed towards the fitting room while I perused the shirts. I didn't know him well enough to have much idea of what he liked, so it was a bit tricky. There were a couple of work shirts, pale and nondescript, and I pulled out the freshest one of those, wondering about the sizing. It was a farming town, so there were heaps of flannelettes and a bunch of plaid, checked things. I chose one, but secretly I hoped he wouldn't like it. Those kinds of clothes made me think of everything that was ordinary about the world, and I didn't want Hamish to fall into that category. At least, not yet. There was a plain dark-blue button-up shirt, fine and cottony. If it was me, that's the one I'd choose. I moved across to the fitting room, the shirts I'd picked hanging over my arm.

'How's it going?' I asked from outside. Hamish grunted in response.

'That good.' I laughed.

'They all come up so high. I look like a primary-school teacher.'

I knew what he meant, even though I'd never been to school. But it was a step up from a madman, I guess.

'Let me see.'

There was a shuffling around and then Hamish opened the curtain. He was standing there in jeans, no shirt, and even though I'd seen him less clothed than that, it made me suck in a breath.

'They fit, you know, they're not too small or anything,' he said, looking down and bending a little at the knees. He seemed comfortable enough, but even in the dim light I could see a hint of red rising up his neck. I wondered if it was my looking at him that made him blush.

'Once you've got a shirt on, you won't see they're high-waisted,' I said, looking at the jeans with a seamstress's eye. I could adjust the waistband—it'd take twenty minutes max. 'Wouldn't be too hard to change with the sewing machine, but probably not before tomorrow. If you're going to stay with Frank.'

'Really?'

I nodded, holding up the shirts. 'I didn't know what kind of thing you were going for.'

He gazed at the shirts carefully. 'I guess I want to look like I've got it together.'

'Like you haven't just escaped death and lost all your worldly possessions?'

Hamish laughed. 'Yeah, that about sums it up.'

'Well,' I said, holding out the pale work shirt, 'there's this.'

He took the shirt and held it up against his body.

'Do you think this colour makes me look washed-out?' he asked, straight-faced. It was a funny comment, coming from him. I didn't know whether to laugh, but when he glanced down at the shirt he was grinning.

'No, seriously. It's a bit pale. What'd you reckon?'

'It's not my type of thing.' I shrugged, looking down at my outfit. I liked my colours bold.

'What else?'

I held the plaid shirt in one hand and the blue in the other. He reached out and touched the checked sleeve. 'This one reminds me of my dad. On a bad day.'

I let out the breath I was holding.

'The blue one is okay.' He took it from me. 'I'll try it on.'

He did up the buttons and turned to look in the mirror. The fit was alright.

'It covers the school-teacher jeans,' he said, looking back at me.

'It's good.'

It was odd how much clothes could change you. Hamish looked completely different. Older, more capable. I felt like a child in dress-ups beside him.

'How much are they?' he asked.

We searched around for the tags. The jeans were eight dollars, the shirt was five.

'Thirteen dollars all up!' Hamish said. 'That's a steal.'

We approached the counter and the old lady spoke to us softly. She was watching my lips as I talked and I wondered if she might be going deaf—if she talked so quietly because she was afraid of speaking too loud. I handed over the money and she fished me out some change. I smiled and she leaned across and took a plastic rose from a vase on the counter, handing it to me.

'Thanks,' I said in surprise.

'It's charming to see a young couple in love,' she said, her words tumbling out unsteadily. Grasping the rose, I saw her fingers trembling in that old-lady way against the counter.

Hamish made a choking sound beside me.

'That's sweet of you,' I stuttered, 'but …' I didn't know how to finish the sentence.

'We're not a couple,' Hamish piped up. 'Just friends.'

The old woman seemed to take this in gradually, her face blank for a few seconds before registering.

'Oh, I am sorry, dear. You look so … well matched.'

I tried to hand her back the rose but she wouldn't take it. 'No, it's yours now, dear.'

We put the new clothes straight into the backpack and nodded our goodbyes. At the last minute the old lady stopped us and threw in a couple of doilies for nothing. Sophie would be pleased.

Out on the street we were quiet.

'That was awkward,' Hamish said, looking anywhere but at me.

'Let's get some food.' I couldn't help it, I was hurt.

'You lead the way,' he said, glancing up and down the street.

I strode off and he followed. It was rare for me to get angry. I guess I didn't know where to put my feelings.

When we reached the teashop I walked straight in but Hamish stood on the street for a second looking at the display in the front window. The Savoy was this funny old place full of meringues and vanilla slices, run by the same people for years. Old-style wooden booths along the walls, not a piece of wholemeal banana cake in sight. My mum hated it with a passion. I suppose that's why I found it appealing. All their cakes and things sat behind curved glass in the front window. The display was meant to entice you indoors, but usually the food looked like it might have been there for days. The Savoy didn't have to work too hard when there was nowhere else to go.

I headed straight towards the back, past the other patrons, out of sight of the street. Sitting down, I glanced up at the menu. There was never anything new chalked up on the big blackboard, so I don't know exactly what I was looking for. Hamish stepped inside and the other customers all stopped still and watched him. He walked towards me in the booth and sat down, ignoring the scrutiny, his eyes on the blackboard.

'Wow, this place is totally old school,' he said, shaking his head. 'They even have banana splits.'

'Yep.' Sometimes Anja and I shared one. Ice-cream and that cream that came out of a canister. Chocolate sauce. All in a long glass-cut oval bowl. We always giggled 'cause it came out looking like a dick and balls, though no one else seemed to appreciate that.

'What are you getting?' Hamish asked, pulling out a table menu to double check.

I didn't know what I felt like eating. I was still rattled by the old lady and the rose.

'I'm thinking, a milkshake and a banana split, just to try the house special.'

The waitress came over. She was a little older than me, hair bleached to a dead white, but she had a pretty kind of face. Big warm brown eyes. I'd seen her in here before but I didn't know her name. The bones were showing through her cheeks in a way they hadn't last time I came in. I looked at her closely wondering if she was okay. There was that line that skinny girls crossed where suddenly they looked as though they could be dying. We'd had a girl in town a few years back so thin she looked like a walking skeleton. Sophie told me they sent her off to some special clinic in the city, but I hadn't heard how she was going. I hoped the waitress wasn't starving herself too.

'So, what'll it be?' she asked Hamish with an easy smile. A dimple flashed in her cheek, and I could see him staring at the place where it appeared. Dimples are a bit mesmerising, springing out of nowhere like they do. Even so, his interest in it made something dip inside me. Hamish ordered and then they both turned towards me.

'I'll have the fruit salad.'

Most of the time the fruit here was out of a can, but that in itself was a novelty. I watched the waitress jot my order down on her little pad.

'You don't want a drink?' Hamish asked, but the thought of a giant milkshake made me feel a little ill.

'I'll just have some water.' I nodded at the dimpled girl and then looked around the room.

I was used to being watched when I came into town, especially with Anja. Anja alone was quite a sight, all long legs and swishing hair, lips as bright as berries, and whenever I was with her people really stared. She was funny about it. A mixture of self-conscious and defiant—daring people to say something. They hardly ever did. I knew most of the gawking was in her direction, and that was fine with me. But the way people stared at Hamish was different. Anja and me, we were known entities, we'd always hung about on the periphery of town, but Hamish was fresh and people couldn't keep their eyes off him. I could see the ladies in the booth opposite whispering—the speculation had begun.

'They're an inquisitive bunch,' Hamish said quietly, trying to hide his smile.

'You mean nosey.'

'Half of them will already know I'm the stupid tourist who washed off the bridge, right?'

'Frank Brown knows everything. Not everyone's like him. Well, there's Rosie at the post office, she knows everyone's business. But she's the postmistress, has been forever, so that makes sense.'

'That'll change soon. No one sends mail anymore.'

I shrugged my shoulders. Mum still paid all the bills with her cheque book.

'It's alright, I'm used to being the foreigner. It's worse in countries where you actually look different—you know— distinctly.'

'You travel a lot?'

'Yeah, for my job. It's here, there and everywhere.'

It was strange thinking maybe this town was just another one of Hamish's exotic adventures. He hadn't said anything about the places he'd been, but I was already imagining.

'You like it—the travel?' I asked. Now we were talking, the rose incident was fading from my mind.

'The thing is, whatever you do, you're missing out on doing something else,' he said. 'That's just the way life is.'

I'd never really considered that. What I did with myself always felt like the only thing I could do. 'Give me an example.'

'Well, when you travel a lot you don't really put down roots in the way that other people do.' He paused for a minute, studying my face. 'I like the variety of it, though. I hardly ever go to the same place twice.'

It felt like a warning, like he was letting me know that he wouldn't be back. I shrugged, twirling the rose around in my fingers.

'What do you think you're missing out on?'

'All that settling-down stuff. Wife, kids, house.'

'You're not that old. You could still do all of it if you wanted to.'

'Maybe,' he said. 'But most of my friends are already there. I'm not even close.'

I didn't even know anyone who was married.

'You don't want any of it,' I said quietly. I didn't know much, but I knew how to read a face. 'You don't think you're missing anything.'

It was odd, but I felt my stomach lurch.

He shook his head but the movement was half-hearted. 'I used to get depressed when I was younger ... I really struggled.' He sounded hesitant. 'And now all I know is ... I seem to function better with exposure to an array of new things.' He looked around the room. 'I feel stimulated that way, and happier. It's taken me a while to realise it's how I work. Travel is good for that.'

I stared down at the plastic flower in my fingers, then sat it against the wall. I didn't think I wanted to keep it.

'My mum did some travelling when she was young, after she finished uni,' I said. 'She talks about it sometimes.'

'You never thought to go? Just head off?'

I shook my head. I didn't want to be like my brothers.

'You should come to the city, Mema,' he said. 'Come and see how the other half lives.'

'What do you do for fun?'

He thought for a few seconds. 'Well, you know, I go out. Pubs and stuff.'

'Drinking?' I didn't much like alcohol. My brothers had given it a good go before they'd run off, and as far as I could see it only made people more stupid. We'd tried it a few times, Anja and me, but it just made us sick.

'Yeah. I kinda thought I might have grown out of it by now. The other day I caught myself thinking maybe there's just people who like to get drunk, and maybe I'm one of them.'

It didn't sound too inspiring. I wondered what else there was. 'What do you like best about living there? What's your favourite thing?'

Hamish was checking out the décor, as though storing up all the particulars to tell someone later. I wondered who he'd tell.

'There's heaps of stuff, Mema. Cafés and restaurants, galleries and music, all that jazz, but it's mostly the feel of it, you know, that buzzing feel of so many people doing so much stuff … I like it.' He paused, glancing back at my face. I wasn't really convinced.

'I just like to go out at night and walk, all those strangers bustling around me. I don't know … I guess I like the anonymity. Something about it is … invigorating.'

This was hard for me to conceive.

The waitress came out then with the food, placing it carefully in front of us. Hamish kept his eyes on his order, as though if he looked up he'd burst out laughing. I smiled at the girl and she wandered back to the counter. He turned the bowl so it was facing me. I think they'd chosen their biggest piece of fruit especially for him. It was a giant-sized banana dick and balls. I laughed and he laughed too. What else could we do? We were trying to keep it quiet but that was making it worse. Giggling like that builds on itself. It's hard to stop once you start. Finally we calmed down and he had a spoonful.

'Mema, that is one of the funniest things I've seen. It's made my day.'

'It's always like that. No one ever says.'

'Really?'

'Yep.'

'This place gets weirder every day.'

Sitting there with Hamish in my town's dingy teahouse, spooning up my canned fruit salad, felt like something special. Sometimes you only appreciate things like that when they've already past, but I knew it right then and there. Soon Frank Brown would come and find us. Hamish would climb back onto the ute and they'd drive away. This moment would never come again. I wondered how to hold onto it, to stretch it to its limits, but then I saw Frank's big body in the doorway and I knew that it was over. It was already gone.

14.

The next day I headed up to Anja's. Mum doesn't like me to go up there anymore, and usually I don't. But Anja doesn't normally stay away long and I was worried about her. Sometimes when I'm awake late at night I worry her dad will do her real harm.

Her place is on one of the hills behind mine. There's a winding dirt road that crisscrosses up the mountain, but you need a four-wheel drive to get up there and I didn't drive anyway. Anja's so used to trekking up and down the mountain that she's fit as an athlete. At school she used to win all the cross-country races by such a big margin that even though she's weird-as-they-come the other kids gave her grudging respect, especially around race time. My brothers used to think it was hilarious 'cause Anja would hardly raise a sweat while everyone else jogged in half an hour behind her—chests heaving, looking half-dead. By that stage she'd be off somewhere making daisy chains, hardly even needing a drink. I liked to think about that—Anja's once-a-year day of cross-country triumph.

I didn't walk up the dirt road 'cause it was harder on my bung foot. I went straight up the mountain. It was steep but I wasn't in a hurry. I took it real slow, zigzagging a little. Moving from tree to tree. When Anja was small she'd had names for them, all the trees. She'd take me for long walks and introduce me to her favourites.

'This here's Lucinda,' she'd say, and wrap an arm around the trunk.

When you were with her it was easy to feel the life in everything. Back then Anja didn't distinguish between people and other things. This seemed wacky for the first few minutes, but after a time it became natural. Being with her was like stepping into another world. The life in everything seemed heightened, the air almost glistening. Your blood pulsed in a way you could feel. It was hard to explain, but there was a magic in it. I guess there was a magic in her too. She didn't talk to the trees anymore, but I felt those possibilities inside her lying dormant. Sometimes I wished they'd come out.

The house Anja lived in was a half-made thing—a real hippie bush shack, everything scavenged from the tip. Sheets of black plastic still filling in gaps, windows with cracked glass, taped over. All the walls were made from second-hand doors that didn't quite match up. Anja's dad used to call them the 'doors of perception', after some old book he'd loved, but there wasn't anything illuminating about the place now. I glimpsed it in the distance and dreaded what I'd find within. Approaching it sideways, out of sight of the windows, I tried to get a feel for her father's mood. If I wasn't sure, or couldn't see any sign of him, I'd make a whistling sound—a special noise we'd assigned years ago, close enough to be mistaken for a bird, but not so like one that she'd miss it—and Anja would come and find me. I could see Anja's father off to the side. He was rearranging the woodpile. That's what he did on a good day. Anja and he had the neatest woodpile in town. I looked around for Anja but couldn't see her anywhere.

'Jim,' I said, stepping up to say hello.

He turned around to face me. 'Mema.'

He was a bit bleary-eyed, but that was normal. Mum told me he'd been a handsome man in his youth, but there was no trace of that left. His beard was long, way past his chest, straggly and grey. When he spoke I could see the gaps where his teeth were missing. His face was sunken beneath his eyes, his skin speckled with brown liver spots. Ever since I was a child he'd frightened me.

'Anja around?' I asked, wondering why she wasn't coming out to rescue me.

'She's up at the hut,' he grunted, going back to his woodpile. 'Been up there for a while.'

The hut was where Anja was born, where the family had lived while Jim worked on the door-house. It was further up the mountain. Just a few walls and a dirt floor. Nothing else in there except her mother's old piano. Anja only went there when she was feeling really blue. I'd coaxed her out before, but not since we were younger.

'She's got a bee in her bonnet,' her father said over his shoulder. 'I don't know what's gotten into her.'

I watched him for a second, pottering there. There was nothing in his stance to suggest the loss of temper that sent Anja running down the hill at full speed, shaking and wordless. It was easy to hate him then, thinking of her, of all the things she'd seen. My hard thoughts darted against his back, but he didn't flinch.

'I'll go and see,' I said, and moved on up the hill.

The hut was hard to find. Covered in vines, over the years it had been absorbed a little into the mountain, indistinguishable from the surrounds. The forest was thicker this high up, and it took me a while of climbing to see anything familiar. Finally I saw Anja's hollowed-out tree trunk and I knew I was getting near. When she was little her parents were fighting so bad, taking her blankets out there must have seemed like the safest option. I walked over and peered inside remembering her child's body, once as small as mine, curled up inside. There was nothing within, so I turned and studied the forest looking for signs of her.

'Anja?' I called out, hoping that she'd give me a cooee. I listened for a minute but except for all the soft bush rustling I didn't hear a sound. Wandering around some more, finally I saw the hut.

'Anja?' I whispered as I crept up to the door. There wasn't anywhere to hide. She was sitting inside on the piano stool, leaning her back against the keys, as though she'd been waiting. I thought she might be bruised up from a scuffle with her dad, but she wasn't. She stared at me, eyes all flinty, but she didn't speak.

'Anja?' I looked at her, searching for signs of trouble. 'What's wrong?'

She looked down at the ground.

'Anja?'

She didn't usually give me the silent treatment.

'You didn't bring him up here, then?'

I didn't know what she meant.

'Who? Your dad?' I asked, standing in the open doorway, confused. 'I wouldn't do that.'

'You didn't bring the flood guy?'

'Hamish?'

It had never occurred to me that Anja might have a problem with Hamish.

'You took him creek-riding, didn't you?' she said, standing up. 'I knew the boards had been moved.'

I nodded slowly, watching her stricken face.

'How could you?'

'Anja.' I was still standing in the doorway, unsure which way to move. I hadn't known it mattered.

'That's our thing. It's our secret, and you shared it with him.'

'He won't tell anyone.' I shook my head. 'I'll ask him not to.'

Her eyes narrowed. 'He's still there?'

I'd seen Anja angry, but not usually with me.

'He's staying with Frank Brown,' I said. 'He'll be in town a little while. He's here for work.'

'You've got a thing for him.' Anja hissed. I could see her biting the insides of her cheeks. 'Haven't you?'

'What?'

'I can tell.' There was no hiding from her.

'Well … it's not comfortable.' I guess I had to tell someone.

'What do you mean?'

'I feel edgy all the time, like I'm on high alert. Plus, it's hard to tell if he even likes me.' I shrugged, stepping forward, reaching out a hand to her, but she stretched away from me.

'He said you were built like a thoroughbred.' I don't know why I told her that. It just slipped from my mouth.

'What?'

'That's what he said, when we were rain-running. He said you were very beautiful.'

I suppose it was like I was giving him away, but I didn't know then how Anja's mind would work. That if she was unhappy she'd try to make me unhappy too. She turned around towards the piano, carefully touching a key. She pushed down and a clanging note played out, discordant and dull. We both knew what would happen next. The ants would stream out in their black lines, covering every inch of the piano, spreading out all over the hut. It was a giant ant's nest in there, and it only took one note to disturb them.

'Here they come,' she said softly. 'No stopping them now.'

From where I was standing I could only see the side of her face, so I stepped further inside.

'Anja?' I wanted to comfort her but I didn't know how. 'It's okay.'

'I don't think so,' she whispered, still not turning around. 'Not for me.'

'He's just a bloke.' Only a few days ago that would have been true.

She leaned forward, pressing her head against the puckered wood of the piano. I stood there feeling helpless and she started banging down hard on the keys. The sound was loud but woozy, harsh and cacophonous. I suppose that's how she felt on the inside. The ants flowed over her fingers and up her arms, running up her neck and across her cheeks, but she didn't stop. They wouldn't bite you if you let them alone. I stepped closer and wrapped my arms about her shoulders, pressing into her tall frame. We stayed there a minute, me hugging her back like a frightened child, the ants spreading from her onto me.

'I won't leave you,' I whispered into her neck, willing her to hear. She stopped banging the notes, but the crashing sound still echoed around us in the air. I could hear my own breath. She gripped my arms then, squashing against the ants.

'Everyone leaves in the end,' she said quietly, and I knew she was thinking of her mother. Hanging from the trees like a scarecrow. Anja never spoke about it, but I knew she'd had to cut her down. When she was just a child. Everyone knew. I squeezed my arms a little tighter round her. I didn't know what to do with Anja's pain.

'I won't leave you,' I said again. I could feel a salty wetness welling at the back of my throat.

Swivelling around towards me, she stood up and took my face in her hands, kissing me dead on the mouth, the crushed ant smell wafting in the air. My eyes slammed shut and everything in me stilled. I'd never thought about Anja that way, all the years we'd been together. Sometimes I'd watched her apply her lipstick and admired the bow shape of her lips, the beauty of them, but I'd never expected to feel them against mine. I'd seen her body morph, swelling into womanhood, and she'd seen mine. Everything about her was familiar—her smell, her touch, the twitching of her mouth and the jittery movement of her eyes. I loved her. I'd always loved her. But she hadn't made my heart quicken.

I stood there in the hut while she kissed me, paralysed but trembling. Unsure how to untangle myself, unsure how to be. The ants dashed across us in their startled fashion, from her hands to my face and back again. Her lips parted a little on mine, and I opened my eyes. She was watching me, through her eyelashes, staring at my mouth. I knew I would have to move but something inside me delayed. I guess maybe I wondered what might happen next.

A sudden roar from the doorway startled us, and we jumped together, still locked in our strange embrace. Anja's father stood staring in, his eyes bulging in their sockets.

'You!' he yelled. It was hard to know who he meant. Anja stepped around me, holding out her arms, keeping him at bay.

'Whore,' he growled, menacing and low. 'Nothing but a whore.'

'Dad,' Anja's voice was cracking at the edges, 'don't be like that.'

I couldn't breathe. If there was a window I would have run for it. Taken Anja's hand and made her run too.

'It's not what you think,' I stuttered. 'We were just … trying it out.'

Anja shook her head. He glared at us, time stretching out.

'Come on, Dad,' Anja whispered, taking a step towards him. He stood rigid for a minute longer, then his body seemed to soften. It was faint, the slightest sag of his shoulders, but we both knew it was enough. Anja grabbed my outstretched hand and we shoved past him and took off down the hill.

My foot started giving me trouble part-way down, must have stepped on something, maybe twisted it a little too, and once we were far enough away I had to pull up and stop. Anja and I were both panting. Her eyes were large and flickering, searching for movement behind us in the shade.

'I can't keep running like that,' I said, picking up my foot to examine it. It was bleeding at the side. 'I've torn the skin.'

She looked down at my bare feet, not really seeing. 'Okay, well, let's walk. But fast.'

Gingerly, I followed her, until the rear of my house came into view. The ramshackle gardens that lined its borders, the uneven tilt of the steps. If I squinted I could see the brown shape of the old dog on the veranda.

'Don't tell your mum,' Anja said, keeping up the brisk pace. I didn't know which bit she meant. About the kiss or about her dad. I couldn't see myself mentioning either.

'I never do.'

I limped down the hill towards the back door but Anja didn't follow. I turned around, wondering what she was up to. 'Aren't you coming?' I called out, willing her to move.

She shook her head. My foot was throbbing, and it was hot out of the shade of the trees.

'Anja,' a few stray ants still crawled on my arms and I brushed them off, 'it's not a big deal. Please don't make this more than it is.'

I glanced back up at her there in her miniskirt, all knobbly knees and long legs. She crossed her arms over her chest. She was peering down at the grass, her hair hanging in her face. 'Please.' My voice was low. I needed to go inside.

'I'm not coming in. I'll see you tomorrow.' She flicked her hair back, face all stubborn.

'Where will you go?' I asked.

'I've got other places.' I knew Anja sometimes just holed up in the bush.

'Okay,' I sighed, 'but come round for dinner.'

'Just go inside.' She uncrossed her arms. 'And I'll see you tomorrow.'

I watched her as she disappeared into the bush, rangy and wild like a feral pony. Something in me surged, a kind of fear maybe. I'd known Anja forever, but it was hard to predict what she might do next. Anja was a little like dynamite. Once you lit the fuse, who knew what kind of blast you were in for? I didn't like the feeling of her sitting up on the hill. I was afraid my whole world might explode from one little spark.

15.

When I limped up the crooked back steps I realised Sophie and the babies had come for a visit. Rory came running to meet me at the door.

'Mema!' He wrapped his arms around my legs, nearly knocking me over. 'Where were you?'

'Just up at Anja's place,' I said, putting a hand on his solid little back and pressing him in against me. 'What's been happening?'

'We came to play,' he gazed up at me, 'but you weren't here.'

I couldn't move with him attached to me like that, so I squatted down and gave him a hug.

He pulled away and looked me in the eye, real close.

'Daddy's gone.' He said it as though it was something he'd only just learned. As though I might not know it either. 'And he's not coming back.'

I wasn't sure how to answer. I didn't know what Sophie had already said. Pushing the wispy strands of his hair back off his forehead, I leaned forward and breathed in the smell of him, looking for comfort.

'He's gone.' He said it again.

I nodded, but my foot was hurting, and I was still reeling from what had happened at the hut. I felt off balance, my bearings had slipped. I wanted to steal off to my room, but there was no way Rory would let me. Sophie came round the corner then, Lila on her hip. She had colour back in her, like she'd finally gotten some sleep.

'Let Mema in, sweetheart,' she said to Rory. 'She might need a cup of tea.'

I stood up, but I was having trouble steadying myself. Sophie looked down at my foot. 'Mema, you're bleeding. What have you done?'

'Stood on something, I think.' I couldn't meet her gaze.

'Rory, help Mema inside so we can look at her foot.'

Rory lifted his arm and wrapped it around my waist, as though he was my crutch and the strength of his small body might hold me up. The tenderness of his touch made me want to cry.

'Okay, sit her down on the couch so we can have a look.'

Rory led me into the lounge room and we sat down, huddled together. Beside me, he was wide-eyed and quiet.

'You hold bubs while I get a washer,' Sophie said, handing me down the baby. Lila wriggled in my lap, but then she seemed to settle. I rubbed my chin on the top of her head, slowly from side to side. Sophie came back in with a clean, wet washer. She looked at me and the babies, taking us in.

'Something happen, Baby-girl?'

I shook my head, but she knew I was lying. She just raised her eyebrows, crouching down at my feet.

'Mema, it's really bleeding. You should have said you were hurt. Called out or something.'

'It's okay.' I could feel the tears welling up in my eyes. Rory peered around at my foot, his eyebrows pushed together in a tight frown.

'Hurts?' he said, patting my arm. I don't think he'd ever seen me cry. His bottom lip started to quiver. Sophie looked from me to him, putting a hand out to squeeze his foot.

'It's alright, little man,' she said. 'Mema's okay.' His lip kept trembling, but he was holding it all in. 'Mummy's going to clean it up and put a Band-Aid on, then it'll be fine.'

Sophie picked up my foot gently, wiping away the blood. 'You haven't done this to yourself in a while.' She peered at the skin. 'You pushed it too hard.'

I nodded, my foot throbbing in her hand. 'I think I've sprained it a bit too,' I said. 'It feels all wrong.'

She inspected it, testing my joint.

'Yeah, it looks a little swollen.'

I glanced around the room. There was no sign of Mum. 'Where is she?' I asked.

'Just ducked out to the shed. We've been here a while already.'

Rory jumped off the couch then, caught by a new idea. His bottom lip was still wobbling, but he was choosing to ignore it.

'Nanny got some flowers!' He ran to the kitchen table, pointing. I twisted my head around to look behind me. There was a bunch of red crucifix orchids in a jug on the table, stringy but vibrant. I looked back at Sophie.

'Someone left them at the end of the driveway, under one of the big trees.'

For a second I thought they might have been for me and my heart jumped. Sophie must have seen it in my face 'cause she looked down at my foot, saying, 'They were for Mum. There was a note. I think it was Frank Brown of all people.'

I felt a rush of disappointment. Never before had I thought one of my mother's random gifts might be meant for me. The stirring of my hope made me feel ashamed. Frank Brown had left flowers for my mother. It seemed in line with him and his gentlemanly ways. I wondered how long he'd been pining after her.

Behind me I could hear Rory clambering up onto one of the chairs to get a better look at the flowers.

'Careful, sweetpea,' my sister called out to him. Those sorts of statements had slipped out of Sophie's mouth for as long as I could remember, comforting in their familiarity. She got up to find a bandage, patting my head on the way past. Lila started fussing on my lap so I turned her around, bouncing her gently on my knee. Her face had changed a little since the last time I'd seen her. Eyes more focused, nose more pointed. She was taking shape. I thought maybe there were glimpses of Sophie that I hadn't seen before. Usually I enjoyed holding the baby, having her stare with those big blue eyes right into mine, but after what had happened with Anja, Lila's gaze seemed uncomfortably discerning.

My sister came back in carrying an assortment of bandages. 'Soph, it's not that bad,' I said, but deep down I was grateful.

Sophie ignored me, picking up my foot and going to work. Sometimes the skin on the side of my bung foot gets stretched beyond its limits, and it ruptures, so she put some Band-Aids over that. Then she wrapped the whole foot up tight with a bandage, trying to relieve the sprain. We'd done all this in the past, from time to time.

'Okay,' Sophie said, reaching out to take Lila. 'Now just put it up for a while. No more running around.'

'I might go and lie on my bed for a bit.'

I needed to be alone and if I stayed out on the couch Rory would climb all over me. Sophie looked at me carefully, weighing me up. 'You sure nothing happened, Mema?' She reached out an arm towards me. 'You sure you're okay?'

It was the last thing I wanted to talk about, so I just nodded, moving away from her outstretched hand.

Lying on my bed, all the things I had gathered, all my knick-knacks and clothes, the nests and the stones, the books, they all seemed dull, like the sheen had gone off them. I gazed around looking for one thing that would give me comfort, but nothing did, and finally I turned over and stared at the wall. I tried not to think of Anja's kiss, of the softness of her mouth against mine, but the feeling of it came rushing in. I could see us as we'd been, pressed up against each other in the abandoned hut. Anja caressing my face, gentle but firm, as though I was something precious she held between her palms. I covered my eyes with my hands, trying to block it out, but the image of us grew there behind my eyes, the colours even brighter in my head than they'd been in the hut. And the more I tried to force it from my mind the bigger it became, until all I could see was me and her, larger than life—her rough bush hands tender against my cheek, stray ants fleeing along her arms, and her ruby red lips reaching down for mine.

I must have fallen asleep 'cause I sat up with a start when the door opened. It was Mum. She hovered near the doorway and I could tell straight away that something was wrong.

'Mema,' she said quietly. 'Old Dog's on her way out.'

'What?' I was still disorientated by sleep.

'She can't get up.' Mum stepped closer to the bed. 'I noticed her food from this morning was still in the bowl and I just went to check on her.'

I scrambled off the side, landing hard on my foot. My ankle collapsed under me, and I went down on the wooden floor with a clunk. Mum leaned down and helped me up, her lips a grim line.

'She's still breathing,' she said, tucking a loose strand of my hair behind my ear. Mum was usually so unflappable, but her face was pale and drawn. Old Dog had been old as long as my memory stretched, so it shouldn't have come as a shock that she would die, but somehow it did.

'She'll be alright,' I said, hobbling out to the veranda as fast as I could. Old Dog lay in the spot she always did, her brown body still, her eyes closed. If I concentrated hard I could see the faint rise and fall of her ribs, achingly slow and feeble. I crouched down beside her, stroking my hand along her back.

'Old Dog,' I whispered, but there was no movement to show she'd heard, not even the blink of an eye. I glanced back at Mum, but she was looking around at the walls in alarm.

'What?' I said. 'What's wrong?'

'Oh, Mema.' She shook her head. 'The ants are coming. They're coming for her.'

I stood up to see what she meant. There were lines of small black ants streaming across the house, heading towards us. They were coming from all over, inside the house and out. Anja's hut and the piano flashed in my mind, her hands and arms and cheeks crawling with ants. I shook my head to clear it, but the image stuck. Now the ants were marching here too.

'But she's not dead yet, why are they coming if she's not dead?' I asked Mum, my voice straining.

'I don't know, Mema,' she said gently. 'I've never seen it before.'

Squatting beside Old Dog, I glared at the ants marching across the rough wooden floorboards. I couldn't let them get her before she was ready.

'We have to take her to the vet.' Trying to bundle her into my arms, I looked around for Sophie but she must have gone home.

'She's dying, Mema. There's nothing they can do.'

'We don't know that.' My eyes were filling up and spilling over. 'We can't just let the ants have her.'

She was a big dog and it was a battle for me to pick her up. 'Mum,' I held her gaze through my tears, 'you've got to drive me to the vet.'

She looked at me struggling with Old Dog, and I could see she was wavering.

'We don't have the money to pay a vet. You know that.'

'I don't care.' I was hugging Old Dog's body close, trying to keep her with me. 'We'll pay it off. I'll pay it off.'

Mum shook her head. 'She's not going to make it, Mema. She probably won't even make the drive.'

The ants were coming closer. They were nearly at my feet.

'I can't let them have her, Mum. Please. What if it takes days?'

I stood up, grappling with the dog until I had her in my arms. My bung foot was throbbing beneath the extra weight. I wouldn't be able to lift her under normal circumstances, but these weren't normal.

'Okay,' Mum said finally, staring around at the ants. 'We'll go. Do you want me to carry her?'

I shook my head. My mum was strong as an ox, but Old Dog was mine and I wasn't giving her over.

Sitting in the back of the car with Old Dog on my lap, tears streamed down my cheeks. Usually weeping was an effortful thing—there was a blustering, a snuffling, something audible and clogged. But these tears were different—they flowed like a tap left on, limitless and soft. Somewhere inside I knew I wasn't just crying for Old Dog, but for all those others lost to me. For my brothers, and my dad, and all the dads I never knew. Sorrow had burst inside me, flowing out like a stream.

We drove in silence and I kept my palm against Old Dog's heart, feeling for her life, trying to keep it within her. When we pulled up at the vet, she was still breathing. Mum opened the door and I shifted around, trying to get out. Old Dog was heavy and her body was already stiffer than it had been before, as though death was claiming her cell by cell. As though she was in the act of becoming other, the matter of her transforming even then, grasped tightly in my arms.

Mum held the door open and I limped inside, holding her high against me until my arms shook with the strain.

The girl behind the counter took one look at my face and said, 'Go straight through,' and I loved her in that moment, loved her kind, sorry face.

'She's dying,' the vet said, when we walked in the door.

'I know,' I whispered, nodding through my tears.

'No, I mean, she's dying now. Right now.'

I slumped down on a chair in the corner, clutching her. The weight was too much, my arms had turned to jelly and I could barely hold her on my lap. My mum and the vet stood watching us—the dying dog and me—and under their gaze my face crumpled like a child's.

I felt the moment her heart stopped, felt it beneath my palm. Something in the room shifted. The vet crouched down and searched for a pulse, looking up at me with sombre eyes.

'She's gone,' she said. 'It's over.'

I nodded, but I didn't move. The seconds ticked by, stretching into minutes. My tears slowly eased. The vet stood back up and fussed around in the corner of the room, trying to give us space. Finally she faced us, looking from my mother to me.

'Would you like us to dispose of her or do you want to take her home?' she asked, needing to move us on.

Dry-eyed, my mum stepped forward. 'We'll take her, thanks,' she said, and lifted Old Dog's floppy body from my lap.

'Come on, Mema,' she said, 'come on home.'

Back out on the street, the sunlight stung my eyes. Mum put Old Dog in the back of the car, covering her with a hessian sack the vet gave us. I stood on the kerb watching her, sapped and strange. My lips felt cracked and dry, and I wet them with my tongue.

'I've just got to grab some things from the shop, now that we're here,' Mum said, squeezing my arm. 'You wait in the car. I'll only be a minute.'

I pulled the passenger door open and settled down inside, feeling woozy. Sitting in there with Old Dog dead in the back made me think about what it was that rendered a thing alive— what made a heart start to beat? And what made it stop? I sat in the front concentrating on my breaths, marvelling that such a simple thing as breathing could mean the difference between living and dying.

There was a knock on the window and I looked up, startled. It was him, Hamish.

'Wakey, wakey,' he said, grinning. 'What're you doing in there?'

He was dressed in the clothes we'd bought, his face shaved, eyes bright. I stared at him for a few seconds, thrown. I guess I should have got out, but I just wound down the window.

'Look who I found,' he said, stepping aside. Anja stood behind him. She looked at me but she didn't smile. 'She was hitching. Frank and I picked her up.'

I stared up at them from the front seat. Anja tossed her hair and put her hands in her pockets and I knew straight away she was up to no good. Hamish bent down, peering closer in the window.

'You right, Mema?'

I felt my lips tilt as though I was smiling, but no words came out of my mouth.

'We've just eaten,' Hamish said, watching my face. 'Pity we missed you.'

I thought of them sitting there at the Savoy, laughing together about the banana splits. With Old Dog in the back it was too much. I knew I was going to cry. I covered my face with my hands, wishing they'd both disappear.

'What's wrong?' I heard him as though from afar. And then— 'Anja, she's crying.'

There was a shuffle outside, them changing places. I felt Anja's hand grab mine through the window, pulling it away from my face.

'If he's only a bloke, why are you crying?' she growled at

me, out of his earshot, her face looming, tough-eyed. I tried to loosen my fingers from hers, but she wouldn't let go.

'It's Old Dog,' I choked out, my voice muffled. 'She's in the back. She died.'

Anja's face changed then, something about it stilled, like she was folding herself away. She stared at me through the window, releasing my hand from her grip. 'Well, she *was* old,' she said then, as if I wouldn't know.

'But she'd always been old,' I whispered back.

Stepping away, she turned around, muttering something to Hamish, and he crossed over in front of her, his hand on the door frame.

'The old dog? The big brown one?' he asked. 'It died?'

I nodded, wiping my nose with the back of my hand. He glanced from me to the rear of the car.

'Shit, Mema,' he said, face solemn. 'That's bad news.' His fingers tapped against the window, softly, marking time. He peered in at the clock on the dashboard.

'I have to go and meet some people for work,' he said finally. 'I only wanted to come say hi.' He put a hand up to rub across his hair. 'I would have let you be if I'd known about your dog.'

I looked down at my lap.

'I'm really sorry, Mema.' He reached in, placing his fingers on my shoulder, the briefest touch.

I didn't look up. I didn't want to.

'I'll see you soon, hey,' he said, straightening up. 'I'll be here for another week or so.'

I nodded, waiting for him to leave. He waved goodbye to Anja and then he was off. Anja stood on the kerb, staring down the street, not talking, and in a minute my mum was back in a flurry of skirts, carrying some shopping.

'Anja,' she said. 'What are you doing in town?' Anja hardly ever came in without me. 'You want a lift back?'

Anja shrugged, but she opened the door and got in. Mum put the bags in beside her, away from the dead dog, and then heaved her big body into the driver's seat.

'I got some ice-cream.' She looked sideways at me. 'Thought it might cheer you up.'

Mum never bought us sweets. It was her only rule. I leaned over then and put my head on her shoulder, and she wrapped an arm around me like I was just a kid.

'It'll be alright,' she murmured, hugging me close. 'Tomorrow—it'll be alright. It will all be better in the morning.'

16.

We buried Old Dog out near Isis. They'd never been pals in real life, not like her and Thor, but it seemed right that their bones might rest together, two skeletons beneath the earth, stretching out towards each other. Who knew what happened after you died? Maybe there was a communion in it, even if it was just in the slow movement of soil over time, a subtle blending of remains.

Anja took off as quick as she could, gulping down her ice-cream so fast I could see it was giving her brain freeze. She barely said two words to me. When she was gone Mum asked me straight out. 'What's going on with Anja?'

Words sat heavily on my chest. I didn't know how to dislodge them. My mouth was full of pebbles. 'Nothing,' was all I could manage.

Mum had a way of looking at me, as though she could see into my brain.

'You be careful of her, Mema,' she said, picking up our empty ice-cream bowls and putting them in the sink. 'You know how she is. When she cracks, she tears everything down.'

I didn't like it when my mum criticised Anja. It didn't seem worth it to pick holes in the only friend you had. Mum had high standards when it came to friendship, so high she didn't have friends. It wasn't something I wanted for myself, though truth be told, I wasn't far behind. 'She's been through a lot.'

'I know she has.' Mum ran the water over the bowls, staring out the window. 'But we all have, Mema. It's what you do with it that counts.'

Even though Old Dog never did that much except move from sleeping spot to sleeping spot, her absence filled the house. After dinner, as the evening light faded into darkness, I knew I wouldn't sleep for hours, so I hobbled out to Mum's shed, thinking I'd make some mugs.

My whole body ached from scrabbling around trying to hold the dog, so it was hard to isolate the pain in my foot. I knew it must be hurting 'cause I was limping pretty bad. Once I was in the shed I turned on the lamp and sat down under the spotlight. Putting your hands in clay is always soothing, and for a while I just squashed it about with my fingers, enjoying the squeeze and suck. By the time I got the wheel moving, a lightness had entered me. The pebbles in my mouth had dissolved and I hummed a little under my breath. I got the first two mugs out pretty quick, just going with the shape of the clay. But on the third one I started to wonder about the similarities between clay and flesh. I found myself imagining my fingers were curving around the rim of a shoulder, or the swell of a breast.

If I closed my eyes I could see the hard line of Hamish's jaw and feel the sweep of my fingers along it. I breathed out in a sigh, and in the next breath the curve of Anja's hip appeared in my mind's eye, and the slide of my hand against it. I didn't try to quell my thoughts like I had before. I didn't try to brush the images away, but let them drift, eyes still closed, fingers bending and shaping the clay beneath my hands in whatever way seemed best. Before long I imagined other people I knew—Billy—the brown hardness of his forearms, sprinkled with dark hair. But in the end it all came back to him—Hamish, with his pale skin and luminous eyes. I got to imagining what his hands might feel like on me if I was the clay, if he could mould me with his touch. I felt a shuddering within, dark and liquid, and it made me want to switch off the light. It was as though I'd happened upon a secret, ripe for the telling, but precious too, and I didn't want anyone else to see. I thought of all the secret places I knew—Anja's hut, the hollowed-out tree, and the abandoned shack way out in the paddocks.

The memory of that shack began to swell in my mind. Tumbledown walls, rusted roof. All alone in the middle of nowhere. A furtive place, where all my secret thoughts could be housed. Somewhere inside myself I opened a door and stepped into a new place. Where clay could become skin, and skin become clay. I turned off the light and crept into bed, careful not to wake my mother. Once I was there, tucked up in my covers, I conjured the shack and let my thoughts roam.

When I awoke it was with a dull headache, as though all those secret thoughts had pressed heavily against my skull while

I slept. It was cool in the early morning, the thick weight of the summer humidity not yet hanging in the air. I slid on a skirt and a floppy jumper and went to watch the sun rise. The grass was damp beneath my feet, the dew quickly soaking my bandage. Though the skin felt stretched tight across my forehead, my foot was stronger, my limp less pronounced. I always marvelled at my body's capacity to right itself. It was as my mum had said—*It will all be better in the morning.*

Far off in the distance, the rim of the sun was just showing above the mountains, and where I was standing was gradually bathed in light. I could see Bessie a little way off, munching the grass. The calf tottered nearby, stumbling against its mother's legs. It seemed a long time since Hamish had washed off the bridge, but when I looked at the calf, still all wobbly and new, I realised it had been less than a week. I looked across the hillsides rising in front of me, wondering where he was right at that minute. I couldn't see Frank's house from mine, but I knew, as the crow flies, it was just over the way. Cross a couple of creeks, head through some camphors, and in no time at all I could be there.

I let the chickens out and gathered the eggs, scooping up the bottom of my jumper and holding them gently in the pocket of fabric. They were warm, only just laid. I took one and rolled it against my closed eyes.

Sometimes when I woke with a throbbing head I wandered to the creek and tried to wash all the heaviness away. It wasn't a sure-fire cure, but from time to time it worked. That morning, the warm egg pressed against my eye, it seemed worth a try. I set off carefully, mindful of my foot, but once I'd meandered down the paddocks, across those open spaces, I was feeling pretty sure. The stretch of creek I'd chosen was a little way down from the secret tree. A deep spot, just before a bend and some rapids. The water had cleared, but the shadows of dawn made it seem dark and bottomless. I sat on the grass on the bank, arranging the eggs in a neat pile then taking off my jumper and nestling it around them. A Mema nest. It made me smile. Unwinding my bandage, I bent my ankle from side to side, testing it. It was still a little sore, but no longer swollen. I held my bung foot in my hand, looking it over. Sophie's Band-Aids were still stuck on and I didn't touch them. I'd be lucky if they stayed on in the water.

My foot was a deformity, I suppose, but I was used to it. It didn't seem like anything other than another part of me. No different from my knobbly little elbows, or the deep recess of my belly button. A feature on the landscape of my body. I knew that in other places things like that—misshapen feet, or any other slight deviation from the norm—could leave you marked. But my mother had always told me I was blessed, and I had the gap between my teeth to prove it. Sitting there, I wondered how it might be to have been born in a different place. It was hard to imagine being somewhere without this sky and these hills and this flowing body of water. Without my house and family, without Bessie, her baby, the chickens and Thor. Even Isis and Old Dog stayed with us, buried beneath the soil. I lay back against the grass, looking at the morning sky. I didn't know if I'd exist without all these things around me. And if I did, who would I be?

Standing back up, I stripped off and slipped into the creek, plunging down deep. The water was cold and fresh against my skin, jolting me out of my thoughts. I lingered there a while, floating, until my skin began to tingle and prick, and it seemed as good a time as ever to go and face the day. Clambering onto the bank, I wrung the water from my hair, drying off in the soft morning sun. I shivered a little, but already the heat was rising. I liked watching the goosebumps that spread across my arms and legs dissolve into the day. When I was dry enough I stepped back into my clothes, clean and revived, my headache banished.

Staring across the hills, I saw a figure walking. It was him, Hamish, striding towards the bridge. I blinked, not trusting my eyes. I know at times I'm a whimsical girl, dreaming about odd things until to me they seem real. I'd longed to see him, imagining myself crossing those same hills towards Frank Brown's old farmstead, but I hadn't moved an inch. I hadn't let myself. And now there he was, walking right towards me. My breath held in my chest, wedged there, until he was close enough that I knew it wasn't just my fancy. I couldn't help but take it as a sign. I had yearned and he had come. Wasn't there some meaning in that?

Hamish had something in his arms, something big and black. He stopped on the other side of the bridge and I could sense his hesitation. We'd ridden across it in a flash on our bikes a few days before, not stopping to inspect the broken, teetering railing, not reflecting on what Hamish had nearly lost in that wild rush of water. I imagined he was seeing it all again. He lifted his gaze and I knew he had felt me there watching.

He didn't hesitate then, but strode across. My breath rushed from my lungs, and I sucked in another, holding it firmly. Stepping forward, I moved through the air towards him, forgetting my eggs all wrapped in their jumper-nest, forgetting my rolled-up bandage. Forgetting everything. My head was buzzing with a strange noise, my heart thudding in my chest. I felt a stranger to myself, a ghost-walker.

As I got closer, I saw he held a dog. A gangly half-grown pup.

'Morning swim?' he called out, taking in my dripping hair.

I nodded, focusing on the puppy. When he got near, I saw it was squirming, wanting to get down.

'You got a dog?' I asked, surprised by the evenness of my voice. I reached out a hand to pat the dog's head. The pup had big floppy ears, fleshy and soft as velvet. 'He's lovely.'

'It's a she,' Hamish said, wrestling with her wriggling form. 'If I put her down she'll run away. I don't have a lead.' He crouched down and put the puppy on the grass, holding onto her back. I squatted down too, my ankle protesting beneath me. After yesterday—losing Old Dog—it was startling to see a puppy so full of life. Vital, its coat black and shimmery.

'I got her for you, Mema.'

I suppose I should have known it was a gift, soon as I saw it in his arms, but I hadn't. I didn't say anything, no words would come. Reaching out, I rubbed the puppy's ears. She turned her nose towards my hand, licking my fingers. It made me think of Old Dog's scrappy fur, coarse and a little matted.

'To replace the old dog.'

I exhaled then, thinking of her buried under the dirt. Dying was natural, but that didn't make it easier to bear.

Hamish looked stricken. 'I guess that's a bad way of putting it.' I could see him striving to choose the right words, struggling through sentences in his head. 'I didn't mean it like that. I know you can't replace something like a dog. I just …'

I smiled across at him 'cause I knew what he was trying for. I wasn't so daft that I couldn't recognise a heartfelt gift. He pushed the dog's bottom down and she sat, head tilted sideways, looking up at me with her soulful puppy gaze. And behind her, he looked at me too, eyes clear and blue.

'What do you think?' He sounded uncertain. 'Is she alright?'

Even though we'd always had animals dumped at our door, I couldn't help feeling that this was different. That it mattered to Hamish in some particular way. My mind was ricocheting with thoughts, still buzzing with that sound. I was searching for the meaning. A life for a life?

'Do you want her?' he asked. ''Cause Frank said he'll take her if you don't.'

I looked at him then. 'I want her.' My words rushed out, low and slippery.

The pup wasn't going to sit still for much longer. She was twitching all over, ready to take flight.

'I think she'll stick near us, if you let her go,' I said, stroking her fur. Puppies were scatty, but there was no traffic here to run her over, no holes for her to slip into.

Hamish lifted his hands off the pup's back and she bolted off, sniffing around us and then snuffling along the creek bank.

'She's part beagle.' He was watching the pup. 'They're sniffer dogs.'

The dog was exploring, but she was keeping an eye on us, not going too far.

'Frank gave me a list of all the local breeders,' he said. 'I rang around until I found her. We picked her up this morning. She's house-trained, you know. She's already a few months old.' He wiped his doggy hands on the grass.

'Did you buy her?'

I don't know why it mattered but it did.

He smiled. 'Finally got into my bank account.' It felt odd to think of him forking out the cash. 'She's part golden retriever too. Though you can't really see that.'

I shook my head—there was nothing golden about her. 'I've only ever had mongrels. You have to guess what they are.'

'You like her?' They were simple words, but they seemed to hold so much.

Within me was all confusion. I nodded, but just having Hamish close made my insides raucous. All the words in my head tumbled together, coherence lost in a pulsing chaos. I felt my stomach turn, my fingers tremble.

'I can't stay,' he said then, standing up. I stood up too. 'I've got to get into work. Meeting with some guys from the council.'

'How's it been going in the truck?' My words sounded clunky. Since he'd been gone I'd worried about the driving.

Hamish glanced across at me, shaking his head. 'That first afternoon in town I just got in the back. Frank must have thought I was a freak, but he didn't say a word.' Hamish could smile at himself. I liked that about him. 'The next morning I got into the cab. It was the same, couldn't breathe, sweating like a pig, but I held on tight and eventually it passed. When we picked up Anja it was better, bit more of a distraction.'

I felt myself stiffen at the mention of her name. An image of them at the Savoy flashed through my mind. At the back of my neck I felt hackles rise. I was an animal, caught in some uncontrolled biological response. Though I tried to stay still, my shoulders shuddered.

'She's an odd one.' He looked at the ground. It was hard to know exactly what he meant. I imagined all Anja's tricks— the ways she played at being a woman. The bright stripe of her lipstick, the long sweep of her bare legs. I wanted to tell him to be careful of her, but I didn't know how.

'Well, I better go,' he said, whistling for the dog. She came bouncing over, ears flopping in the air. 'You grab her otherwise she'll follow me.'

I picked her up. Half-grown she was pretty heavy. She scrabbled around in my arms, but after a second she stilled. Hamish reached out and gave her one last scratch behind the ears, then he stepped away from me, holding up a hand.

'Let me know what you name her,' he called, throwing out a promise of tomorrow.

17.

Mum wasn't too impressed about the puppy, even when I explained her pedigree. I knew she could see how much it pleased me, how every time I looked at it I thought of him, and how he'd thought of me. I saw the puppy as a sign of affection, and shafts of hope began to rise inside me. Would you buy a pup for someone you didn't care about? I named her Blossom, for all the new things that were bursting inside me, but my mum refused to call her anything but 'that pup'.

On the first day she dug up the garden, eating the hearts right out of some of Mum's most precious plants. Her bromeliads. The house was tense, my mum bristling with annoyance. I tied Blossom up and she was chastened. After that she stayed by me, looking at my face to try to ascertain the rules. There weren't many I could teach her, besides *don't eat the plants*. In my house it had always been a case of anything goes.

Anja didn't come all that day and I wondered where she was. I wasn't game to head back up the hill and face her father, look into his half-crazed eyes and see the kiss reflected back at me. I missed her. She'd known all my unknowns—there hadn't been anything to hide. I thought back on all we'd shared, tried to find those hints of sex, but, in truth, the boundaries between us had always been lax.

When we were very small we'd found a log, half submerged in the creek. Wedged under the stones by one of the floods, it lay there on an angle gathering moss, only the tip of it protruding. We always swam nude and I don't know which one of us discovered it first, but we came to know that if we rubbed ourselves against it, there was a kind of pleasure. It was impossible to do together, so we'd take turns, one of us treading water while the other rubbed herself against the log. It wasn't a secret, we spoke of it openly—'You want to go rub the log?' Too young to know that such things should be concealed. And in any case, when we looked about at the adult lives around us—all the frolicking nakedness, the hopping from bed to bed—how could we have known about such a thing as a private realm.

We didn't see the log as a means to an end. We didn't rub ourselves raw trying to get somewhere, we just liked the feel of it, comforting and sublime. The log washed away one flood, as unexpectedly as it'd come. We'd sat on the bank staring at the place it had been, wondering where it would end up, wondering if anyone would love it the way we had. The mossy log, svelte and lean. We mourned its sudden disappearance, but we soon forgot, moving on to some other curiosity. But maybe it had been there all the time, this shared thing. In the scheme of things it was hard to fathom.

All the next day I waited for Hamish to reappear, knowing that he would. There was a hum inside me, a kind of twanging. He had given me a pup and wasn't that something? When my mum was finished in the shed I took her place, tying the pup to a post outside so she wouldn't get under my feet while I made my mugs. Feeling the clay between my hands, I dreamed of him some more. I didn't see Mum watching me, standing in the doorway, her frown growing deeper by the moment. When I finally noticed her, she couldn't hide her dismay, and the secret sound inside me quietened a notch.

'Mema, it's no good.' Her eyes were fierce and sad.

'What?' I asked, though I knew she saw everything. I knew she always had.

'He's not for you, love,' she said, and I was struck 'cause she never called me that. 'He's just going to disappear. He's been itching for it from the start.'

I think I knew she was right, but the shafts of hope inside me burned bright.

'Mema, I know he seems all smooth and shiny, and you've been starved of some real company.' She paused a second, watching my face. 'And don't think I've missed how much charm he's thrown your way. I've seen him looking at you through those long lashes. But try to pin him down, even for a second, and he'll just wriggle free.'

I could see there was no joy for her in speaking these words. That she'd rather not be standing there breaking my heart.

'You don't know him,' I said, but my hands were shaking.

'I can smell it a mile off, Mema. Call it my area of expertise.'

'But what about the pup?'

'Everyone has moments of kindness,' she said. 'The trick is telling which ones matter.'

I thought about the clearness of Hamish's eyes. That first moment I truly saw them, pushing on the flank of my silly birthing cow.

I nodded, trying to dim that clamour inside me, trying to cover my shards of hope.

'Okay, Mum.' Fear was welling in my belly. I'd let go of the reins and my horse had galloped away. My imagination had jumped the fences—long gone—I didn't even know where to look.

'I know it hurts, Baby-girl,' she said softly. 'But I'm telling you, it can hurt a whole lot more.'

I thought of all the men my mum had known. All the times she'd believed. She stood there in the open doorway watching me, and I wished her gone, and all this bad history gone too, swept up under the rug.

'They're not all like that,' I said, soft but defiant. 'They can't all be.'

She spread her arms wide, like she was holding the whole world, but she didn't speak. She didn't have to say a word. I looked out of the shed to my horizons, taking in the lie of the land—the gentle undulations of those rolling endless hills—and I nodded then, tucking my feelings away.

I was still tinkering at the wheel when Sophie came to visit in the afternoon, carrying a baby on each hip. It looked like they'd all just woken up, even Rory was quiet.

'How's the foot?' she asked, putting Rory on the ground. He clung onto her leg, all sleepy-eyed.

'Alright,' I said. 'It wasn't bad.'

She sighed, looking up at the back veranda—the place where Old Dog used to be. After the vet, Mum had called her, letting her know that she was gone.

'Mum said the flood guy bought you a new dog,' she said, ruffling Rory's hair. 'A fancy one. That's a bit of an investment.' Sophie looked me over, and for once I wished her gaze was not so penetrating. 'Where is it, then?'

'I tied her up out the front. She keeps getting under Mum's feet. She chewed the hearts out of a few of her bromeliads.'

'Really?' Sophie looked around, hiding a smile. 'That's bizarre.'

'I know. What are the odds of getting a dog that likes to eat bromeliads?'

'About a hundred to one,' Sophie said, and I could see it tickled her fancy. Bromeliads were the only plants my mother really loved.

I got up from the wheel to go and untie the dog.

'Come and meet her,' I said to Rory, and he held out his hand for me to hold. When we got to the dog she was sitting, tail wagging against the ground, trying hard to control her enthusiasm. Rory was bamboozled by the new pup replacing the old. He couldn't quite wrap his little mind around how such a swap would take place. He kept staring at her and saying again and again, 'Mema, Old Dog was old,' as if this should explain it, but it didn't, and nothing really would.

Blossom was excited by Rory, recognising that he was fellow young pup. Once I let her off the leash she jumped straight up onto his back and knocked him over. It didn't matter how many times I chastised her, she didn't seem to believe this wasn't great fun. In the end we went inside and sat on the couch. I held her still between my legs so Rory could get his bearings.

Even though I'd heard my mother's words clearly, I found myself listening for the stranger's footsteps on the dirt road, pining for the distant throb of Frank's truck on our driveway, and in the end I heard it. Rory went speeding onto the front veranda, the puppy breaking free and following, running into the back of him and knocking him over so he landed face down on the old wooden slats. There was a graze and a bruise and he screamed, more in outrage than anything else. When Frank and Hamish stepped from the truck it was a general commotion that greeted them.

'Hope she's not already causing trouble,' Hamish said and I could feel my mother's irritation moving through the air towards him.

Frank stood back a little, holding his old hat in his hands, and Sophie took pity on him and asked if he wanted a cup of tea.

'If you've got one on the boil,' he said, and I could see him checking out our rusted gutters and all the peeling paint. I wondered then if he'd come to fix things then see what he could get.

Hamish looked at me, across the crying toddler and clumsy pup, but he didn't step any closer. 'Frank, you should see some of the pots and stuff in the shed,' he said, motioning towards it with his head. 'It's pretty amazing in there.'

'I'd like to see them. Would you …?' Frank asked, looking across at Mum with just a touch of longing. Even though it was a set-up, how could she refuse?

Up on the veranda I stepped aside and Hamish came into the kitchen. The kettle had boiled and Sophie was pouring out the teas, Lila gurgling on her hip.

'I'm sorry, I don't think I met you properly. I'm Sophie.' It was a pretty valiant effort at normality, considering the last time they'd encountered each other.

'Hamish.' He held out his hand to shake.

'This is Lila.' She smiled down at the baby. 'And I'm sure you've already met Rory.'

Rory was standing, clinging onto my leg, tears still pooled in the corners of his eyes, warily watching out for the pup. He didn't bother saying hi to Hamish.

'How do you have your tea?' Sophie asked.

'However. I don't mind.' I guess Hamish knew we had limited options in the tea department.

The teas brewed on the benchtop and I watched the steam rise. Hamish sat down at the kitchen table and the puppy wandered over, finding her way to his feet. She sat right down on his shoe, leaning back against his leg, and he bent down and rubbed her ears.

'What did you call her?' he asked me, breaking the silence.

'Blossom.' Saying that word, I couldn't look at his face.

'Pretty,' Sophie said, glancing between us, swapping Lila onto her other hip. She motioned Rory over for a hug, and he sniffled and let go of my leg.

'Baby-girl, can you take the teas out?' she asked me. 'I can't hold this lot and carry them.'

My nickname sounded odd in company. I nodded, but there was a part of me that felt shunted off like a child.

In the shed Frank was listening carefully as Mum told him how the wheel worked. He'd linked his fingers behind his back, as though to keep from touching anything. I stood a moment watching them. Frank kept breaking in to clarify some minor mechanical working. He asked question after question, keeping up the talk. He listened intently, hanging on Mum's every word. I felt I was intruding, but the teas were getting cold.

'Where do you want these?' I called into the shed.

Mum was startled but Frank turned around slowly, like he was accustomed to any eventuality. He stepped towards me, taking the mugs from my hands, and handing one to my mother.

'And these ones are yours, Mema?' he asked. 'You made them?'

'Yep.'

He picked one up in his spare hand, inspecting it.

'Clever.' He paused, and I knew I was going to be kept there for a bit while he asked me about the process in the same way he'd been asking Mum. All the time I was thinking of Hamish and Sophie holed up in the kitchen, wondering what they'd have to talk about, and getting agitated imagining it. Finally Frank turned his attention back to Mum and I made a getaway.

When I stepped up onto the veranda I fished around a second for the dog lead, thinking if Blossom was still terrorising Rory it'd be best to tie her up. I heard their voices drifting out the door towards me, and I couldn't help it—I stood there and listened. Sophie seemed to be giving Hamish the third degree.

'So, you got a girlfriend, then?' I heard her ask. 'Someone missing you back home?' I sucked in my breath, waiting for his answer.

'No one special,' he said, but there was something unconvincing about it. I could hear what he was leaving out. There *was* someone. Just someone *not that special*. It hit me like a punch in the stomach, even though I knew that, all things considered, it was obvious he would. He'd come from a life full of others—with cups of coffee at cafés, galleries and museums and restaurants and all that other stuff he'd told me about. Of course he had *someone*. Someone to do all that stuff with. I stood there wondering what makes someone special.

'And you travel a lot for work? Other places besides out here in the middle of nowhere?' My sister's voice was chipper, that's how I knew she was fishing.

'Yeah, it's pretty good, really. Lots of different gigs. Sometimes it's small contracts like this one, but other times it can be quite big. And, you know, because it's always to do with environmental issues, often I get to see places off the beaten track.' Hamish didn't seem to mind the grilling. He was going with the flow.

'Like here?' Sophie said. 'This is pretty off the beaten track.'

Hamish didn't answer but I imagined him nodding. A part of me was afraid Sophie might move on to interrogating him about me so I stepped inside.

Hamish smiled as I came through the door. My skin tingled under his gaze. My sister stared so hard I imagined she could see the trace of every minuscule quiver beneath my skin.

'How's Anja?' Sophie asked me suddenly. 'I haven't seen her for a while.'

Blossom was nestled there at Hamish's feet, asleep, without a care in the world. I looked at her, still cherubic and new, and I wished, just for a second, that I could be like that too.

'She hasn't been here for a few days.'

The baby fussed a little on Sophie's hip and she jiggled her around. Rory was quiet on the couch, looking at a picture book.

'That's unusual,' Sophie said, sitting down at the table and pulling up her shirt to breastfeed. 'Hope everything's okay.'

'I've seen her a few times, out and about.' Hamish piped up, looking away from my sister's pale breast. 'She seems alright.'

We both looked at him then, sharply.

'It's weird, she's the main person I seem to bump into,' he said. 'You know, when you see the same person everywhere you go?'

Sophie looked disturbed at this and the baby started up fretting at the breast. She turned aside, whispering to Lila. I didn't know what to think about Anja. She must have been stalking him. It was something she'd do.

'What kind of places?' I asked, trying to sound normal.

'I don't know, just in town, I suppose.' He tapped his fingers on the table. 'It happens all the time in the city. You'll notice some girl in a bookstore and then suddenly you'll see her everywhere. I don't know what it is.'

I tried to ignore how my stomach dipped at this mention of another girl. In the back of my mind I could see their faces. The girl who wasn't special. The girl from the bookshop. All the girls he couldn't remember. I guess Hamish didn't realise that Anja rarely went into town. I could see this development had got my sister thinking. She didn't look up from Lila's face but I knew her mind would be working overtime piecing things together. Lila had settled and was doing her funny gutso sounds. It was pretty loud. Comical, really. Hamish was going faintly pink—that creeping blush poking out of the top of his shirt. I felt sorry for him, stuck in the middle of all this woman-drama.

'You want to go check out the calf?' I asked, and even I knew it was a clumsy way to make an exit. Hamish stood up so quick Blossom toppled off his feet. He bent down to give her a pat.

'She can come.' I still had the lead in my hand. We didn't have a collar yet, so I wrapped the lead around her neck and clicked it back on itself.

Hamish watched me and then he said, 'Resourceful, Mema. That's what you are,' echoing Frank's words that day in the truck. I didn't turn around to see what Sophie thought of that. I just walked with Hamish and the pup right out the door.

18.

We stood on the rise of the hill, the roll of the paddocks spreading out before us. They were empty of cattle, 'cause we only had Bessie. For a period she'd kept breaking the fences, searching out a mate. 'Bulling,' Frank called it, as he herded her back to our side. 'She's just bulling.' He'd managed to say it with a completely straight face, but it was hard not to laugh. She'd gotten herself knocked up—quick smart—and then she'd settled down. And now there was the calf.

Bessie was a little like a dog—she came when she was called—but I waited until we were out of sight of the house before I sang out her name. Nothing moved for a bit, then we saw a flicker of brown in the trees way off in the distance and she trotted slowly up towards us, the calf straggling along behind.

'Wow, it's gotten bigger.' Hamish held up his hand to block out the sun. 'Looks healthy.'

'Yeah.'

As Bessie got closer, Blossom started to fret. I suppose it was only natural, she'd never been close to a cow. She pulled on the lead, trying to get away, and then ran round me, wrapping me up in the rope.

'She's at that silly stage,' I said, and Hamish took the lead and helped me untangle her. Now that I had him alone I wasn't quite sure what to say.

'How's the mill thing coming along?' I asked, thinking work was a safe bet. 'Find out lots of stuff?'

'Yeah, I've talked to quite a few different people.' He looked around at all the hills, taking in their shape. 'The mill guys, the council, and a few of the local environmental groups.'

Bessie came right up, searching for my fingers. The pup rushed out in front of her in fright, pulling tight against the lead. Bessie stumbled backwards and behind her the calf recoiled, skittish and clumsy. They kept their distance then, warily, staring at us, unblinking.

Hamish pulled Blossom back, placing her between us.

'Sit.' His voice was firm, and she did so, no hesitation. He looked across at me, like there hadn't even been an interruption. I was amazed at how calm Blossom was at his command, sitting there, watching Bessie and the calf.

'And what have you found out?' I wasn't so much interested in his answer. I was listening, but I was more absorbed by the deep timbre of his voice.

'There are a few hitches. There always are. Cane is seasonal and there isn't much to burn in the off-season. They've been on the lookout for an alternative source of fuel.'

'Alternative?'

It was like he was telling me a story about another place. Some far-off land where these types of things happened.

'Yeah, something else to burn.'

I couldn't think when he was standing so close.

'If you throw another fuel source into the mix, I don't know if it ends up being all that ecologically friendly. Depending, I suppose, on what it is.'

I nodded, though I didn't really know what he meant.

'It's complicated, Mema.' He turned back to the hills. 'It's so green here. It's amazing. All those trees.'

The camphors. 'They're beautiful, aren't they?' I said.

'They're noxious weeds.'

I looked at him sideways. After our fight about the cane toads, it was hard to tell if he was goading me.

'I love them.' I didn't care what category they fell under.

'I know that.' His voice was soft, gentle even.

'When will you be finished?' I made myself ask him. I didn't really want to think about endings, but I knew that I should.

'I'm not sure. Not too much longer.'

Hearing those words made my chest hurt.

'I've always wanted a dog,' he said, left of field.

I looked down at Blossom, and in that moment she seemed more his than mine.

'Why don't you get one?' I asked, thinking maybe I should give her back. I didn't want to, but maybe I should.

He rubbed the back of his head. 'You know, I travel too much. You can't have a dog when you do that. It's not fair.'

'What about a girlfriend?' The words slipped out of my mouth. I felt my skin prickle. 'Can you have one of those?'

He looked at me and I knew he could feel it. My yearning hanging there between us like some kind of bright flag.

'That's a little different.' He held my gaze. 'The right girl won't hang about waiting for me to come home. She'll be busy, her own thing going on. Not like a dog that just mourns you the whole time you're gone.'

'Have you found one? A right girl?' I felt my voice quaver.

'Finding a girl is easy, Mema,' he said. 'Someone who's fun for a few weeks—but finding one that you want to spend more time with is harder.'

'Have you ever been in love?' It was a small sentence. Six little words.

'A few times.' He looked down at the pup. 'But I could count the girls I've loved on the fingers of one hand.' Blossom looked up at him and he reached out and gave her a stroke. 'It's always hard.'

'Hard?' I don't know why I was surprised, it wasn't exactly new information.

'Yeah, for me that kind of thing has always been hard.'

I thought about that. Love seemed most problematic when it wasn't returned. But what did I know?

Standing out in the paddock—out of sight of the others, the afternoon light beginning to fade—it would have been the perfect moment for him to broach the space between us, but he didn't. I could feel myself shifting a little closer. The shafts of hope still glowing somewhere within, inextinguishable.

'Mema,' he said, and I felt myself tilting towards him. 'You know I really like you,' he said the words carefully, each one clear and precise, 'but ... as a friend.'

Whatever moment I'd imagined was crushed, like a clean piece of paper scrunched into a ball. Even though no one had ever said those words to me before, there was something familiar about them, something bitter and forlorn. My eyes stung, my stomach rolled. I couldn't stutter out an answer, so he just kept going.

'You might not care either way,' he said, 'but I get the feeling from your family that ... they think I'm playing with you.'

I wondered if he could see my hurt. I felt like my skin was splitting, exposing my insides.

'And yeah, we've all done that. But ... you're a different type of girl and ... I really like you.'

Those words again. I must have uttered some kind of sound 'cause the pup jumped up and moved towards me. Hamish leaned over and handed me back the lead. I hung onto it with numb fingers while she sniffed around my feet.

'In a few days I'll be gone,' he said softly. 'I know how fresh you are. I wouldn't mess with that.'

My body was stiff with the effort not to cry. I was stranded, not wanting to go back inside, but wishing I didn't have to stand here, my hurt spilling from my skin. Hamish was quiet, gazing at the trees.

'What if you weren't leaving?' I choked out. It surprised me that my heavy tongue could still form words. 'Would you mess with me then?'

He looked across at me, his eyes scanning my face. 'I don't know, Mema,' he said, 'but I am leaving, so it doesn't matter.'

I guess it mattered to me.

'Me and you, we're funny,' he continued. 'I feel like I've known you forever. Almost from the start. I've never been like that with other people. I guess I'm a bit of a lone wolf.' He smiled, and I could see he wanted to get moving. 'If you had a bloody email address then we could keep being friends.'

I knew he was half teasing me, but I didn't much feel like laughing. The silence hung there like an early morning fog.

'So, Frank's got a thing for your Mum.' He changed the subject, aiming for something light. 'I've been trying to get him to visit since I first arrived there, but he's a very stubborn man.'

I knew he didn't have a clue about Mum, about how the town saw her. Clearly no one had enlightened him.

'Do you think he's got a chance?'

I thought of my mum, her angry back, her silence, and I just didn't know.

'Do you?' I asked him, unsure what else to say.

'Frank's a good sort. Your mum looks like she could do with a good sort.'

Gazing through the green at Bessie, I thought of the day Hamish washed up. All fresh and clean from the tossing of the floodwater but quickly mucky and bloodied from saving the calf. A stranger, turning my world on its head. How could it be that nothing felt the same? I grieved it, this loss of all I had known before.

'I guess we all could,' I said with a shrug, wishing he couldn't see my face.

I turned then, on my bung foot, and headed back to the house. It seemed a long walk, the pup prancing along at my heels. Every now and then she would stop, peeking back at Hamish, tugging against the lead, but I just kept on walking.

19.

All my life I'd heard about the randomness of love. Coming at people sideways like a cyclone, wiping out life as they knew it. But my ears had never been sympathetic to love's secret calling— my heart had not fluttered with want or need. I'd placed no trust in that thing that ripped your roof off when you least expected it. But though I had turned my back on all that love promised, still love came raging in.

I lay awake, looking back on the days since Hamish had washed off the bridge, trying to make sense of how it happened. It had started after the rain-running. From then on whenever he was in the room my breathing had become shallow, my heart clattering around like a pigeon trapped indoors. Next, I'd found myself studying the back of his neck, as though it was a great work of art. Finally, I'd felt those awful surges of anguish when I'd pictured the other girls. All of a sudden I was aware of this terrible force within me, this uncontainable feeling, and wondered how long it had been building. I wondered how much of myself I'd missed.

I didn't know where to put all that misplaced emotion, where to funnel it. And so, once blooming, that love lived on inside me. Trapped and corrosive, it began to eat away at me from within. Hamish didn't come and visit again, but my cheeks stayed hot, my heart tight and heavy as stone. There were times when I could hardly breathe. The days I didn't see him stretched on forever. I knew he would be gone soon—off to the next place—and gradually I became wordless, his rebuff filling me with an irrational grief. How could I have done it? Fallen so hard for someone so unfixed?

Slowly, I began to view myself with a kind of disdain. I took to disappearing with the dog he gave me on long walks down the bitumen road, boot-clad and sweltering, hoping I could stamp out my feelings. Hobbling along, I was desolate and unfathomable, even to myself. More disturbing, I could feel a pulse between my thighs that seemed to radiate upwards, making me burn.

On my walks I tried not to examine my feelings. Tried not to analyse his every word, his every past look. But what else to fill my head with? I counted my short, hot breaths. I looked aside when the farmer's trucks passed me, not meeting any of their prying eyes. None of them were his, so I held my face away. I focused on the green swell of the mountains around me. But I was blinded. I was disabled. For the first time, I was truly lame.

And meanwhile, like a signal to the town at large, little Blossom came on heat. It had been so long since we'd had a young dog, we missed the first signs—the sudden spots of blood on the veranda, the late night howling of dogs in the distance. It was only when the town's mongrels started hanging at our fence line that we began to understand. The pup herself seemed at a loss. Blossom watched the dogs pacing on the borders with uneasy eyes. She made no attempt to approach them, and in the evening we locked her indoors while we listened to the mongrels howl.

But the days were steamy, and my love sat like a rock in my belly, so I took my little pup on those long walks, heedless of her spots of blood, and the pattering steps of dogs in the distance that didn't dare come nearer. Like hyenas, they prowled just out of our sight. I walked and smouldered, hoping against hope I could burn my love out.

On the third day one of the trucks slowed and crawled along beside me. I could see the bloke inside winding down his window, getting ready to ask something.

'Hey, sweetheart,' he said, cocking his head to the side. 'Nice day for a walk.'

This surprised me, usually they just drove on by. 'Yeah.' I nodded, wondering what he was after.

'Fine dog,' he added. 'You gunna breed her?'

He wasn't old like Frank, but he was older than me. Maybe Sophie's age. I didn't know him.

'I'm not sure yet,' I said, still walking, the pup at my heels.

'She's a good mix, you wouldn't want to mate her with any old mutt.' He inched the truck along slowly. 'I got a beagle at home. He's sired a few litters in his time. Nice pups they were.'

It seemed odd to talk about mating dogs with someone I'd never met.

I shook my head. 'She's still just a pup.' I knew Blossom was on heat, but she seemed like just a baby to me.

'Not for much longer.'

I suppose that was true.

'Let us know if you do want to breed her.'

I nodded, cheeks hot, wishing he'd drive away.

'Well, see ya,' he said, glancing one last time from me to the pup.

I lifted my hand in goodbye but I didn't say a word. He took off then, his wheels spinning on the loose gravel at the side of the road. Blossom whimpered beside me. Out in the open I felt suddenly exposed. I cut across the paddocks and walked along the shady creek, trying to wash the feeling away. Tucking my skirt up, I carried my boots, cooling my legs in the still, crisp water. Blossom sniffed happily at the bank alongside me, looking up now and then to check things were right.

When I walked back to the house I felt soothed. I picked a few weedy-looking dandelions from the grass and put them behind my ears. Blossom sniffed at the hem of my tucked-up skirt and I wondered if she wanted flowers too. I couldn't place stems behind her floppy ears, so I linked some dandelions together and hung the chain about her neck.

'So pretty, Blossom. Such a pretty girl.'

She seemed to shimmy in response to my words. Maybe she was trying to shake the flowers off, but I didn't think so. Every girl wants to look pretty sometimes.

When I got up the top, Frank Brown's ute was in the front yard. I started trembling on the chance he'd come. *Hamish.* And instantly the throbbing heat was back.

Walking inside, all bare legs and flowers, I came face to face with Frank. His cheeks were red, and at the sight of me a rough noise spluttered from his throat. He took a step back, but he touched his hand to his forehead in greeting. I nodded in response. There was no sign of Hamish and I could feel my spirit droop.

'What's going on?' I asked. There was something I was missing.

'You've got to tie the dog up,' Frank said, his voice steady. 'A couple of the blokes in town have asked me to have a word.'

Mum never lets anyone tell her what to do, but this time I saw her hesitating. She looked at Frank and shook her head, ever so slightly.

'I don't believe it,' she said. 'I don't fucking believe it.' Mum rarely swears. I glanced from her to Frank and back again.

'She's spreading her scent all over the place. Everyone's going crazy. I don't want there to be trouble.'

'She?' Mum said, glancing over at me with a sad smile. 'And by that you mean the dog?'

I looked down at my legs, all muscular and brown in the afternoon light, singlet strap hanging down my bare shoulder, hands full of flowers. I could feel my heart fluttering uneasily in my chest.

'You're all disgusting.' Mum held out her hand to me and I crossed the floor towards her, a kind of alarm sounding in the back of my mind. 'Just fuck off.'

Frank looked bewildered, like he'd taken a knock to the head.

'The bitch is on heat,' his voice was slow, choked.

'Well, why don't you tie up *your* dogs? It's a simple solution, Frank.'

My mum's body was quivering with rage. I'd never seen her so angry. There was a tic at Frank's temple, his eyes darted from Mum back to me. The dog was nowhere to be seen.

'The dog hasn't done anything. It's not her fault,' I said, knowing somewhere deep inside that Frank wasn't here about the dog.

'A whole town can't tie up their dogs just because one bitch is on heat.' Frank's forehead was gathering sweat and he wiped at it with the back of his hand. 'It's not practical.'

Mum shifted towards him and Frank stepped back until he was almost standing in the doorway. It was hard to tell what Mum would do from the way she was moving, but it looked like she wanted to give him a whack. When she got close, Frank held up his hands as though warding her off.

'You scared of me, Frank Brown?'

He shook his head real slow, but I could tell he was.

'Just get out of my house and don't come back.'

Frank's mouth opened and closed, but nothing came out. Then he turned on his heels and walked back to his truck.

'Mum, what's happening?' I asked, moving towards her, but she stepped away from me and out the door, heading to her shed.

I followed her, my alarm rising.

Once she got there she moved quietly between her pots, surveying them one by one. The white ones still to be fired and the coloured pots that were already done. I stood outside watching her, the fluttering, uneasy feeling in my belly only getting stronger.

'Mum?'

She didn't even seem to hear me. The pup came slinking out from wherever she'd hidden herself and sniffed around my feet. I crouched down to give her a pat, pulling off the chain of dandelions. The flowers were a bit wilted and squashed. I knew Blossom was only a dog, but her eyes were so full of feeling—I could have sworn she was as confused as I was. The sound of the first pot smashing took me completely by surprise. I tumbled backwards from where I was squatting, the breath jolting out of me. I sucked in air and called out to Mum, but my voice came out strangled.

Pulling myself off the ground, I stumbled into the shed. Mum held another pot high above her head, ready to slam it on the ground. There were fragments of pottery lying around her feet. A scream was building deep inside me but nothing came out. Mum's face was red, her arms trembling under the weight of the pot, but she threw it onto the ground with such vehemence that when it smashed I could feel the earth vibrate beneath my feet.

'Mum, stop!' I yelled.

She didn't even look my way, but just took another one off the shelf and threw it on the floor. It always feels bad to break a plate, something that you've eaten off for years, wiped down at the sink and stacked carefully on the rack. And then with one clumsy movement it cracks apart and becomes useless. A broken thing, and there's nowhere much for it but the bin. I mourned those fragments, but this was much worse. When my mum made a pot, it was taking something shapeless, a giant block of clay, and making it whole. To see her smash pots into pieces made my heart squeeze and my throat close.

I tried to cross the floor towards her, but my feet were bare and there were so many broken pieces. I was stranded, stunned. Blossom started whimpering beside me, pushing in between my legs, trying to hide beneath my skirt.

'Mum.' My voice was raw. 'What are you doing?'

She didn't answer me but hefted another pot into her arms.

'Please, Mum,' I cried out. 'Please stop.'

'Mema, baby, you don't know anything about the world,' she said finally, her eyes filling up. 'You don't know anything at all.'

And she threw the pot, but without as much force. When it hit the ground it cracked and splintered open, but I could see the fire was gone. Mum swiped at her eyes with the back of her hand.

'Mum, you've got no shoes. Let me run inside and get you some.'

I bolted into the house to find her sandals. When I got back she was sitting on the floor of the shed, head buried in her hands, sobbing. I froze at the doorway. Mum never cried. Blossom had found a way through the shards and was standing close, trying to lick her tears. Mum didn't even bother pushing her away.

I stood staring at the broken pots, shards lying upturned on the dirty floor like there'd been an earthquake. The air around me felt different, stilled somehow, like it feels after a storm. I picked my way through the wreckage. Putting my arm out, I called off the pup, and Blossom tumbled towards me, knocking against my legs.

'Mum?' I said, holding the dog tightly, my voice strained.

She looked up at me, wiping her eyes with the heels of her palms. Her movements were rough, her face red and patchy. She looked utterly different from the mother I knew—vulnerable and broken.

'Can you get up?' I asked. There were so many things I could have said, but nothing was coming out. 'Come and I'll make you a cup of tea.' It was a feeble offer, but it was all I had.

When I was small, my mother's body was a welcoming place, but now I had no concept of how to touch her. I stood, holding back the dog, unable to do more. Mum pushed herself forward onto her knees and slowly she rose. I passed across her sandals and she slipped them on. She still hadn't spoken. Gripping the edge of one of the shelves for a few seconds, she steadied herself and then stepped forward. I helped her across to the house and into her room, pulling back the covers of her bed. She clambered up as though her body was made of lead, curving her head against the pillow.

'Come on, pup,' she said, looking down at Blossom, who was trailing us around, still jittery from the smashed pots. She patted the bed with her hand. 'Come and lie with me.'

The bed was high and Blossom jumped up, her two front paws on the edge, her back legs scratching around on the wooden floors. She stretched her neck out to get closer to my mum, but she couldn't quite reach.

'Mum, she's in heat. She might get blood all over your bed.'

Mum shook her head, as though my words meant nothing. 'Help her up, Mema. Give her a boost.'

I lifted the pup's wriggling body up onto the bed and she bounded over to lie against Mum's belly. She snuggled right in, and whenever Mum tried to pat her, she'd start crazily licking her fingers.

'It's okay,' Mum said to me from across the room. 'You'll be okay, Baby-girl.'

I nodded, but I wasn't worried about me.

'I'll go make a cup of tea,' I said quietly, moving over to the bed and pulling off her sandals. She didn't shift an inch, just closed her eyes. Once Mum was still, Blossom stopped licking her hand and settled down. My mum never let the animals into her room, let alone onto her bed, and even though Blossom was just a pup and hadn't been with us long, she seemed fully aware of the exception. She lay there quietly, as if any second it might end, any second she might be banished back to her mat on the floor, or even shoved outside onto the veranda. She might have been only a dog, but she knew how to savour the unexpected. I watched them for a minute feeling suddenly like an outsider.

Stepping through the bedroom doorway and down the hall, the walls of my home seemed to push in against me. I looked around at the old flaking paint, the skirting boards filled with borer holes, the worn scratches on the floor, and I knew I had to get out. The sun hit me in the face as I walked outside, stinging and bright. I squinted at the long road that ran towards the bridge. The road Hamish had washed off. The road Frank Brown had driven here on, and then driven away on. The only road in here and the only road out. And for the first time in my life I longed for the leaving.

20.

You get a feeling when someone is watching you, the skin at the nape of your neck prickles. It's like your body has an extra sense, some other way of seeing. After Frank Brown came that afternoon, telling us to tie up the dog, I started to feel like I was being watched. I knew it could have been Anja, skulking around at the edges of things, unable to make herself come in, but I wasn't sure. I'd glance up quickly, hoping to catch a glimpse of some shadow, a pair of eyes, but there was never anyone there.

Sophie had come and given me the talk. The one where she tells me that Hamish is a bad bet, that he probably has a girl in every port, that men who kept all their worlds in separate compartments were always the ones to watch out for. I wasn't sure where she'd gathered this knowledge from, but I assumed it was true enough. I didn't know how to tell her she didn't have to worry. That Hamish had already saved me from himself. That I wasn't a girl in a port, that I didn't have my own compartment. I just let her words wash over me and fretted about the unseen eyes I felt at my back. I thought about the dogs hanging at the fence line, waiting for little Blossom to slip up. There was an ominousness to it, this kind of mating. A harangued sort of endurance. I wondered if I should turn things on their head. If I should go out bulling.

Mum lay pretty low for a day or so after Frank's visit. Staying in her bedroom, keeping to herself. Sophie and I fussed over her, but it didn't do much good. I'd never seen her like that, although Sophie had. We were worried, but what could we do except wait?

On the second morning she appeared for breakfast, sitting down at the table, while I made her some toast. She was watching me fondly, the way she used to, and then she let out a little laugh.

'What?' I didn't know if I was ever going to fully understand her.

'I keep thinking of your name,' she answered, massaging her knee beneath her skirt. I could see she was stiff. 'I called you after the huntress. You know, the one who doesn't tussle with love.'

I'd never heard her explain it that way before.

'But I'm thinking now maybe I should have called you Aphrodite, that maybe I got it all wrong.'

'What do you mean?' I'd pretty much ignored mythology, as best as I could manage.

'Aphrodite is the goddess of love, you know that. She has this belt, and when she puts it on she's in her full power.'

I felt my nose crinkle. I didn't much like it when Mum tried to talk to me about sex.

'But she can take it off when she's had enough. She can even lend it to someone else.' She pushed her crumpled fringe back off her forehead. 'She doesn't have to be that way all the time, it doesn't have to define her.'

I knew she was trying to tell me something, but I wasn't quite sure what.

'But who would I be then?' I asked, thinking of how the name would shorten. 'Dity? I'd be Dity. That's not much of a name.'

Mum laughed again and the sound was sweet to my ears. I half wanted to ask her about the bulling, about whether I should turn things on their head, but I didn't know where to start. I buttered her toast, spread it thickly with jam and then put it on the table in front of her. She reached out and squeezed my arm.

'You're spectacular, Mema,' she said. 'Don't let anyone tell you you're not.'

I suppose I shouldn't have been surprised that she'd known exactly where things stood. All those hidden thoughts, rising up and finding an open space. I wondered if she knew I'd been imagining the abandoned shack. The thought of her seeing it— all my desires shunted off into that deserted house—made me redden. It was hard to know if I would ever have a private place.

Mum disappeared into the shed to clear up the mess she'd made, and I took the dog on her lead to see if I could find the watching eyes. I figured if it was Anja she might as well come inside. It was only a kiss, I reasoned, not the end of the world as we knew it. My first port of call was the secret tree, the spot where we stashed our boards. It would be just like Anja to haunt the place where she saw herself betrayed. I headed down the hillside, Blossom tugging at the lead. My foot was better, the torn skin almost healed, my ankle sure and strong. The sun was hot against my head, but I knew I'd soon hit the shade.

My love still sat in my belly, starved and hungry, bellowing to be fed. I did my best to kill it off, careful not to feed it titbits of care, sliding my thoughts away. But in the night it came back to haunt me and I opened the doors of that abandoned shack, trying to shove it all inside.

Watching the pup as I walked—frolicking about me in her careless way—I went back to counting my breaths. In and out, an oscillation, that point in the middle when everything is still. Finally, I stepped into the shade of the secret tree and my reverie ended. Instinct had told me where to look and I'd followed it blindly, but peering along the banks of the creek, I didn't see any trace of my observer. I wondered if I was going mad, if my body had been so short-circuited by this deluded love that it was starting to feel things that weren't there. That all that tingling at my nape was just another expression of the thwarted desire I carried inside. Was I so scrambled that now nothing worked as it had?

I stood pondering for a few moments, staring out at the empty space, but then I saw them, on the other side of the creek, a little way off to the left. A pair of men's boots, brown and mud-splattered, with crumpled dirty socks spilling out the top, and I knew I was right. There *was* somebody else out here. I stared at the shoes, wondering about the man who'd worn them. I'm not a fool, there was a part of me that was afraid, that understood I was putting myself in danger. I thought about the way Blossom whimpered when she got too close to those restless mongrels patrolling the fence line. She was torn between fear and wanting, animal instincts kicking in. When it came down to it, I knew it was only me locking her up at night that kept her away from them. She was a dog, after all, and without me she'd do what dogs did. Slink off to find a mate in the night.

I couldn't see any signs of movement, so I sat down under the shady camphor and waited. It takes two to play cat and mouse. In a little while Blossom stopped sniffing around and settled beside me, chewing her paws. Every now and then she'd glance up, hold my gaze for a sec, checking in. I didn't know what to tell her. We were waiting it out. There was no way whoever left those shoes wouldn't come back for them—a fine pair of work boots like that.

Finally I heard it, a faint shuffle in the bushes on the other side. Blossom heard it too and she sat up, alert, floppy ears shifting around, trying to ascertain the source of the rustle. She barked then, a high-pitched feeble sound. I'd never heard her bark before. Obviously she needed some practice. I guess I could have called out, but I didn't. What would I have said? When I saw him, it seemed natural enough, like I'd expected it all along.

'Mema,' he called across the creek, 'whatcha doing?'

It was the question I should have asked him.

'Watching you,' I called back. It was easy to feel relaxed with a body of water between us.

Billy stopped still then, peering at me, squinting like he couldn't quite make out my face.

'What are *you* doing?' I asked, and I knew if he tried to tell me it was something to do with Old Gordon's driveway he'd be talking shit. But he didn't answer, not right away.

'Hoping I might see you,' he said finally, and I liked him for telling it straight.

'How many times have you come here?' I asked. You couldn't see our house from the secret tree. I wondered if he'd been crossing the creek a little further downstream where it was shallow and coming up closer to the house. I guess he must have if he'd taken off his shoes.

'A few.' He kept squinting at me through the sun. He wasn't the type to look away. 'I got used to seeing you walking, but then you stopped.'

I hadn't walked on the road since Frank came. It didn't seem quite so soothing anymore.

'Where's your place, then?' I didn't know exactly where Billy lived.

'My dad's farm is further out that way,' he pointed across the paddocks, 'but, you know, along the main road. I been living in the caravan. Just for now.'

As far as I knew, Billy's mum had taken off when he was small, but his dad remarried, had a couple more kids. I was hardly going to judge him for still living with his parents.

'I used to hang out with your brothers quite a bit. Sunny and me, we were pretty good mates. How come you never came to school, Mema?'

It felt funny having a conversation like that, half yelling across the creek. A part of me wanted to ask him to come over, but I wasn't sure whether I wanted him up close. There was no easy way to answer the question about school.

'I was always curious about you,' he admitted, still not looking away. 'Your brothers never tell you?'

I shook my head. I knew nothing about their friends.

'You ever hear from him?' I called out. 'You ever hear from Sunny?'

Billy shook his head. 'When he comes home, he'll drop by. But he hasn't been home for a while now.'

'You know where he is?' I asked, and it suddenly hit me that I could go and find them. Take off on the road, follow their trail. But then I thought of Mum and Sophie, Rory and Lila, and Anja too, and I just didn't know. I'd promised Anja I wouldn't leave her, but now it felt like she'd left me.

'Last time I heard, Sunny was somewhere up the coast, you know? Half of those boys, they do the snowfields in winter. Work real hard, earn some good money. Then sometimes they go out to the islands and stuff for the summer, or do some fruit picking.' His voice carried across the water. 'Sometimes I think I should go too.'

I thought of Billy leaving like the rest. 'Why don't you?' In my mind I could already hear the sound of his footsteps walking away from me.

'I like it here,' he said, looking around at the trees. 'It's home.'

There was something warm about those words. They sounded small but they weren't. That heavy feeling that I'd been carrying loosened a little.

'Did you ever go to the abandoned shack?' I asked, knowing in my mind it was a beginning. Knowing I was starting something.

'With the boys, yeah. Not much left.' He was standing over there, baking in the sun.

I didn't know how to tell him what I wanted, with that wide stretch of creek between us. Maybe I didn't even know.

'Your friend Anja, she's been on the wander,' Billy said out of nowhere. Maybe they'd bumped into each other, snooping around. Maybe Anja was shadowing me too. 'She's always been a weird one.'

'She's alright,' I said, my old habits kicking in.

'Back at school, the kids used to kill ants right in her face just to watch her scream. She'd scream like it was murder, till she was red in the face, and then she'd go and tell the teacher. Teacher'd just laugh. No one cares about an ant.'

Something about this story reminded me of the chook joke. 'Anja does.'

I couldn't help thinking that there was nothing wrong with that. Caring about ants. Who decides what things matter, anyway? Sometimes when we were small, I'd step on an ant by accident and Anja wouldn't talk to me for days. Ants were big to her, spiders too. At one stage, every spider in her house had its own name. I loved animals, but Anja loved them more. It all became complicated when she started with the snakes. She had to breed the mice to feed them, and I guess she got accustomed to the cycle of things. When she'd kissed me there'd been that smell of crushed ants. It hadn't seemed to bother her then, those ants dying under her palms. I hated to think of her screaming at school while everybody laughed.

Now we'd started up talking, I wasn't sure how to stop.

'What's she doing? Hanging around your place, not coming in?' he asked.

'You can talk, Billy,' I said, and it seemed ludicrous suddenly that they should both be prowling about.

He looked away then.

'But you and her, you're friends,' he added, moving across to pick up his shoes. 'You don't know me from a bar of soap.'

I didn't know which was weirder. Stalking a friend or stalking a stranger. It would be easy to sit back and think I was above all that, but if I'd been able to stalk Hamish I would have. I just never knew where he'd be, he wasn't a fixed target. I couldn't see myself out thumbing rides like Anja, when I didn't even know where to.

'I don't know what she's doing out there.' What could I say about Anja? 'If you see her, tell her I said hello. Tell her to come visit me.'

I wondered if I should invite Billy too, but somehow those words wouldn't form on my tongue. I got up from where I was sitting, brushing off my clothes. Blossom got up too, ready to go.

'She's a pretty pup,' he said, watching her. 'She looks like a good breed.'

'Yeah.'

'Bit of beagle in her?'

I nodded, leaning down and adjusting her lead.

'Heard that fella bought her for ya, that fella that washed off the bridge.'

Sometimes the strangest news travels the fastest.

'My old dog died,' I said, thinking of how Old Dog's ears had stood straight up, exactly the opposite of Blossom's, and suddenly I missed her real bad. I wanted to turn then and go, back up to the house. See if I could nudge Mum out of the shed so I could throw some mugs. Lose myself in the clay.

Billy didn't say anything for a bit. I could see him watching my fingers restlessly wind the lead.

'Well, nice to see you, Billy,' I said, always awkward at goodbyes. Sometimes I wished we didn't have them. That a conversation could just be over without this staggered winding down. 'Bye then,' I fumbled on, rushing towards the end.

He held up his hand but he didn't speak. I guess I was doing a runner before he could hold me to something. The funny thing was—I knew he'd be back. I wouldn't have to search hard to find him. I walked in my crooked way towards the house, and all the while I felt his eyes burning into my back. It made me stiff, being watched like that, all my looseness gone. I wondered what Billy saw in me, what image he held in his mind. My bung foot seemed bigger then, something that stuck out. When I got to the front garden I tried to shake the feeling off. I looked down at my foot, bare and imperfect in the grass, and I couldn't help but imagine what life might have been like if I'd been born without it. Standing there, my foot felt like a *wrongness*, and for the first time in my life, I wished I was right.

21.

It was late and I was still wide-eyed, musing in my bed. I guess I'd often thought of my brothers at night, guessing where they might be, but lately I'd been imagining other things too. I started picturing the city, what it might be like. In my mind it was all tall buildings looming, people scurrying like ants, but if I went down to street level there were coffee shops and bookstores, teeming with life. Galleries and restaurants and all those pretty girls. I didn't really know anything much, but that was the sketch I was forming. I tried to shake my thoughts away, just a flick of my head, but then I started up imagining my home.

I thought of it with a circle around it, like the ring that forms on the water when you throw in a stone. And in my mind the ring was growing wider. I started thinking what it would be like if the ring spread so it included my town—all the old shops, even the sad motel right on the outskirts. And then if it got a little wider, stretching even more, it would include the sugar mill too, and all those other farms and things farther out that I'd never really seen.

I lay there trying to calculate how wide the circle would have to get before it included the city too. And all the things between here and there that the circle would encompass. All the paddocks and scrub, the houses and cars, the factories and mills. Everything. I kept thinking of those rings, expanding over the water until in the end they disappeared. And then was everything one? It was the type of question that had no answer, or not one that I could grasp.

I wondered about that sugar mill in my vision of trees and farms and hills. I pictured it at night, lit up and eerie, huge metal pillars sputtering smoke into the dark sky. Under my covers the whole thing seemed ominous. Imagining the sugar mill made me think of Hamish and that place between my breasts started up its aching. I pressed there with my fingers, like I had the nights before, trying to soothe myself, release some of the hurt.

There was a tapping at my window then, and I jumped up, thinking it was Anja. Sometimes she'd sneak down in the middle of the night, but usually she just crept inside. The window was too high to reach from the ground outside.

I got up and peered out the glass. It was Billy, holding up a stick. I opened the window a little further so I could poke my head out.

'Mema,' he called up, trying to be quiet, 'you're awake.'

I had to smile. If I hadn't been awake his tapping would have woken me. I didn't want my mum to get up, so I pointed to the door. 'I'll come out,' I whispered down and he nodded, letting the stick drop.

I slipped on a skirt and crept out, down the front steps till I was standing on the grass.

'Whatcha doing?' It was a funny enough question the last time he asked. I didn't answer, just stood there watching him struggle with what to say next. I could hear Blossom shifting around in the laundry, and I didn't want her to start whining, so I walked away from the house, out of earshot.

Billy didn't say anything, he just followed.

We stood there in the darkness, staring out into the black. There was a slender moon, and though I could see the outline of the hills in the distance I couldn't see Billy's face.

'How far away is that shack on Old Gordon's place, do you think?' I asked, alert to all those feelings I'd tried to shove inside. I wondered if they could come out with Billy. If it didn't much matter who caused them, if they could be spent with someone else.

'Don't know, fifteen minutes maybe.' I knew he was trying to see me through the dark. 'Why?'

'I want to go there.'

'Now?'

'Yeah,' I whispered back, reaching out and taking his hand. He stood there a minute, his fingers in mine, like it wasn't a development he had planned for. My heartbeat started up, quick and lively, and it made me think that it might work. Maybe I could transfer all that feeling from one person to another.

'Lucky I brought my torch,' he said after a few taut seconds, switching it on with his spare hand. And without another pause we set off.

Once we'd entered the shack I knew things would go wrong. Under the beam of the torchlight, we looked around at what we'd found—broken windows and sagging floors. Furniture so damaged it had been abandoned years before even by wild, rummaging children. Pieces of debris, so long forgotten they weren't even sentimental. Everything was utterly without life.

All the humming in my veins—the deep heat that I couldn't stop rising inside me while we walked—was dissipating in this place. Glancing across at Billy, I wondered what to do. I knew so little of seduction, the ebbs and flows of passion.

'It's no good in here,' Billy said, dropping my hand. 'It's no good.'

I nodded and suddenly felt I couldn't breathe, like all the oxygen had vanished. I could see Billy's expression darken, even in the dim torchlight.

'You're scared of me,' he said, out of nowhere. An accusation. 'Nothing's even happened.'

He crossed the room and was out the slumped frame of the door, all before I could even turn. I followed, stumbling through the dark, wondering what I had ever seen in this shack, wondering how I'd created it as some sanctuary in my mind. Billy stood outside in the moonlight leaning against a crooked wooden post, his face in shadow, torch switched off. I could only see the outline of him against the dark sky. Watching his supple body, the silhouette of his jaw, I felt that flicker of heat rise inside me.

Again, I wondered what it was that I was supposed to do with it.

'Billy ...' It was strange to be standing out in the bare paddocks at night trying to throw myself at a man I barely knew. 'I ...'

I didn't know how to explain it. All those things I'd seen from the outside for so long but never been within. The slide of a finger against my skin, a breath at my neck. I was perfectly capable of putting two and two together, but lost as to how to actually begin, even there under the cover of night. I willed him in my silence to step towards me, but he didn't. I wondered if it would always be this way. If I would always be filled with longing and never assuaged. I wondered if all women were like this. Filled to brimming with need, but always left wanting.

'It's not that big a thing, Mema,' Billy said, kicking at the dirt. 'No big deal.'

I didn't know what he meant. I could feel my breath inside my chest expanding as though I was only breathing in.

'It's not?' I choked out.

'Just a bit of fun, you know?'

Even though he kept his face down, I could see in the moonlight he was glancing up at me. Eyes hidden but watchful.

I didn't know. I knew nothing. 'Maybe for you.'

'Who you saving yourself for?'

Hamish came into my mind, unbidden. I closed my eyes, trying to shut out his form.

'It's him, isn't it? The stranger.'

It was as though he could smell my need upon me. I shook my head. It was a private thing. The insides of my mind my own.

'He's not right for you, Mema,' Billy said. 'It's all wrong.'

I knew that but it didn't help.

'He's so slick. You know how many girls he'd have up his sleeve?'

I nodded there in the dark. I knew that too.

'Does he even want you?'

He stepped towards me and I faltered then, needing something to lean on. I moved backwards until the rough wall of the shack was behind me. He stopped a second, watching me, and then he stepped up closer, breaching the gap.

'I want you.' He said it real quiet, quiet but sure. 'And I don't care about any of the stuff he would.'

I didn't understand what he was getting at.

'I don't care about your mum, all that shit she does.' I felt myself stiffen but he kept on whispering. 'I don't care about Sophie and whatever crap about me she whispers in your ear.' He was suddenly very near. 'I don't even care about your fucking dodgy foot. I *like* it.'

His words were rough and they rubbed against my heart like sandpaper, but in that moment it didn't seem to matter. I wanted something and I wanted it bad.

'Billy,' it was hard to get the words out, 'I don't know what to do.'

I could hear his breath in the quiet moonlight. He was right in front of me, holding out his hands and grasping onto mine. His fingers were dry, and I couldn't help but imagine them as I had before, touching me like I was clay. Even though it was dark, in my mind I could see every black hair on his knuckles, every furrowed line that crisscrossed his brown fingers. It struck me that maybe I'd never really looked at his hands. Maybe all the images I held in my mind had come from some other place. Maybe nothing inside my head was real at all.

Slowly, I pulled my hands from his and looped my fingers around his wrists. The skin on the top of his hands was rough beneath my thumbs but the underside was soft. In my mind I could see his blue veins pressing against his skin. I slid the pads of my fingers along his wrists, trying to learn him with my touch. His face was still in shadow, but I could feel something within him shift. He seemed suddenly kinder. I ran my fingers down the undersides of his forearm, imagining his strength. He juddered a little, but he didn't pull away.

'Ticklish,' was all he said, and I wondered if he was impatient. I wondered if he'd done this all a million times before.

'I've never done it when I'm not drunk.'

I knew I didn't need to say that I'd never done it at all.

It was irksome, that pause before action, that endless, stilted moment of waiting. I wanted to help him but I didn't know how. Almost millimetre by millimetre he bent his head towards me. The scrape of his beard against my skin was soundless, but it felt loud in my head. I wished I could see him, then maybe I wouldn't be so scared. He moved his cheek against mine, tenderer than I'd expected, and then inched his mouth closer until his lips brushed the tips of mine. He breathed my name, a whisper, but the humming in my mind seemed to swallow the sound. I'd lost my moorings and I felt myself gripping his arms.

'Don't be frightened,' he whispered. 'I won't hurt ya.'

There was no reason to believe him, but there I was doing just that. He twisted one of his arms free of my grip, slowly, so I wouldn't get a start, and then he moved his hand across me, in a lingering sort of way, touching me in places I'd never been touched. I was holding my breath, still stuck in some kind of waiting. Hoping against hope that it was worth waiting for. He slid my skirt up, and I stood there still clinging to that one arm. He groaned then and pressed himself against me, and I could feel all his hardness at once.

'It's different when you're not pissed,' he whispered against my ear. 'You can feel it more.'

I was glad for him, but I didn't know if it was true for me, having nothing to compare. I could sense his pleasure, as though through glass, but I couldn't feel it myself. He tugged his arm free of my grasp and lifted my skirt there in the darkness, pushing my underpants down. I didn't do a thing to hinder him. He pushed himself against the bareness of me and then he pulled back a little and unzipped his pants. Tussling around, he struggled to get himself free. I tried again to imagine I was the clay and his hands were shaping me, but now he'd gotten this far, he'd stopped touching me, there was only the press of his hardness against me and the rough wall at my back. I let go of something in my mind, something I was holding, and I let his body do its thing. All the tugging and pressing seemed outside me, I floated somewhere above. There was a tearing kind of pain, but I don't think I made a sound. He'd lost me along the way to the starry night sky. I don't know how long it took, maybe a few minutes, maybe more. But I knew when he shuddered against me that he was done.

'Sorry, Mema,' he whispered, voice all raspy. 'I didn't mean to … come inside you. It just … happened.'

What could I say? I'd been around sex long enough to know far better. It wasn't entirely his fault. He stayed pressed up against me and I could feel his bristly cheek brushing my neck. It was suffocating, that feeling, and I fought the strongest urge to push him away. Finally he stood up straighter and adjusted himself in the dark. Whatever had been between us moments before was gone. My skirt collapsed back down around my legs and I could feel the wet stickiness of what he'd left dribbling down my thigh. I didn't know where my underpants were and I couldn't see anything much in the dark. I had a vision of them, abandoned outside the shack, strewn amongst all the forsaken things, and I couldn't help feeling that if anybody saw them they'd know in an instant they were mine.

'Maybe we should go to the chemist. Get that morning-after pill?' Billy said. 'I could take you in tomorrow, before work, soon as it opens.'

I imagined walking into the pharmacy to ask for such a thing, all those eyes upon me. The knowns and unknowns colliding there in that small-town store. Every face familiar and all of them reflecting back at me who they thought I was. The lame girl needs the morning-after pill. You know, the one with the potter mother? I couldn't see Billy's face in the dark, but I could picture it. He was holding firm. I knew it was a brave thing to offer. To take me to the chemist. It made me see he was a certain sort of man. I leaned forward and hugged him then, just gave him a big squeeze.

'It'll be okay,' I said. 'It's not the right time.'

I thought of my cycle, when I would bleed, and I hoped I was right.

He stood there holding me, gingerly. 'You sure?' he said, but I could sense his relief.

There was no way I was hobbling into that pharmacy, even with Billy at my back. I nodded against his chest. It was comforting, the size of him. His heart beat beneath my ear. After a bit he pulled himself free and I wished again that I could see his face.

'We better go.'

I shrugged, 'cause in that moment everything seemed fleeting.

'I'll walk you home.'

I shook my head, I didn't need that. 'I'll be okay.'

He peered at me in the dark. 'Alright, but you take the torch,' he slipped it into my hand.

I nodded. Now he'd moved away from me, I wanted him gone.

'Well, see ya then, Mema,' he said, leaning down to kiss my head.

Standing there, I felt like a child. Baby-girl again. And in a minute he disappeared, lost in the darkness of those paddocks, a shifting shape against the night.

I walked for a bit, away from the shack, disorientated and shivery. It was hard to comprehend that all the feeling I'd stored within—the heat, the longing—could lead to those few minutes with Billy. It seemed a violation somehow, though I'd brought it on myself. I wandered in the dark, empty and aimless, my belly churning and raw. Inside, I was all commotion, but on the outside I felt numb. Stopping a second, I touched my fingers to my face, tracing its familiar contours, pinching the skin on my cheeks until the numbness receded. Then I lay down on the ground. The grass was prickly beneath my back, stars bright, sky black and vast. The smell of earth and growth and darkness was all around me. And despite what I'd done with Billy, I closed my eyes and thought of the stranger.

In that place behind my eyes all sorts of things were possible. Images could rise and fall, spaces could fill and empty. Words could trail across the sky. I could call him to me and he would come. I could bid him to stand naked and he would heed me. I could press my tongue to the hollow of his throat and feel the shudder of his body against mine. Behind my eyes he was not retreating. He was upright and fearless, and he didn't look away. I imagined him holding up his hands in surrender, his pale body gleaming in the night. And in that secret place, I wasn't stymied by my lacks.

I could reach out for him and my hand would find his touch. He would speak words to me, soft and low, and I would laugh in the face of time and all those who had gone before and failed.

When my eyes opened, my body was alive. The ants had found me even in the dark. I could feel their light tread upon my skin, see the flicker of their movement. I thought of Anja and the kiss. It played on me uneasily, an anomaly, tricky to define. In another time and space I might have reached down and brushed the ants away, but on that night I welcomed them, blending into the dark. Spreading my arms wide, I surrendered to the ground beneath me, to its accommodating touch. And suddenly I wished I was naked, that I could feel each blade of grass—that the bristly edges of things would relieve my need.

Quickly, I pulled my singlet free, slipped my skirt off. Turning over I felt the roughness of the paddock on my breast, against my pelvis, my belly, my knees. I pushed down against it, willing the earth to conform to the curves of my body. Stretching myself out to feel every undulation. My hands slid out into the grass, feeling the strands between my fingers. My nakedness pressed into that midnight paddock. I lay face down, breathing against the earth, and I conjured him again behind my eyes.

He was beneath me and I could surge hard against his form. It didn't matter the force with which I pressed, or the weight of me, he took it all and then some. And when I opened my eyes, his were right there in front of me, blue and bright and clean as the day we met. I had never been absorbed by his mouth, it wasn't lush and soft like mine, but behind my eyes I was drawn to it, and slid my cheek against his lips.

Scraping there against the grass, I felt the tide of my body swell. Pulling to some external point, humming with need. My nipples grew hard against the blades, and I raised myself so I could move my breasts against the green tips. Swaying there a while, I savoured the touch.

I turned over, naked and open, and sat up a little to look down on my form. In the dim moonlight I was lovely, no stains or marks or defects, though the imprint of the grass pressed against my knees. I gently rubbed them. And then, without another thought, I finally touched myself, wet and mysterious in the dark. It was sore down there, tender, and I steered clear of where he'd been inside me. I thought of the water hole, and all the pockets and crevices of the creek bank. I imagined the swell of the flooding creeks, the way the water rose to fill spaces that were invisible before the rain. All those secret hollows. I touched myself and in my mind the velvet of the water ran all around me.

In an instant the darkness of the sky was illuminated by a lone strike, and I knew with certainty that it would storm. The clouds would roll in and the clear, starry night would turn wild. I waited a few moments, my fingers stilled, and then it came. A strike of lightning and the rumbling echo of thunder. My fingers sought that wet place. I watched the sky and the lingering image of him dispersed into the air, though my body sat hungry and heavy with pleasure, my breathing short and light. I had found my rhythm. A drop landed on my cheek, then my belly, and I smelled that deep lushness that comes just before the rain.

My body quivered with readiness, my breathing harsh. All at once the rain crashed around me, an avalanche of sound. I opened my mouth to receive the drops, the water rushing across my face in lines. I felt it slide against my body, smooth and slippery, and then it was upon me—the shuddering spasm of ending. I heard myself moan. Sitting in the rain, quenched and dripping, I threw back my head and laughed.

22.

That night I slept like I hadn't in years. Tucked up and naked under my doona, my pile of wet clothes hidden in the corner, I didn't even think about my lost undies, not once. But when I woke up it was the first thing that popped into my mind, and I hoped they weren't in some obvious place turning starchy in the sunshine. Though on reflection, the shack was a lost kind of place, and I couldn't imagine who might pass by it to see.

The storm was over, come and gone fast in the night, and I lay there for a few minutes, just enjoying the feel of my skin on the sheets. Lifting the doona, I peered at myself, and in the cool morning light I seemed unchanged from yesterday, but I knew I wasn't. My body, so familiar, had become new. I sniffed at my arm and it smelled like the rain, clean but with a touch of the earth. I rubbed the back of my hand across my face, and I don't know why but I touched it with my tongue. It didn't taste like anything much and, truth be told, I was a little disappointed.

Even though it was Billy who'd had me at the shack, I didn't think about him. I didn't even think of the stranger. I just lay under those covers and thought about me, and all the ways I could have my own pleasure. I thought of the coolness of the creek water on my skin, how when I plunged down fast and burst back out, my whole body tingled, and if I sat in the sunshine afterwards the goosebumps on my arms and legs would spread out, hairs standing on end. Those dots would sweep from my extremities in towards my core, and I could watch them stretch up my thighs in a wave until the gentle kiss of the sun would smooth them all away.

I thought about the places in the creek where the ochre rocks had been ground down to pebbles, where it was soft and pliant under my feet, and how, if I sat in the shallows, the pebbly soil would shape itself to my form, accommodating me like the palm of a giant hand.

And I was held.

I thought about Anja's trees, how they seemed to reach out their branches to her, and when I was with her, to me too. How if we stretched our arms out and touched them, then maybe as the branches overlapped in the canopy, we'd be touching them all. I wondered if Anja would come back inside. If she would ever slip into my bed in the night like she had in the past, but most of all, I wondered whether, if she did, I would tell her these things about my body in those secret waking moments. I'd thought we'd shared everything, but now I knew we'd only shared what it was we'd known about ourselves, and all those deep-down unknown things—just as startling, just as true—we'd shielded each other from, as we'd shielded ourselves.

The day went by in a haze, and if Mum noticed anything she wasn't saying. It started off sunny, but by the afternoon the sky looked grey. Yet the rain had changed its meaning for me and I was looking out for those first fat drops, filled to the brim with longing. Images of Hamish still flashed inside my mind, but I pushed them away. I concentrated on what I'd learned of Billy—the soft undersides of his wrists, the scrape of his beard against my cheek. I was waiting for the night 'cause I knew he'd come again. I knew how we'd done it wasn't good, the muffled fumbling, his breath against my neck, but I was hopeful. When I pictured the shack, stowed full of my desires, it was in a rainstorm, the pounding rhythm of the rain hard against the busted-up tin roof, and my secrets washing away, washing down the hillsides in rivulets. I wondered where we would go, Billy and I, and I wondered whether his hands could become like the water in the creek, finding my invisible places.

By lunch time my body was humming, but I was feeling anxious too. Anxious about Anja and how she was holding up. I hadn't seen her since Old Dog died. Seven days at least. A week was the longest we'd ever been apart. Even when she went to school, we'd always seen each other in the afternoons.

I took a walk up to the door house, careful to keep out of sight. I'd tied up the pup beforehand, not wanting her to give me away. I was worried about Anja's dad, worried about what had gone down. The closer I got, the more uneasy I became. Jumping at shadows and the rustling of leaves. When I saw the house I stayed in the cover of the trees for a minute, listening, but I couldn't hear a thing. There was no sign of life at all. Hesitantly, I made the bird sound, our secret call, and I half expected to see Anja's form shuffle out from somewhere and come towards me but there was nothing. Not the slightest movement from within.

After a while I crept closer, poised for flight if Anja's dad should rear up out of nowhere, but he didn't. In the end I inched forward and peered in one of the windows. Inside, the house was in disarray, broken plates, bits of food, clothes everywhere. No sign of Jim. I figured he must have taken off to get supplies. There was only so long he could go without a drink.

From when she was real little, Anja had kept that house in order—she said it made her feel like the insides of her brain were less crumbly. Judging by the mess, I don't think she'd been there for a while. I snuck away and headed further up the hill to see if she was at the hut, but it was deserted like the house. There was a sleeping bag on the floor, and a make-up bag on top of the piano, so I figured she'd been using it as a base. I looked around for a piece of paper—or something—to leave her a note on, but I couldn't find a thing. In the end I got a stick to scratch a message in the dirt of the doorway. I didn't know what to say, what could possibly cover the appropriate ground, so I settled for—*Anja, I miss you.* Thought it was best to keep to the one thing I knew. Then I hobbled back down the hill, staying in the shadows of the trees and thinking of how to go about bringing

Anja back. I fretted about it all afternoon, but as dusk came, and the dogs started up their howling and Blossom whimpered and snuffled around my feet, the only thoughts I had were of Hamish and Billy and how all the secrets I'd stored in the shack had finally broken free.

I was wide awake when he tapped on my window, already dressed and ready to go. His tap was quiet and I slipped out noiselessly so the dog didn't even stir. Together we drifted across the grass till we were out of earshot.

'You came,' I whispered, once we were far enough away.

He looked at the ground and nodded. I'd left his torch behind in my room 'cause I rarely used one, even on the darkest night. I seemed to know my way round in the dark, like there was a map in my brain of the lie of the land, and my body followed it instinctively. I wondered if Billy was the same.

'I forgot your torch,' I added. 'Sorry.'

He flicked a switch with his thumb, lighting up a patch of grass, but looking up at my face. 'Got another one,' he said, and I supposed then that he didn't know my place well enough to have the map.

'Alright,' I said, but even I wasn't really sure what I meant.

The torchlight on the grass was stark, washing out the colour, and even though I could see him better I wished he'd turn it off. There was something in the way he was looking at me, something weighted and full. I wondered again what he saw in me, what vision he held behind his eyes.

'You want to?' He pointed the torch out towards the paddock, towards the shack and what had gone before.

I hesitated a second 'cause I wanted it to be different.

'Let's go somewhere else,' I said, and I stepped out of the torchlight into the darkness, wondering where my feet might carry me.

'Where?' he asked but he stepped along behind me.

I shrugged in the blackness and kept moving forward, the grass flattening beneath my feet.

'Turn off the light.'

He flicked the switch and blackness engulfed us. I could hear Billy's tread behind me, not too close but not too far. I stopped a second, getting my bearings, and he stopped a second too.

'You listening?' I asked. 'You listening for my steps?'

He was still, not making a sound, holding his breath, and I knew that was his answer.

I walked downhill, slowly across the paddocks towards the creek, Billy at my heels. The moon was slender, the stars dimmed by clouds, but after a while my eyes adjusted and I could see the silhouettes of the trees in the distance, the soft undulating shape of the land. In any case, I didn't need my eyes—I could hear the lilting tinkle of the creek, and that was where I was headed.

Night swimming was a particular kind of pleasure. Our summers were so agreeably warm that it was perfectly lovely to swim in the night if you could brave the unknown blackness of the water. In the day, the creek shimmered with sunshine and you could see through the glassy water all the way to the bottom. The world you were moving through was known, the perimeters visible. But at night there was none of that, you could vaguely make out the lines of the waterway but nothing much else. The water seemed mysterious, bottomless even, and everything had to be sensed. It was easy to get caught up thinking of critters—eels, catfish and the like, even things as weird as bunyips, or some other kind of creatures of the deep.

Anja and I sometimes came down here for a lark. After the sun had set. It was a part of the creek we didn't normally swim in, surrounded by trees, less exposed. We'd head down at night and scare ourselves silly. So maybe there was some part of me that was testing Billy, seeing how he'd hold up.

When we got to the water, Billy stepped up silently beside me. I looked across at the shadow of him and then I dipped a toe in. It was fresh and cool and the thought of stripping down and wading in got my heart banging away in my chest. Billy bent down to take his boots off. The moment was closing in around me. I pulled my singlet over my head, stepped free of my skirt and undies and hung them carefully over a baby-sized palm tree that had grown up on the creek bank. I was naked there beside him then, but I didn't wait to see if he'd noticed.

The rocks in the shallows were rounded and soft, but with my wonky foot, one wrong step and I'd be over. Arse-up. The thought of such an inelegant entry made me giggle a little, and I heard Billy startle behind me at the sound.

'You right?' he asked.

I turned around and smiled at him, still stranded on the bank, but I knew he couldn't see my face.

'You coming?' I asked, wading out further into the deep.

He hesitated a moment, watching me, then pulled off his shirt, yanking it with one hand at the back of his neck, like my brothers used to, and then in a flash his pants were gone too. I could see the outline of him against the hills, poised and ready, and I wondered if half the reason for my clattering heart was just fear. What did I know about Billy anyway? I swam further into the deep, out where I couldn't stand.

'You can't dive,' I called, treading water. 'It's shallow till you get out here.'

Billy felt his way forward, wary as a cat. I dipped my head under the water, feeling it rush over me, and then slipped back to the surface.

'Marco.' His voice was husky, unsure. He must have lost sight of me. I watched him for a second, the water slapping softly against his thighs.

'Polo,' I called out, finally, my voice high in my ears like a child's.

He pressed forward, coming nearer, but disappearing further down into the darkness too.

'Marco,' he said again.

He was close now and I quietened, hovering there in the water.

'Polo,' I whispered. He stretched out his hands towards the sound of my voice, but couldn't quite reach me.

'Marco.' This time his voice was soft. He knew he was near.

'Polo.' I said it under my breath, but he inched closer, until his fingers grazed my cheek. He cupped it softly in the dark.

'I can't see a fucking thing.'

I smiled beneath his fingers, turning towards the shape of his hand.

'Come here,' he said, simple as that. 'Come on.'

I moved towards him in the water, slowly, and he slipped his hand from my cheek, down my neck and along my shoulder. I got so close my knees bumped into his beneath the water. He slid his hand down my back, holding me there before him.

'You right?' he asked. 'You right, after last night?'

I nodded, but it was dark.

'Mema?'

'I'm right.'

I edged a little closer, felt my nipples brush his chest. The humming inside me was getting loud. I wondered if Billy could hear it.

'Go under,' I said, and reaching up I pushed my wet fingers into his dry curls. He had a bush of hair, Billy did. I suppose it's no surprise that I liked it. I pushed his head down, gently but firmly, and he let me. Beneath the water he smoothed his hands along my sides, resting them on my hips, and slowly his head went under, all the way. I leaned my body into his face, my submerged breasts against his closed eyes, and the hum of me grew and grew. When he needed air, he came back up, and I let him, wrapping my arms around his neck. Even in the water he smelled of wood shavings. I suppose it's no surprise that I liked that too. He moved one hand up along my side, smooth as a fish beneath the water, brushing his thumb against my nipple. I had to turn my face away. That's when I started trembling.

'You're slippery as an eel,' he said against my cheek.

'You ever caught one with your bare hands?' I'd never done it, but I knew some of the boys had.

'Yep. They wriggle like hell and you've just got to hold on tight.'

He squeezed my breast in his palm and pulled me in towards him, slipping a hand along the small of my back.

'They make good eating if you cook 'em up right.'

I didn't like to think of a cooking eel. The image disturbed me. I could feel his erection against my belly and it made me want to get moving.

I slipped from his grasp and he let me. I swam towards the bank with the pebbly ochre rocks. Crawling a little way up, I turned over, feeling the pebbles sink beneath my weight like a sponge, the bottom half of my legs still in the water. I leaned back on my palms, shivering all over, but not from the cold.

'Come on,' I said, like he had to me. 'Come here.'

I could hear the sluicing of the water as Billy moved towards me, the shadows of his shoulders visible in the moonlight. I wanted to reach down and touch myself like I had the night before, feel all that velvet wetness envelop my fingers like the waterhole itself, but I waited. He climbed out of the water and sat beside me. After a few seconds he leaned over and kissed my shoulder.

'I don't know what you want, Mema.' He sounded stranded, alone.

I didn't know how to explain it. I was humming so bad by then I couldn't fathom he didn't hear it.

'You got to touch me,' was all I whispered in the end, but it seemed to be enough.

I sat there, quivering, feeling all those pebbles beneath my skin, the water lapping softly at my legs, and he reached out a hand and ran it along the length of me. From my collarbone all the way down, over my breast and belly, across the patch of my hair and down further still along my leg, until his fingers hit the water. In my mind I could see his hand, brown and firm with its bristly dark hairs.

'Like that?' he asked, his breathing hard. He leaned over to kiss me, tentatively, like I might become like that slippery eel and slide away.

'Like that,' I said against his lips, 'but more.'

He slid his fingers back up my leg, stopping then at the base of me, where all my liquid pooled. He pushed the back of his hand against me, firm but questioning, and then he turned his palm over and pressed his fingers inside.

'You're so wet,' he groaned against my neck. 'Fuck.' But he didn't touch me the way I wanted, so I shifted a little, wiped the pebbly soil from my fingertips against my thighs, and touched myself, his fingers there beside mine, pressing still into my wetness. He turned on his side towards me and I could feel the hardness of him against my leg. It had bothered me before, his erect flesh a kind of intrusion, but in that moment I liked it.

He pushed his fingers deeper inside, and as I touched myself everything built around me. The feel of the bank beneath my body, the air against my breasts, the water slippery against my legs, and the darkness of the sky above. It all pressed in against me, and his body too, until I was lost somehow in the feel of things.

'Baby,' he sighed out, all low. 'Baby.'

It was a little odd to hear my nickname in amongst that eddy of feeling, but it didn't bother me.

'Climb up on me,' he whispered.

And I didn't see why not.

In no time at all that hard part of him was inside me, and I looked up at the sky, dark and starless, my fingers still touching that nub, his breath coming hard and fast against my breasts, and somehow, despite the absurdity, it felt right. I rocked against him, and the humming built, and I could hear myself making sounds like his, until it all burst, like it had the night before, even without the rain.

He quietened then, as I sat on my knees astride him, my body liquid and shuddery, him still hard and throbbing inside me. He listened, his breathing unsteady. Running his hand down my side, he grasped my foot, my wonky misshapen foot, holding it like a treasure in his hand.

'I don't want to come inside you, Mema,' he murmured. 'That was bad of me last night.'

I wasn't sure what to do about that—it not being my area of expertise.

'I brought condoms this time.' He squeezed my foot between his fingers. 'But I left them in the pocket of my pants.'

I looked towards the bank where our clothes were and I didn't much feel like swimming across. Neither, I guessed, did he.

'Up you get,' he lifted me off him and lay me back on the pebbles of the bank. My limbs were heavy and the feel of the stones against my back was soothing. He knelt between my legs, looking at me under that sliver of moon, running a hand down my body just like I was the clay.

'I'll pull out,' he said, before he pressed himself inside. He moved hard and fast then, shoving against me like I was a keyhole he couldn't unlock. And I waited, sated and still. A little sore. In the end he pulled out, like he said he would, sprinkling himself over my belly in a final groan. And I hugged him, 'cause it seemed a small miracle in that moment that he should care about me so.

When his breathing slowed he lifted his head. 'I don't want to get you in trouble.'

I thought about that, just for a second. 'Us, you mean. It'd be *our* trouble.' But I knew it wouldn't, I knew it would only be mine. 'We'll know in a few days.' I pretty much bled like clockwork.

I slipped out from beneath him and back into the water. It was colder the second time around, less welcoming, and I ducked under, trying to brush all the sprinkles and pebbles from my skin. Hamish's ochre-painted face flashed in my mind. I felt hollow when moments before I'd felt full. I thought back to the press of the pebbles, Billy's hand stretching down the length of me, trying to hold it all in my mind.

Scrambling up the bank, I shook off the drips, pulling on my singlet, shivering a little.

Billy clambered up beside me, shaking the water from his ear.

'Don't rush off,' he said, reaching out a hand. 'I'll walk you home.'

'It's alright.' I leaned forward and gave his fingers a squeeze. 'It's in the wrong direction.'

He pulled on his clothes, not looking at my face. In a minute he was ready.

'Mema?'

I couldn't think what he might possibly want to say.

'I could cook you up that eel. I know how to cook them right.'

Fishing was one of my least favourite things.

'I don't eat meat.' Around here it was hard to explain that particular aversion.

'Vegetarian?'

'Yep.'

In the moonlight I could see him shake his head. That had put a spanner in the works.

'They're just animals, Mema.'

I nodded. 'We all are.'

I thought of the way he'd held my foot, held it like it was the best part of me. It made me want to give him something then, something nice to say goodbye. I patted my pocket, the secret one sewn into my skirt. There was a rock, a little heart-shaped stone I'd found somewhere on my travels. I unzipped the pocket and pulled it out.

'Here.' I pressed it into his hand. 'I'll see you tomorrow.'

He turned it in his fingers in the dark, bemused.

'Thanks,' he said, though I don't think he knew what it was.

I turned around and headed up the hill. And on my way I thought of how everything had pressed in against me, how it had seemed for that moment that some kind of barrier had collapsed, particles had merged between the world and me, and I wondered if Billy had felt like that too.

It was very hard to tell.

23.

When I rose from my bed the next day, there was a mound of fine brown pebbles on the pillow that must have fallen from my hair as it dried. I looked at it in the bright morning light and a part of me felt faintly disbelieving. It was as though I had split into two people. My days and my nights somehow coming unhinged. After I'd dressed I pulled the sheets from the bed and put them in the washing machine. I'm not sure why, but it bothered me, this evidence of what I'd done.

I started my morning rounds—feeding Thor and the pup, sweeping the floors, letting the chickens out—and by the time I came back inside, Mum was already in the shed, pottering. In a week or so we'd head off to the market, sell some mugs and pots, replenish our supplies. I looked out the window of the kitchen at the roll of the hills, wondering about Anja and where she could be. There didn't seem to be anything else for it, I'd have to go into town. Hunt her down. I needed to get a lift, but I couldn't decide who I'd rather ask—Mum or Sophie. I was pondering it when I heard Rory's voice, bright and springy at the back door.

'Mema, I'm here!' He liked to announce himself. I picked him up to hug him and he snuggled in against my neck.

'You smell funny.' He wrinkled his nose.

Still holding him, I sniffed at my arm, same as yesterday—creek water with a touch of earth.

'Do I?'

He wriggled out of my arms and onto the floor as Sophie stepped through the door with Lila.

'Mummy, Mema smells funny.'

Sophie laughed at that. 'You little bugger, leave your auntie alone.' But when she looked across at me, I felt caught in her gaze. I held out my arms for the baby and Sophie handed her over, leaning in towards me to take a sniff.

She smiled then, kind of sad-eyed. 'Mema's like a flower.'

'What?' Rory said, peering up at me.

'She's in bloom.' Sophie said, scuffing up his hair.

My face was suddenly hot.

Rory seemed to consider Sophie's words, but he didn't say any more.

'Maybe I better have a shower.' I leaned down and kissed Lila's plump little cheek, and she smiled all gummy mouthed.

'I'm coming!' Rory cried out, jumping on the spot. It was one of his favourite things, to watch me in the shower.

'Do you mind?' Sophie asked, studying my face. 'You can say no if you do.'

I'd never minded before so I couldn't see how this time was different.

'It's fine.' I handed Lila back to Sophie. 'Come on boy-o.'

There was a small stool in the bathroom, just the right size for Rory, and he rushed inside, snatched up a couple of his toy dinosaurs from the edge of the bathtub, then perched himself on the stool, ready to go. I'd never really thought much before about Rory seeing me naked—it had never felt strange. Just a natural progression from him being the baby I took into the shower with me, to him being a toddler who scrambled about in the bathroom, watching the whole affair. Part of the fabric of things as they were. But suddenly I felt self-conscious. I turned on the water, letting it heat up before I took my clothes off.

Rory chatted away to himself, doing the voices of the dinosaurs. I stripped down quickly and climbed under the spray. The cane toads were back, squatting in the corner. They made me think of Hamish. I wondered where he was, if he was still in town. I wondered if he'd leave without saying goodbye. I wondered if Anja was still stalking him, like some kind of starved dingo. And deep down I wondered what he thought of her, whether he'd be able to resist. It was bad enough imagining him and all those invisible girls, but thinking of him with Anja was unbearable. It made that place between my breasts start hurting, and I pressed it hard, pushing against the bone.

'Mema?' Rory called out then, still sitting on the stool. 'Can't *see* you.'

I guess I'd pulled the shower curtain too tight. Usually I left it open a little and we chatted. I turned around and smiled but I wasn't feeling much like playing.

'You sad?' His little voice was croaky, his fingers clutching at the dinosaurs, turning white.

I shook my head but it was a lie. Standing there, exposed before him, I could have dissolved into tears.

'You're a flower, Mema!' His eyes were big and black, widening as he watched me under the spray. 'Mummy said.'

I nodded as I soaped up my hair. I could feel the bits of pebble there, gritty against my fingers. I thought of the weight of Billy against me, his fingers pressed inside, and my nipples tightened there under the shower spray. It felt wrong then that Rory should be watching, but I didn't know how to get him out. I turned my back, washing away the soap and fumbling with the conditioner. Glancing around, I saw Rory had taken up his game with the dinosaurs, distracted for a few seconds at least. I finished up as quickly as I could, wrapping myself in a towel.

'You ready?' I said to Rory and he looked up at me in surprise.

'Finished?' He didn't much like a break in routine. 'You didn't do the swirly bit.'

'What swirly bit?' I asked, but I knew what he meant.

'The swirly.' He dropped the dinosaurs on the ground and smoothed his hands across his little body, demonstrating. 'That bit.'

'You missed it. You were too busy playing.'

He looked forlorn. 'That's the goodest bit.'

I held out my hand. Reluctantly, he took it.

'Next time,' I coaxed. 'I'll do the swirly bit next time.' I said it, even though I didn't know if I should.

When I came out, Sophie was standing at the window, baby on one hip and a steaming cup of tea in her opposite hand. She was watching something, staring.

'Mum told me she'd been walking down the driveway every day. Trying to get her knees working properly, but I wasn't sure I believed her.' She motioned out the window. 'But there she is, heading down. Mum. Doing *exercise*. I never thought I'd see the day.'

I walked over and stood beside her, still wrapped in my big old towel. Rory let go of my hand and attached himself to Sophie's leg.

'I missed the swirly bit,' he said, and burst out crying.

'Aw, baby,' she murmured, hiding a smile. I reached out and took Lila from her so she could give him a hug. 'Did Mema go too quick for you?'

I guess it was a bit comical. Lila was smiling too.

'She's happy today,' I said, bouncing her on my hip, hoping I wouldn't lose my towel.

Sophie picked up Rory and he wrapped his arms around her neck, snuffling.

'I know.' Sophie looked at me over Rory's head. 'What a little trooper she is. This one's been all over the place.' She kissed Rory on the head. 'Guess he's missing you know who.'

The mongrel. 'You heard anything?'

Sophie looked at the floor, shaking her head. 'Guess I could have held it together better,' she said quietly. 'Probably made it worse for him.' She squeezed Rory tighter. 'I just didn't see it coming. I mean, he only went to the shops.'

I nodded, bending my head to give Lila an Eskimo kiss, rubbing my nose against her nose. The baby swiped out at my wet hair with her dimpled fingers. I thought of my sister's bruised forehead, the night I first brought Hamish home.

'Rory's alright.' I didn't see that Sophie beating herself up over things would make them any better.

I glanced out the window then, still snuggling Lila, and suddenly there were two figures walking back up the hill— Mum and Frank Brown.

'What do you know,' Sophie said with a sideways smile at me. 'He's come back for another try. He's keen, this one.'

As they got closer I could see Mum was holding a bunch of crucifix orchids. It was my guess she'd busted him trying to leave the flowers down the bottom, like he had the time before. In the spot he always used to leave the bags of avocados, near the letterbox.

Frank was clutching his hat in his hands, and even from this far away he looked a little nervous.

'Poor guy,' Sophie said, but she was grinning now. She gave Rory one more squeeze and then slid him back down to his feet. 'You had brekky yet, Mema?' she asked me. 'I might make Rory some toast. Bit of distraction. You want some too?'

I nodded, but I was still watching Mum. There was something about her I couldn't quite place, some kind of agitation. I wasn't sure, but I didn't think Frank could be the cause of it. When they stepped up onto the veranda and through the door, I saw she had something else besides the flowers in her hands. There was a card, a postcard, and she passed it to me without saying a word. On it was a beach scene, some far-away town. Still jiggling Lila on my hip I flipped it over, scanning the handwriting quickly. It was from Max. My oldest brother. And there was a return address. None of them had ever sent us something in the post.

'He's up in North Queensland,' I said and Mum nodded, holding that big feeling tightly inside her.

'He says we should come and visit.' We hadn't heard from him in years. I was having trouble believing my eyes.

Mum turned then and started fussing with the flowers at the sink. I was worried she might break down and start sobbing.

'Who?' Sophie was preoccupied, looking in the fridge. 'Hi, Frank,' she added as a kind of afterthought. 'You want some toast?'

Frank stood awkwardly in the kitchen, like he didn't know where to be. I realised I hadn't even said hello, but I was thinking of my brother and that card, and what it all meant.

'Max,' I replied to Sophie, grasping the postcard hard between my fingers. 'Max sent us a card.'

Sophie stood up straight then and looked at me, forgetting the fridge and the toast.

'Max?'

He was the brother closest to her in age. They had the same dad. There must have been a time when it was only those two.

'Yeah.'

My sister stepped over and took the card from me, quickly scanning the back. We both looked across at Mum, still tussling with the flowers.

Frank stepped towards Mum then, taking them from her hands. He pulled down a vase from the top shelf, and standing there beside her, filled it up with water and carefully placed the flowers inside. He did it real slow and then he put the vase on the kitchen bench, just out of Mum's reach.

'Naomi,' he said, steadily enough. It was the strangest thing to hear my mother's name. She still didn't turn around, but stood, back to us all, clutching the sink.

'Mum?' Sophie's voice was high, worried. 'It's good, isn't it? We know where he is. He probably knows where the rest of them are. Maybe they're all there?'

'He says we should come and visit.' I heard myself saying again. I'd forgotten about Rory but he was there, pulling on my leg.

'Toast, Mema!' He looked up at me with pleading eyes.

I handed the baby back to Sophie, and holding my towel in place, I leaned down and looked in the open fridge. All the jars of things right where they always were—Vegemite, peanut butter, honey, jam, but I couldn't seem to make sense of them. I kept thinking of the white sands on the postcard and Max's scrawled words. His address. I don't know why something so small should seem so important but it did.

'Naomi?' Frank said again behind me, and I could hear Lila start up grizzling.

'Jam, Mema, jam!' Rory insisted, standing close and pulling a little on the corner of my towel.

'Okay.' I nodded down at him, getting out the jam and butter and moving across to the toaster.

And then it happened, that thing I thought I'd never see. My mum turned and Frank opened his arms and she leaned into him, and he hugged her there in the kitchen, everyone standing around. He held her and she cried a little, her big body soft in his arms. There must have been something between them already, some progression of events I'd been too distracted to perceive.

I didn't know where to look so I concentrated on the toast. Sophie had sat down at the table to feed the baby and we were all quiet, even Rory, while Frank whispered to my mum in his soothing way, slow and gentle.

I buttered the toast and smothered it in jam, then cut it into triangles, the way Rory liked. And when I was done I put it on a kiddy's plate we'd picked up from the markets and set it on the table, delaying the moment when I'd have to look up and see her, my mum, held like that in such a loving embrace. There was something Frank knew about my mum, something vital and deep. It seemed like the most private of moments, and it made all that I'd done with Billy feel pale. Suddenly I felt cold and exposed just wrapped in that towel, and leaving them all there I took off to my bedroom to get dressed.

When I came back out, the bright beach postcard was stuck up on the fridge with a magnet and Mum was off in the garden showing Frank Brown our attempts at growing vegies. I peered out the window to see Rory bouncing along beside them, pulling out the odd weed, chattering away. I figured I'd best ask Sophie about a lift into town.

She took one look at me and sighed, swapping Lila from one hip to the other. 'Mema, what's going on with you?'

I stood there in the kitchen looking from Lila's bright little face to hers, trying to figure out how to begin.

'Something happened with Anja and now she's not coming around.' I didn't know where to start but Anja seemed as good a place as any.

'What happened?'

I told my sister about the kiss, my cheeks getting hot even saying the words. I thought Sophie might laugh but she didn't. She didn't even smile.

'And now she's out stalking what's–his–face, right?'

I nodded. That was about the size of it.

Down on the floor beside me, Thor had climbed into an empty cardboard box just a tad too small for him. He was always squeezing himself into places he didn't quite fit, and usually this sort of display had me grinning, but not today. He looked up at me, yellow eyes defiant, and then sank his teeth into the cardboard ripping off a piece and coughing it onto the floor.

'He thinks he's a dog,' Sophie said, looking down. 'What a duffer.'

He kept on tearing away, till the floor was littered with scraps of cardboard.

'He likes that box,' I said, watching him. 'Why would he destroy it?' It made me think of Anja, of how Mum said she'd tear everything down.

'But she's barking up the wrong tree, isn't she, Mema?' Sophie asked, like she could read my thoughts. 'Anja? You haven't seen the flood guy for days.'

I nodded, but I didn't want to talk about Billy. I didn't have words to describe what we'd done. 'She kissed me, Soph.'

Stepping up closer, I smoothed my hand across Lila's downy head. The baby flapped her arms out towards me. She'd never done that before. She'd never had the coordination. It was plain remarkable how much babies changed every single day.

'I don't really understand.' I took Lila from her, snuggling her into my shoulder.

'I dunno, Mema.' She was considering it. 'You and her were always so close. Like an odd pair of twins. Maybe she's just being possessive. I mean, she *is* possessive. You know she is. Half the time she doesn't even like me hanging about.'

'But did you … ever think she liked me like that?'

'Nup.' Sophie didn't even hesitate. 'Never crossed my mind.'

Leaning my cheek towards Lila's head, I breathed in her scent, and she burrowed in towards my neck. I swayed then, moving my weight from foot to foot, thinking she might sleep.

'Did you … like it?' Sophie looked down at Thor in the box. 'The kiss, I mean.'

I thought of those ants swarming from Anja's face to mine. I still didn't really know if I liked it. Sophie looked back up and I shrugged. 'It was okay. I'd just … never thought about it.'

Sophie nodded, watching my face. ''Cause if you did like it, that'd be alright, you know, Mema.'

I guess I realised that. In these parts, falling in love with a woman might be considered the pragmatic choice. Especially in my family.

'Her dad busted us.'

'Jim?' Sophie's body shifted, she was listening in a different way. 'Fuck, that's not good.'

'I'm worried about her, Soph.' My eyes filled up. 'You know how it is for her. He's unpredictable. When I went up there to check on her, there was no one around. I think she'd been sleeping in the hut. Who knows what Jim's been doing?'

'Oh, Mema, you know you can't go up there.' Sophie put a hand on my arm, just for a second, her grip tight. 'I mean it. Don't go up there. Jim's a nutter.'

'But she *lives* up there. I'm not supposed to go up there 'cause it's too dangerous, but she hasn't got anywhere else. That's her life.'

'Does Mum know what's going on?'

I shook my head. 'Anja asked me not to tell her. I wouldn't anyway, though.'

'I can't take you into town today, Mema. I don't have enough petrol to get back. But it's payday tomorrow, so we can go in then and look for her. Okay?'

Sophie got a parenting payment so at least there was that.

'Maybe I should ask Frank?'

'He would have come out here on his way back from town already. You know how he is, always heads out early. Probably dropping the flood guy in town.'

I nodded, knowing she was right. We all knew Frank's movements, in a roundabout way. Same as he would know ours. Mum's little walk down to the bridge must have really thrown him. I imagined him then, standing there self-consciously with his flowers, not expecting to have to face her.

'You could ask Mum,' Sophie said, looking across to the postcard on the fridge.

I thought of my brother Max, of what he might be like now, of how it would feel to see him. Lila's body was going limp against mine, sleep seeping in. I shook my head, kissing the skin just above her ears. I didn't want to tell my mum anything. Not today.

'Look at you, the baby whisperer,' Sophie said gently, glancing back at me. 'It'll be alright, Baby-girl. Anja will be okay for one more day.' Sophie sounded far away—she wasn't thinking of my predicament anymore.

I nodded, wandering towards the couch.

'You sit there with her for a bit while I do the washing up. She sleeps better if someone's holding her.' Sophie stepped up to the fridge and slipped the postcard out from beneath the magnet, peering into the glossy photograph as though it might reveal something more than glaring sands and rolling waves.

I sat down with the baby's soft weight against my shoulder, Sophie and the postcard at my back, and I wondered then if we all slept better—like Lila—tucked up in some other person's arms.

24.

I guess I could have hitched into town, or ridden the bike even, but I didn't. I wanted to find Anja, but there was another part of me that was scared. She'd never stayed away so long, and every minute that passed I imagined her anger growing, until somehow it was swelling, taking up all the room in my mind.

That night I waited for Billy outside on the sweep of the hill below our yard. Mum had gone to bed early and I was so itching with thoughts I fled outside. I saw the faint glow of Billy's torchlight flickering across the paddocks below me, but once in range of the yard he switched it off. The stars were bright and my eyes had already adjusted to the darkness. The silhouette of him stepped from a pocket of trees.

I liked the way Billy stood so straight. He had a quiet kind of grace, and it was easier to observe from a distance. He didn't see me at first, so I got to watch his steady stride towards me, taking all of him in. Well, all that I could see. There was nothing so appealing as a man, in the right sort of light. For a second I thought of Hamish, walking across the paddocks with the pup, but I banished the image of him from my mind.

When Billy got close I called his name. His whole body shifted at the sound, aware of my night-time gaze. When he was right in front of me, I held out my hand and he took it, sitting down beside me on the grass.

'You right?' He was like that, straight into it, as though there'd been no time between then and when he saw me last.

I nodded, but I was concentrating on the feel of his rough fingers in mine. It got me thinking of the clay.

'You ever throw a pot?' I asked him, sliding my free hand along his forearm, sort of wishing he would slide it along me.

'Nup.'

It was soothing to have his body so close. All the thoughts that had been clanking around inside my brain began to quieten.

'You want to swim?' he asked me, squeezing my fingers in his.

I thought about that for a moment. My body had already started up its whirring. I could feel the wetness pooling, waiting for his touch. I hadn't bothered with underpants, knowing they were only going to come off, and I wanted to lift my skirt and show Billy my nakedness, but I didn't. I couldn't stop thinking of his hand stretching up my leg, slowly. The feel of each blade of grass was suddenly spiky beneath me and I shifted a little on the ground.

'Not tonight,' I said, wondering about what I wanted.

I felt him glance across at me in the darkness, waiting, I suppose, for some kind of clue.

'Let's go into the trees,' I said finally, standing up and letting go of his hand.

He seemed to spring up beside me, effortless and light. 'I'm listening,' was all he said.

I led him sideways, the opposite direction from Anja's place, but still uphill towards the bush. All the hills around our place were forested. Camphors and the occasional gum, leaf litter thick on the ground. Dried camphor leaves are slippery underfoot, rustling like paper, but after the floods the soil stayed moist. Once we reached the trees and stepped under the canopy, the leaves beneath our feet were quiet, sinking slightly into the dampness as we walked. The camphor smell of the earth rose up around us.

The darkness was different in the forest. Thicker. It seemed to carry more weight. I stretched my arms out in front of me, feeling my way between the trees. I wanted to be deep inside, in the heart of the forest. I could hear Billy's step behind me. In my mind I could see him pause to orientate himself. I tried to imagine his face, but all I could think of was his hands.

'Billy?' I whispered, grasping a tree trunk and feeling my way amongst its roots.

'I'm listening.' His voice came from behind me.

'You coming?' I reached the tree and rested my cheek against the bark.

I felt his fingers brush my shoulder in the dark. Holding my breath, I waited for him to step up against my back. For a moment there was only stillness and then in a heartbeat he was there. He pressed against my body, sighing into my hair. The bark of the tree was corrugated but not sharp and I liked the feel of it against me, rough and smooth at once, the woody smell of it lingering in the air.

'Press me harder,' I whispered, leaning in against the bark.

He lifted his hands from me to the tree, a palm on either side of my head, and then he pressed himself into me, the contours of his body following my back, his breath heavy against my ear. I wanted to feel his bare skin, but I wasn't sure how to go about it. He pushed himself away from me and I closed my eyes, feeling suddenly lonely. Even though the air was warm, I felt goosebumps spread up my legs and across my back, and I quivered there against the bark, wondering how to let him know.

'I've got it this time,' he said. 'The condom.' And I could hear him digging in his pocket.

I nodded against the tree but I didn't say a word.

He unzipped his pants, and I tried to block out the sounds of him tangling in the dark, readying himself in whatever way he knew.

'Mema? You right?'

Murmuring some sound, not words exactly—an affirmation—I pressed myself further into the trunk. I could hear the crack of Billy's knees as he crouched behind me. And then the feel of his fingers grasping my ankle beneath the hem of my skirt. First one, and then the other. He squeezed softly, rubbing his thumb against the skin of my bung foot. I felt a sudden wetness in my throat, tears welling up in my closed eyes. He moved his hands up my calves, his hold firm, and I sank a little into his touch, sliding down the bark towards the roots, my singlet and skirt rolling up as I slid down, until I could feel the tree's rawness against my skin. There was a root between my legs, thick and knobbly, and I thought of the mossy log and all the pleasure it gave.

His fingers paused on my skin. 'You like that, don't ya?'

I didn't want to speak.

'The feel of that tree?'

I liked it as much as I liked him. I liked all of it together. And then I was kneeling, the root between my legs and him behind me. He lifted his hands high against my thighs, pushing my skirt up.

'No pants,' he whispered, sliding his fingers across my skin.

The whirring in me was rising, loud in my ears. I reached down to touch myself, my fingers between me and the hardness of the root, and he breathed out against my shoulder, a trembling breath. Then his fingers were inside me, and he groaned, shifting around till his body took their place, the plastic sheath between him and me. He tugged my singlet over my head, pushed the skirt up my body, and I sank into him a little further, pressing my fingers against the place I liked, and letting him press against me, while the tree rose up in the centre, bark smooth and hard against my breasts, the smell of crushed camphor filling the air. Far above, I could hear the sound of the leaves brushing against each other in the breeze.

It didn't take long and I was done. Inside my mind was black like a starless night, and I pushed my forehead against the bark, listening to my own breathing.

'You don't really need me, do ya?' Billy said into the darkness, and I could feel the throb of him still hard inside me.

I turned a little, looking over my shoulder, knowing his face was right there in the blackness. 'Maybe not.' I couldn't deny it. 'But I like you … some.'

He laughed then, more gently than I'd heard him.

'*Some?*'

I nodded, moving to turn around, and he slipped out from me, shuffling back into the darkness through the dirt and leaves.

'You find your tree.' I told him, lifting my skirt up over my head, wanting to be free of it. I crouched there naked, peering into the black.

'I'm gunna.' His voice was soft, just a little way off. 'Okay … I got it.'

'I'm listening,' I whispered, and my whole body stilled waiting to hear the soft inhale and exhale of his breath. I crawled then towards him, my fingers and knees pressing into the soft earth, the camphor smell still thick in the air. When I was close, he reached out a hand and felt for my face, lifting my chin. He was sitting, back against the trunk, waiting for my touch.

'Mema, at my tree you gotta look at me, okay?'

'I can't see you,' I said. 'I can't see a thing.'

'I don't care.'

I felt my way up his body, pulling up his shirt to feel the skin of his belly, and he leaned down and kissed me, straight on the mouth.

'You gotta be thinking of me,' he whispered against my lips, 'and not that bloody tree.'

I smiled, nodding, and clambered up over his lap.

'I got it.' I pressed my cheek along his face. 'Billy, I'm listening.'

I'd forgotten to get my sheets off the line, so when I crept back inside in the middle of the night, my bed was bare. Even in the dark I knew I was grubby so I just lay out a towel that was hanging on the back of my chair and hoped that'd be enough. I pulled the doona up over me, imagining all the leaves and dirt and twigs I'd gathered on myself with Billy. I imagined lifting my body from the towel in the morning and seeing a map of what we'd done, each leaf and stick a landmark.

I thought it'd be impossible to sleep but it wasn't. I knew tomorrow I'd seek out Anja, find what kind of rage she was carrying, see if I could shoulder some of the burden. But somewhere inside I knew that everything would be different, that I couldn't do these things with Billy and expect nothing would change. And just before I slept I thought again of Hamish, of all the feelings I'd had and where they'd gone. It seemed wrong that it could be so easy to extinguish the flame I'd carried for him by smothering it with another person. And deep down I wondered if it was still there, a few smouldering coals, ready at any time to ignite.

25.

Sophie and I were quiet on the way into town. Both the babies had crashed out in their car seats almost as soon as we got going, so maybe she was enjoying the peace. I'd gotten up early to have a shower. I didn't want to risk Rory watching the show. I don't know what I thought he'd see that he hadn't seen before, but it bothered me. It was odd that having sex with Billy should make my body a private thing. I didn't understand it, but it seemed to be true.

I stared out at the rolling green of the trees lit up in the morning light, the new leaves of the camphors glowing against the sky. I breathed in deeply, and then slowly let the breath go.

Sitting there, in Sophie's battered little Honda, babies slumbering in the back, the breeze blowing softly against my cheeks and the trees flickering by, it didn't seem that anything much could be wrong.

We pulled into town and Sophie parked beneath the shopping centre in the shade. It was an ugly cement box of a building, twice as high as everything else, with a giant-sized supermarket inside. Built before I was born, it was the newest thing in town, rising up out of the street like a misplaced puzzle piece. Someone's dream gone bad. We all went in there from time to time, but the fluoro lights and skid-marked floor were a little depressing.

Sophie transferred Rory into the stroller without waking him, and then hung her bag over the handles. She was adept at this sort of thing by now. Lila woke up as soon as we stopped, but she still had that dreamy look about her. I helped Sophie fasten the baby-pouch and then we slipped Lila in. It was amazing how, when you had little kids, even doing the simplest task—like the shopping—required so much preparation. Looking at Sophie in the dimness of the car park, it struck me how encumbered she was. So weighed down it was a miracle she could move.

'Okay.' Sophie nodded at me and I resisted the urge to tweak one of her curls. 'I'll probably be an hour or so. Go to the post office and ask Rosie about Anja. If anyone knows where she is, Rosie will.'

That was true enough.

'When I'm finished I'll take the little ones across to the park.' She jiggled Lila in the pouch, trying to get comfortable. 'Come find us there when you're ready.'

It was hard for me to imagine where Anja would hang out in town without me. I supposed the first place to look was the Savoy, so I headed in that direction. Out of the car park into the sun. I walked across the pedestrian crossing, staring down at my feet in my special boots, remembering how I used to jump from white stripe to white stripe when I was just a kid. When all of your experiences are in one town, everything you do points to something you used to do, and then it's layer upon layer of memories built up around the same place. Everything becomes personal, even the pedestrian crossing.

I was looking down so I didn't see him at first, standing at the other side.

Hamish.

When I raised my eyes the breath caught in my throat. It startled me, how my body responded to the sight of him, all racing heart and jittery limbs. He was talking with a couple of men in button-up shirts and ties. They must have been from the council to be dressed that way—clean and scrubbed, ironed even. Hamish saw me then and he lifted his hand, motioning at me to wait, but he didn't stop his conversation. The men were finishing off, about to say their goodbyes. I stood off to the side, feeling silly, listening in to the last of their talk. Something about sending documents, nothing that meant anything to me. I looked down at the skirt I'd chosen that morning, all bold blues and reds, hanging long against my boots. Next to these men I felt like some exotic parrot, and I could see them trying not to stare at me. Finally they held out their hands for Hamish to shake and headed across the crossing, just the way I'd come.

'Thanks for waiting,' Hamish said and I nodded. We were awkward, standing there in the open street.

'You got a minute?' He had new clothes, shop-bought. They were only clothes, but they made him seem even more like a stranger. 'Want to get a coffee?'

I looked at his face, familiar from all the time we'd spent together. Even though it had only been a week or so since I'd last seen him, everything about him seemed more remote. I suppose it was because of Billy. Billy felt strong and real to me, the shape of his fingers lingering on my skin, while Hamish seemed like a vanishing dream. But my body didn't seem to think so, doing its juddery thing. I shrugged, a touch ashamed. I wanted to make a quick exit, but I was in town to search for Anja and Hamish was as likely to know where she was as anyone else I might bump into. Maybe more so.

'The Savoy?' He pointed up the street and we headed off together in silence. I could feel him glancing at my face. It would be hard for him to know—I suppose—why I was so quiet.

We sat at the booth at the back, me staring down at the laminated menu even though I knew exactly what was on it. Something beeped and I looked up, startled. Hamish ignored it but the noise repeated, insistent and loud. Glancing away from me, he pulled a phone from his pocket and checked the screen. I wondered what it said.

'So ...' He tucked the phone back in his trousers. 'What's new?'

It was hard to know where to start.

'Nothing,' I said at last. 'Nothing, really.'

'You look good.' That surprised me. Hamish scanned my face and added, 'Healthy.'

I nodded, not sure what to say. I wondered if the way Billy touched me had changed me somehow, brightened my skin.

'Glad I spotted you.' Hamish flicked the corner of his menu between his fingers. 'I was going to ring you today 'cause I'm leaving tomorrow and I wanted to say goodbye.' Since the moment I'd first met him, Hamish had been in the process of leaving, but his words still felt wrong inside my head. 'There's some stuff I need to tell you.'

I don't know why, but I thought Hamish might try to tell me about his girlfriend, the girl who wasn't that special, or something equally as unhappy to hear. I guess I must have looked like I was bracing myself.

'It's about the mill.'

'The what?'

'The sugar mill. The one I've been investigating.'

This was left of field.

'What about it?'

The waitress came across then, the same skinny girl with the dimple. She stared down at Hamish unsmiling, the dimple nowhere in sight.

'Just a coffee,' he said, motioning to me. 'What'll you have, Mema?'

'A tea.'

'What sort of tea?' The girl asked me, cheeks pink. I looked at her closely then and saw what I hadn't straight up. She was jealous. Burning like I had burned. I wondered if Hamish had been sprinkling some charm her way.

'Just a normal tea,' I said, feeling sad for her. 'Just white thanks.'

'She likes you,' I said, when she'd walked away.

'We have a bit of a thing.' He shrugged. 'It's not going anywhere, it's just … there.'

My eyes narrowed. I was wondering about the size of the thing, and whether it was bigger for her. It looked that way from the outside.

'She'll get over it,' Hamish said. 'They always do.'

That got my hackles up. 'How would you know that?' I hadn't thought of him as careless. 'You're never there to see.'

I must have sounded sharp 'cause he looked at me real close. He was silent for a minute then, like he was sorting out the right words in his mind.

'Mema,' he scratched his fingernail against the surface of the table, 'you seem … put out. You want to get it off your chest?'

'She looks pretty fresh to me.' I wondered what the difference was, the difference between me and her.

He shook his head and I thought of the time after the creek-riding when he'd painted my face and told me I was pretty. All the times after that when I'd felt something between us. In my whole life I'd never been such a fool.

'Why did you say all those things?' It came out a whisper. 'Why'd you tell me you liked my hair?'

Even in the darkest corner of the Savoy I could see a familiar redness creep up his neck, slow but sure. He stared down at the table and I wanted to cry, shame rising inside me.

Finally he looked up. The waitress came and plonked down our cups, my tea splashing over the rim. Hamish nodded to her, lifting his coffee and taking a sip. She stood there a second and then turned on her heel.

'I dunno, Mema.' I could tell he thought it was a tiresome question. 'It's just … habit, I guess.'

I felt myself flush, knowing it was true. I watched the prickly back of the waitress banging around behind the counter. Maybe I shouldn't have, but I felt a kind of relief that it wasn't just me. That I wasn't the only one who had misread intentions.

'Boy meets girl. Boy drops a line in the water to see if girl bites.' He sighed, shrugging. 'We all do it.'

A game. 'Fishing?'

He was getting impatient. 'I guess.' He had another sip of his coffee, looking down into the brown liquid. I wondered how many different lines he had in the water.

Hamish wrapped his fingers around the base of his cup. 'Mema … I thought we were friends.' He looked back up at my face. 'I mean, I thought there was something different between us. It just seems … a bit pointless to argue over stuff as small as this.'

I didn't know what to say to that. I sipped my tea but it tasted dirty on my tongue.

'Anyway,' Hamish said. 'I want to tell you about the mill. The big picture. It's important. More important than all this relationship stuff.'

Relationship stuff. I glanced at the door, thinking about Anja. 'Mema?'

'Have you seen Anja lately?' I asked him, done hearing how small the stuff between us was. 'Do you know where she's hanging out?'

Hamish turned around, following my gaze to the door. 'I haven't. For a while I was seeing her everywhere, but then not.'

I must have been frowning 'cause he asked what was wrong.

'I haven't seen her for a while, that's all.'

He tried to catch my eye.

'Mema, it's about the trees.'

'What?'

'The mill is going to start burning the trees.'

I had no idea what he was talking about.

'I mean, in the cane season they'll burn the cane waste, but out of season they're going to start harvesting the camphors.'

I still couldn't comprehend it. 'The camphors?'

'Yeah, they're considered noxious weeds—I know you know that—so they'll pay contractors to come in and knock them down and chip them in the paddocks. Then they'll pay the farmers for the woodchips. Burn them up for green energy.' He drummed his fingertips against the table. 'Everybody's happy.'

'The trees?' He'd got my attention now. 'The camphors?'

He nodded. 'Well, wood is considered a renewable energy, 'cause trees can grow back. I think it's a loophole myself, burning wood is more polluting even than coal, but I'm not in charge.'

In my mind the hills were on fire.

'I mean, it might be different if there were plans to regenerate the native forest, but of course that isn't on the table.'

'But …' I stuttered out, '… how can that happen?'

'Well, if there's money to be made …'

'Why didn't you tell me?'

'I'm telling you now.'

Around me the land dissolving in smoke. It was too much all at once—Anja missing, Hamish leaving, my brothers so long gone. It felt like everything was slipping from my grasp. I covered my eyes with my hands.

'Mema,' he said, 'I'm going to be gone tomorrow, so it'll be your fight. I just wanted to give you a heads up.'

'My fight?'

'It's a tricky one 'cause the environmentalists don't like the camphors either. The cane toads of the forest, so to speak. So it'll be hard to get them onside.'

Hamish reached across and pulled my hands from my face.

'Mema,' his voice was soft, 'this is important.'

I tried to look at him but it was a lot to take in.

'They're going to chip them in the paddocks?'

'Yes.'

'But there'll be nothing left.'

'Well, technically even bush regenerators don't advocate clear-felling trees, even if they are noxious weeds—damage to waterways, loss of seed stock, all that stuff—but because there's money involved I don't think anyone will make too much noise.'

'Why?'

'Except maybe the animal activists.'

'Who?'

'Well, animals find protection in those forests. Natives. A few koalas, possums, smaller marsupials. Some people won't like that.'

I felt like I'd been whacked on the head from behind. My ears were ringing, my brain slow.

'Mema, you've got to pay attention.' He tapped me on the arm, gently. 'There's this guy, he lives in one of the next towns along, and he's an expert on endangered frogs.'

His words seemed to come from far away, but I nodded.

'He's one of those bio-nerds, been studying this particular species for a while. I haven't met him but we've been emailing.'

'Bio-nerds?'

'University types that specialise in one animal or plant, something so obscure no one's ever heard of it.'

'Oh.'

'So, he's been studying this frog that only really exists in your region. And guess where it lives?'

I didn't answer, just sort of shook my head.

'In the creeks around your place ... and in the camphors.'

'Frogs?'

'Right. I mean, they wouldn't have originally been camphor dwellers, but they've adapted,' Hamish continued. 'So, I've got his number here, and his email, and a printout of our correspondence. I've been carrying it around, hoping I'd see you.' He pulled out a couple of folded pages from his pocket. 'I think you are going to need him.' He handed me the papers. 'I told him you'd get in touch.'

'Me?'

'Mema, no one cares about the camphors. Only you. If you want to stop this mill thing, you're going to have to get out of your comfort zone.'

'And do what?'

'Well, talk to this guy first. Tom's his name.'

I shook my head. I couldn't imagine ringing up a stranger to talk about frogs.

'I know it's not your thing,' Hamish said carefully, 'but I think you'd be good at it.'

I didn't quite know what he was referring to. 'What?'

'Mema, you got to love the world to want to save it.' His eyes glowed, lighting up his face, almost evangelical.

'When will they start?'

'I'm not exactly sure, but it could be as early as next week. The burning won't start yet, but they're going to start felling the trees and stockpiling the woodchips.'

'How come no one's talking about it?'

'They are, Mema.' He fished the phone from his pocket and checked the time. 'There's a lot of talk about it around town 'cause of the potential to generate cash.'

I guess we hadn't heard.

'Mema, I've got to go. I thought I'd be done days ago but I've still got things to sort out.' He fished some cash from his pocket, handing me three tens. 'Here's the money I owe you from the other day. I meant to pay you back when I brought the dog but I forgot.'

I had the notes in one hand and his printout in the other. My throat constricted, it was hard to swallow.

'You'll tell your company it's no good?' I stammered out. 'The ones you consult for?'

'That's why they pay me.' He looked at my face. 'They won't buy in, but they aren't the only possible investors.'

He moved to stand. I followed, tucking all the stuff he'd given me into my pocket. Hamish paid at the counter. I didn't even think to offer him my share. He had a few words with the dimpled girl and I walked out to stand on the street. When he met me on the pavement we both looked at the ground.

'You know what the funny thing is?' he asked me, and I shook my head, still all foggy and slow like I'd taken a knock.

'Those little endangered frogs, they don't look much different from cane toads when they're small.'

I watched his face then, focusing in, and he glanced up a bit shy.

'He emailed me some pictures. To compare. When they are little they look almost the same.'

I don't know why, but I felt this was Hamish's way of saying sorry. A sideways, lopsided apology.

'Well, goodbye Mema,' he said, and I could tell he was trying to decide whether to hug me. I didn't much feel like having him that close. I lifted a hand to wave and he lifted his, mirroring me.

'Come find me in the city if you ever get out.' He nodded, looking grave. 'My email's on the page.' He pointed at my pocket. 'Come find me. I want you to.'

I waved my hand and just like that he turned around and walked away. I watched his shiny new shirt from behind, but he didn't look back. Not even once.

I stood outside the Savoy, stunned and blinking, as if the sun was shining in my eyes, though I was well under the front awning. I couldn't get my bearings. The street of my town rose around me, buildings large and surreal.

Tomorrow Hamish would be gone. Anja was still missing. And the trees were going to burn.

I stumbled on towards the post office, not knowing quite why. I didn't see the man till he was right in front of me.

'Hey, Mema.'

I looked up, startled, 'cause I didn't know his name.

'Wanna come for a walk to the river?'

He was youngish, stocky, dry lipped and greedy looking. Something about his eyes disturbed me. I shook my head and tried to walk past.

'What? Too good for me?' He grabbed my arm.

'What are you doing?' My voice came out quiet, swallowed.

'Heard you been fucking Billy's brains out.' The words dropped from his mouth like they were nothing special, but my cheeks stung as though I'd been slapped. He stepped up real close. 'Thought you might be up for it. Like mother, like daughter.' His grip on my arm tightened.

'What?' I tried to twist myself free but he held on.

'I'd give ya something,' he hissed. 'I heard Billy doesn't even pay.'

I stared at him a moment, seeing the hardness in his smile. His fingers were digging into my skin. I tried to wrench myself free but he held firm, pulling me even closer.

'Don't fight it,' he whispered. 'I know ya want it.' He stepped sideways off the edge of the footpath, tugging me along after him. 'Come on, Mema,' he urged, and I realised he was prepared to drag me.

Must have been instinct, but I kicked him then, in the shins with my old black boots, and he grunted, loosening his grip. Jerking away, I stepped around him real quick and ran. I loped down the street, everything blurring with tears. When I burst into the post office I couldn't breathe. The air was stuck in my throat. I was clogged with tears.

'Honey,' Rosie said, taking me in. 'What happened?'

I could feel the grip of the man's fingers on my skin, the force of his hold. His words echoed around in my head.

Like mother, like daughter.

I lifted my arm to cover my face.

Heard you been fucking Billy's brains out.

What Billy and I had done was so private, so unspeakable, I'd never thought he might talk about it. Or how those words would come to light. What they'd sound like once they moved from the cover of night. The morphing of something beautiful into something plain and ordinary, dirty even.

I heard Billy doesn't even pay.

I pressed the heels of my palms against my eyes and Rosie carried a chair out from behind the counter and hovered beside me making comforting sounds. I sat down, but I couldn't speak, only cry, odd hiccupping sobs. Her husband stood against the back wall, sorting mail, envelopes in hand. He peered at me, detached but curious.

'I'll go check the street,' he said after a minute, stepping outside.

'Something give you a fright?' Rosie asked, tentatively touching my shoulder.

I nodded, but there was no way I was talking about it.

'Snake?' she asked. 'Or something else?'

Rosie had worked in the post office as long as I could remember, but I'd never been physically close to her. She'd never come over to the other side of the counter. I'd only ever seen her from the waist up. As though she was half a person. She was bigger than I'd thought. Solid and hearty.

I shook my head, my sobbing slowing. Embarrassment creeping in.

'Not a snake.' My voice croaked. It was an odd thing to get precious about—but I would *never* be scared like that by a snake.

'You have a run-in with someone?' Rosie asked, looking me up and down.

I shook my head, snuffling my nose against the back of my hand.

Rosie passed me a tissue. 'I've known you since you were just a little thing and I've never seen you do anything but smile.'

I blew my nose a little and rolled the tissue into a ball, looking around for a bin.

'Your mum used to come in here in all those pretty clothes, bells tinkling round her ankles, pop you right up on the counter. Such a happy thing you were, always holding out your little arms for a cuddle. Used to make my day.'

I remembered a lot, but I had no memory of that.

'I always used to watch you tagging along behind those big brothers of yours.' Rosie stood beside me talking, lightly rubbing my shoulder. 'Saw you got a postcard from one of them. That's good news, hey? Nearly broke your mother's heart to see them go, one by one like that. She just plain wilted.'

I nodded, still holding the tissue.

'She wasn't your classic beauty, your mum. But she had something.'

This took me by surprise.

'When she first moved here with that fella of hers—Sophie's dad—all the blokes in town ... well, they all went wild.' Rosie sighed. 'But that was a different time, all that fresh blood flooding in from the cities, everyone trying new things. They shook things up around here, I can tell you.'

'Bloody hippies ...' I muttered, knowing that's how the town saw us.

Rosie smiled. 'It was a good thing, Mema. Town needed a shake-up.'

I couldn't help remembering how big the world had once seemed. Full of people, full of promise. They'd all moved on to some other more forgiving place.

'You remind me of her at your age.' Rosie said that like it was a good thing. 'I guess people must say that all the time.'

'No one,' I sniffed. 'I'm all dark, like my dad was.'

Rosie raised her eyebrows. 'No, you're pretty in just the same way as your mum. Colouring's a little different, but that's nothing. People get fooled so easy.'

I felt like she was trying to tell me something but I didn't know what.

'She's strong, your mum. Took care of the bunch of you all on her own. You never see her turn to drink like half this town, even when life throws her a bum deal.'

That was true enough.

'And the way she took on Jim's girl after the mother died. Tried to keep her safe. No one else lifted a finger.'

Anja.

'You seen her lately?' I asked, remembering why I'd come.

Rosie's fingers stilled on my back.

'The wildcard? She's usually with you.'

'I haven't seen her for a bit.'

'Oh.' Rosie peered out the window behind me, checking the street. 'Well, she was hanging about in town making eyes at that newcomer, but I haven't seen her for a few days. Jim's been causing trouble at the pub, but that's nothing new.'

Rosie's husband stepped back in from the street. 'Couldn't see nothing. That Tony what's-his-face was lurking around, though.' He looked at me sharp. 'I told him to fuck off. He say something to ya?'

I shrugged. 'I don't know who he is.'

'Best to stay away from him,' Rosie's husband said. 'He's …'

'A bit of a fuckwit,' she finished for him. 'Let's not beat around the bush.'

I guess that much was true.

'He hightailed it,' the man said, watching me real close. 'He didn't touch ya, did he?'

I thought of the man's grip on my arm, the way he'd pulled me. No one had ever touched me like that.

'I just—' The wrongness of it made my belly roll. I shook my head to try to clear it.

'You want a glass of water?' Rosie asked, gesturing to her bloke to go and get it. They lived out the back and he went over and came out with a glass, handing it across the counter to Rosie who gave it to me.

Sipping the water, I wondered about Anja. Where she could be. 'You haven't seen Anja in town? For a few days?'

She shook her head.

'Child services should have done something,' Rosie said. 'Not left her up there. She needed protection.'

I knew Rosie was right, but if they'd taken Anja away I'd never have gotten to know her.

'Your mum tried to take her in, you know, as a foster carer, but it wasn't far enough away, she just kept on running back up the hill.'

No one had ever told me that. Funny the things you didn't know, even when it was your own mum. I sat there sipping water, imagining Anja really was my sister. We'd always pretended to be related.

'I hope she gets away someday,' Rosie said, moving back behind the counter. 'This place isn't right for a girl like her.'

I took a last sip of the water, wondering what sort of girl this place was right for.

'Thanks, Rosie,' I said, standing up and putting the glass on the counter. My hand was still shaking. 'I better go. Sophie'll be waiting.'

'Alright, sweetheart. You take care now.'

From the doorway, I peered outside, scanning for Tony, but there was no sign of him. I looked back at Rosie one more time before I stepped out the door. It was odd, but I felt like she could see inside me, all my secrets. Like I was suddenly laid bare.

26.

All the way home I could smell smoke. I was so dazed I was thinking it was inside my brain, but then Sophie wound down the car window and sniffed the air.

'I think there's a fire,' she said, peering along the road. 'Strange, when it's been so wet.'

I sat up straighter, looking around. The air was a touch hazy.

'Maybe someone's burning off,' she added.

Sophie hadn't said anything when I'd arrived at the park all puffy-faced. I'd run the whole way, watching out for Tony, but no one stepped into my path. I was out of breath when I got there. Sophie just put her arm around me and gave me a squeeze. I didn't know how to tell her what had happened.

'No Anja?' she asked, now we were back on the road.

'Rosie hasn't seen her.'

'You see the flood guy in town?'

Nodding, I felt my chest tighten.

'Bumped into Lorraine.' Sophie paused a second, I could feel her weighing her words. 'She said he had a thing going on with that waitress girl.'

I looked back out the window. What could I say?

'That sucks, Mema.' I guess it was sweet of her not to say I told you so.

'It's alright,' I said, thinking of the smoke and what was going to happen to the trees. They hadn't started chipping the camphors yet, so it couldn't be those that were burning. And the mill always had a smoky plume. Surely if they were already camphor-burning it wouldn't make the whole sky hazy.

'He wasn't right for you.' Sophie said that real quiet, tentatively. I didn't know if it was true. I didn't know anything. 'Baby-girl,' she whispered, 'the first one's always hard.'

That made me think of Billy. I wanted to cover my face again but I didn't. The haze was getting thicker, the sky white not blue. 'Shit,' Sophie said, 'I hope it's not close to us.'

Suddenly it was plain smoky and we wound the windows up.

'It must be close,' I whispered, peering towards home. We were quiet then and I turned to check the babies. They weren't asleep yet, but hypnotised-looking, eyes all misty.

Sophie switched on the local radio to find out if there were any reports, but there was just an old country song playing. She put her foot on the accelerator and we surged forward. I could feel her anxiety mingling with mine. It seemed airless inside the car, but I didn't want to wind the window down.

In the back, Lila started to grizzle. I turned around and clutched her foot.

'It's okay, little one,' I murmured, but I was worried. 'We're nearly home.'

Sophie was pale as we drove up our driveway and saw how thick the smoke was, but we both breathed out when we saw the house come into view.

'Baby-girl,' Sophie said absently, looking around for Mum, 'I better drop you here and run. Check that my place is alright.' I still couldn't see any sign of fire, just lots of smoke. 'I'll whip over and come back.'

I stepped out.

'Alright.' I nodded, shutting the door and peering down at her through the window. 'But don't be long.'

Watching her drive off, I wondered if I should have tried to make her stay, but it was too late now, she was gone. I looked around for Mum and found her out the back, up a ladder clutching the hose, filling the gutters with water.

'Mema,' her voice was shaky, 'can you hold the ladder for me?'

Rushing over, I grabbed the metal sides. Mum didn't much like heights.

'What's happening?' I called up to her.

She didn't answer, just adjusted the hose.

'We never get fires in the wet season. It only flooded two weeks ago. Everything's still soggy—'

'Mema.' Mum cut me off. 'You got to stay here with me.'

I nodded. I was holding the ladder, where else would I go?

'You promise me?' She looked me hard in the face. 'Promise.'

'I promise.'

'It's Jim's place, darling.' It might have been the smoke, but Mum's eyes looked teary. 'It's got to be deliberate.'

Anja.

My whole body started to tremble. I was clutching the ladder so hard my fingers turned white. I couldn't let go. Mum started clambering down towards me and when she got close to the bottom she turned around and tugged me free and into her arms.

'The forest's still damp, hopefully it won't take. Frank's gone up there. The fire engine's coming.'

I couldn't speak. My face was frozen.

'Jim's in the lockup in town. Frank said he got in a brawl last night at the pub.' Mum was staring at the mountain behind us. 'The wind's blowing up the mountain now but the minute it changes, we've got to get in the car and drive.'

'Anja?' I choked out, hanging onto my mum like a life buoy.

She couldn't look at me, but the lines on her forehead were hard and deep.

'No one's seen her,' Mum croaked. 'Come on, you got to help me pack stuff in the car. I've got Thor and the pup in there already.'

It was Anja's fire. That much I knew.

'Where's Sophie?' Mum asked, still holding on to me. She peered over my shoulder, like she'd expected her to be right there.

I shook my head, trying to clear my brain. 'She went back to check the cabin. We didn't know how close it was.'

I could feel Mum's body tense around me. 'Why would she do that?'

'We didn't know where the fire was,' I stammered out.

'The wind's blowing it the other way from her.' Mum stared in the direction of Sophie's cabin even though you couldn't see it from our house.

'Do you think she's in it?' I whispered.

'No, she'll just grab the photos and get the kids out. She's got her head screwed on right.'

'*Anja.*' My eyes brimmed. 'I mean *Anja.*'

I pulled myself free of my mother's hold.

'Please don't go up there, Baby-girl. *Please.*' I'd never heard her plead. 'Frank's already up there. You can't do more.' Her voice was breaking at the edges. 'I can't have you all scattered. You stay here.'

I looked up the mountain. The bush was so thick, there was nothing to see. Just the smoke around us, filling the sky. I didn't say a word, but the tears started slipping from my eyes. Mum reached out and swept them away with the flat of her hand, rough, like she used to do with my brothers.

'She'll be okay, she's as wily as a cat,' Mum said softly. 'Maybe it was time she burned that place down.' She pulled me up the steps and inside the back door. 'You got to grab what you want. We don't have time to dilly-dally.'

I looked around the house. All our things scattered about. There was nothing I needed. Mum started rushing around but I just stood stock still. Then I went to my room. My clothes all hanging where I'd left them, my unmade bed with the dirty towel, all my sticks and rocks and nests. I couldn't make any kind of decision. What to take and what to let go? I looked out the window, the rolling green of the hills, smoke settling like mist, and then I saw it. Smoke drifting up in a new column. And straight away I knew what it was.

The shack.

I was out the door and running before Mum could think to stop me.

'Mema!' I could hear her yelling behind me, but I didn't even slow. I knew she couldn't follow with her bung knees.

The smoke spiralled in the distance, billowing up in curls. I focused on it as I ran, the heat of the day bearing down on me, nothing but Anja in my mind. When I got closer I saw the glow. Panting, my face slick with sweat, I ran towards the fire till I could see the lick of the flames.

Stopping then, I watched the burning shack. Even from a distance it radiated heat. Fire flickered out from the crooked windows, caressing the edges of the open door. Parts of the roof thudded to the ground, all the debris hissing and crackling within. In the distance I could hear the wail of the fire engine heading up the hill, but it barely registered.

The burning shack stood on open ground, not hemmed in by the bush like Jim's place on the hill. There were a few big old camphors along the fence line, but not close enough for the fire to spread—it'd just burn itself out. I scanned the paddocks for Anja and saw her sitting a little way off, clutching her knees.

From this distance she looked lost and small, crushed. Keeping well clear of the heat, I moved towards her. When I got close I saw she had a big metal petrol container. She was perched beside it on the grass. They were heavy, those things, hard to carry. I had a vision of her dragging it cross-country.

'Anja,' I called out softly. She turned towards my voice, eyes a little glazed. She was smudged with black and at first I thought it was soot, but when I reached her I realised it was bruising. All along the side of her face, her arms. One black eye, busted lip.

'He gotcha real bad,' I said, rage rising inside me. If Jim was here I swear I would have struck him down. I wanted to touch her but I didn't know how. I stood there, hot and helpless beside her. She seemed to focus on me then, take me in.

'All along I thought it was him,' she whispered, 'but it wasn't.'

I crouched down. 'Who?'

'The flood guy.'

I didn't know what she was getting at. Her blonde hair was sticking to her cheeks. I stretched a hand towards her but she flinched away from my touch.

'It was *him*.' She was twitching a little, eyes large and spooked. 'Billy.'

'Billy?' I guess I mustn't have been thinking straight to ask that. Her fist clenched, gripping something.

'What you got?' I asked, holding out my palm.

She looked at me, face brittle, and then she uncurled her fingers. I could see them there, sun-bleached and stiff, my crumpled undies. The ones I'd left at the shack days before. I was hot already, half-baked by the fire and the sun, but I could feel my face start to burn. I leaned forward to grab them but she sprang away out of my reach.

'How could you?' She choked on the words. 'With *him*?'

I had no answer to that. All I'd done with Billy flashed before my eyes. It seemed a world away, in the cool of the darkness. It didn't hold up in the light of day.

'Anja …' I didn't know how to set things right. 'I just …'

'We were happy, weren't we?' she asked, eyes filling up.

I nodded, holding out my hand, willing her to move towards me. She looked away, staring at the fire. I stepped up a bit closer and she took off then, straight down towards the shack.

I could hear myself scream and then I was running too, right into the heart of it. Up close the heat was blistering and we both stopped short. I grabbed at her arm, clinging on hard, but she wrestled with me, elbowing herself free. Losing my balance, I crumpled sideways onto the scorched grass. From the ground I watched as she lobbed my undies straight into the fire. They were swallowed up without a sound—a millisecond in time— and the shack began to slowly sag and collapse inwards, a new blast of heat bursting out. Anja stood there mesmerised, watching the whole thing burn. I tried to scramble up, but the way I'd fallen I was struggling, the heat pulsing against my face.

'Anja,' I called to her, and she pulled me up, tugging me backwards along the grass towards the petrol container. Once we were there, we carried it further back, under the shade of the nearest tree, and collapsed together onto the ground. The container was empty now, so it wasn't so heavy. The shape of the shack had vanished. All that was left was a bonfire.

Anja turned towards me, her fury gone.

'I can't stay here, Mema. Dad'll kill me.'

I shook my head, curling on my side to face her. 'No, he's in the lockup.'

'I burned his place down. You know how long he's been building that.' Her lips turned up at the corner. The smallest smile. For the first time I noticed there was no lipstick. I don't think she was wearing make-up at all. 'When he gets out he's going to fucking kill me.'

'You can live with us.' I smoothed her hair back from her face. Up close, Anja had freckles. I couldn't usually see them under the foundation. She looked young, just a girl. 'Mum won't mind.'

'I should have left years ago.'

I knew I'd cry then, even if she wouldn't.

'There's something wrong with me, Mema,' she whispered. 'I can't stay away from him.'

'He's your dad.'

She grasped my hand, holding my fingers to her lips. 'No, it's more than that. It's like a sickness. I fight it but I never win.'

I didn't know what to say to that. I could feel them, all the tears welling up in the back of my throat.

'They'll charge me with arson.'

'They'll know he deserved it. They'll take one look at your face.'

Anja shook her head slowly. 'I have to go. Today.'

She leaned towards me then, kissing me softly on the mouth. All I could do was cry.

We both sensed him before we could see him. Sitting up we watched as he materialised at the side of the paddock, walking slowly towards us. *Billy.* He glanced at the burning shack, but he didn't stop. We sat there huddled together, Anja and me. I didn't bother trying to wipe away my tears.

He stopped at the edge of the shade, just looking at us.

'Burning shit?' he said finally, and Anja flicked her sweaty hair half-heartedly, staring him down.

He looked at the ground for a minute and I took in the contours of his face. He was beautiful, even in the hot sun, even in the broad daylight. My stomach dipped strangely.

'So, you guys lezzos or what?' He asked it straight up, but I could see he was hurting. Then I thought of the man on the street, of what he'd said to me. *Heard you been fucking Billy's brains out.*

I shook my head, lips trembling, mouth wet. 'We just … love each other.'

Anja gripped my hand hard.

'You fucking around with me, were ya?' he threw at me. 'Why'd you do that if you loved her?' He kicked at the dirt, tearing up tufts of grass. 'You playing with me?'

A game. I wriggled free of Anja's grasp. 'I …'

'She was just trying it out,' Anja said, looking at me sideways. I knew that's what I'd told Jim in the hut. Out there in the open paddock it shamed me.

There was silence between us, stretching out.

'But weren't you?' I asked Billy, finally, stumbling to my feet, pulling Anja up beside me. 'Isn't that what you were doing? Trying it out?'

He shook his head, real slow. 'I always had a thing for you. Ever since I was a kid. But I couldn't even get near.'

It was odd hearing those words. It was as though I'd known it all along, but somehow pretended I hadn't. All the years Billy had been watching me.

'Why'd you have to tell everyone?' I asked, the feel of the man's grip still on my arm.

Surprise flashed across his face. I could feel Anja shifting beside me, taking in my words.

'I didn't tell everyone, I only told Johnno.' He hung his head then.

I shrugged. Telling Johnno was telling everyone, he knew that. 'You know what that makes me, don't you?'

There was no way he couldn't.

'Slag,' Anja whispered. 'The town bike. Whore.' All those words we'd been hearing for years.

We stood there, the three of us, Billy still kicking at the dirt. My head was starting to throb and my throat was dry. I needed some water. Anja flicked her hair again, like she'd made a decision.

'You think you could get me out of here?' she asked Billy, standing up straighter, trying to tug her clothes right. 'Put me on the bus? Out of town?'

'Anja, please don't go.' I felt like I was cracking right down the middle. 'You don't have to.'

Billy looked from her to me and back again. I could see him checking out her bruises.

'Her dad's a fucking nutjob,' he said to me. 'She should tell the police.'

Anja shook her head, tilting her chin up, defiant. 'Will you take me?' She didn't look across to me, not once.

Billy turned around, watching the smoulder of the burning shack. I guess he was thinking it over. The flames were lower now, it was burning down.

'I'll take ya,' he said finally.

I felt myself sag, like I was crumpling inside, but Anja was jittery, ready to go.

'You want to come?' Billy asked me. 'For the drive?'

All I could do was shake my head. I thought of my mum back at home, filling up the gutters on her own.

Anja grabbed my arm then, pulling me towards her, bending down so her forehead touched mine. She stared at me hard, like she was scorching the image of me into her brain.

'Don't go,' I whispered, even though I knew once she'd made up her mind there was no way to change it.

'Butterfly kiss,' she murmured back, bending down further to blink her lashes against my check, just like when we were kids.

'You got money?' I asked. 'Where will you go?'

She stepped back, pulling some twenties out of her pocket. 'I'll head north, like the boys. I'll find them.'

I nodded, unsteady. That was as good a plan as any.

'You got money?' I asked Billy. 'You'll give her some?'

I was crying again, wiping my eyes with the back of my hand.

'I'll give her what I got,' he said with a nod, and in that moment I nearly loved him.

Billy picked up the petrol container as though it didn't weigh a thing. 'Better get rid of this while we're at it,' he said, motioning for them to get going.

And just like that they headed off across the paddock. Back the way Billy had come, wary of each other, their backs bristling like a couple of stray cats. I watched them till they were out of sight, my heart heavy inside my chest, and with one last look at the smouldering shack I headed home.

27.

When the house came into sight I could see they'd been watching for me. Sophie and Mum and the babies sitting on the steps, Frank standing off to the side, the pup at his heels. Rory scrambled up and ran towards me, full-pelt, and I braced myself for when he threw his little body into my arms.

Thirsty and hot, my head pounded, but I caught him and held him tight against me.

'There was a fire,' he said against my ear. 'Mummy was scared.'

'Did the fire engine come?' I whispered back. There was nothing Rory loved more than trucks.

He nodded. 'Nanny was scared too.'

'Did you see it?'

He pulled back, looking up at my face, eyes large and dark, searching. I guess he was trying to figure out if I was scared too.

'Fire's hot, Mema.' He smoothed a finger along my arm. 'You can't touch it. Mummy says.'

I rubbed my chin along the top of his head and leaned down to kiss his cheek. He squirmed away from me and I let him slide to the ground.

'I know … no kisses,' I said, but I held out my hand and he took it.

We walked together towards the steps. Though the air around us was still smoky, I could tell the fire up on the hill was out. I wondered what was left up there. Bits of Jim's rickety door house? Anja's hut? Or nothing but a bunch of ashes?

Sophie and Mum stood up as I got close, making room for me to come inside.

'You didn't bring her back?' Sophie asked, sliding Lila from one hip to the other. 'She alright?'

I hobbled up the steps and straight inside. I needed a drink of water. The others followed behind me. Standing at the sink I filled a glass and gulped it down quick.

'Mema?' Mum asked from behind me.

'She's a bit bruised,' I said turning around, voice all broken. 'But she's gone.'

Frank remained in the doorway. I watched him slowly put on his hat. He nodded to my mum and then he made to go. He'd waited to see me home safe. It was the smallest thing—him caring about me—but it made me feel like my chest might burst right open.

'She took the postcard,' Mum said once Frank was gone. 'I noticed it was missing this morning but I thought it was you.'

I gripped the glass in my fingers, trying to conjure up the address on the back of the card. I didn't even remember the name of the town. Sophie stalked over, looking down the cracks on either side of the fridge, leaning right over and poking her fingers underneath. For a minute she looked like Rory does when he's about to blow. Eyes fierce, lips quivering. Rory stood beside me tugging my skirt.

'How could she?' Sophie snapped out, and Lila started to wriggle in her arms.

'She must have come in here last night when we were all asleep.' Mum sighed, glancing around the kitchen. The sight of my empty bed flashed inside my mind. Maybe Anja had come looking for me but I wasn't here. Out with Billy. I hung my head, trying not to think about it.

'Soph, it's alright, stop growling. I remember the address,' Mum said, holding out her arms for the baby. 'I could never forget.'

'I bet she raided the cash jar too.' Sophie handed Lila over to Mum and started rummaging in the cupboard. In a second she pulled out the jar Mum used to store our market money in. It was empty. 'She took the lot!'

I swallowed another gulp of water. I couldn't say it out loud, but inside I was glad. Rory lifted the hem of my skirt and crawled beneath it. I could feel him huddling against my leg, trying to block us all out. Sophie was pacing now. On Mum's hip Lila was gearing up for a full-force squall and Mum jostled her around so she was facing over her shoulder.

'Sophie,' Mum said, 'it's alright.'

'How could she steal from us?' Her voice was getting loud. 'We were her family.'

I shrugged, the air in the kitchen pushing in against me. 'She needed it more than us.' I held the glass of water up, pressing it against my forehead. 'We won't starve.'

Mum looked at me real close, like she knew there was something she was missing.

'It doesn't matter anyway,' I added, suddenly thinking of the trees coming down, the sound of them cracking. 'Nothing lasts, does it?'

I realised then how angry I was. Scorched and sore, hemmed in by babies, facing the women in my family, all the men long gone. All the things they'd never told me came bursting in.

'Baby-girl?' Sophie stopped pacing.

'Don't call me that.' And it struck me that I'd always let them. 'You can't call me that anymore.'

Sophie crossed her arms in front of her chest.

'Mema?' Mum quizzed, gently patting the baby's back.

'How can you … not know?' I said, biting down on my lip. 'The whole world's at risk.'

Sophie's eyes narrowed.

'Well,' the words felt heavy on my tongue, 'maybe not the whole world. How would I know anything about that? But *our* whole world.'

'Mema.' Sophie sighed. 'What are you talking about?'

Mum kept patting Lila's back while she watched me. 'Just tell us, Mema,' she added softly.

'All my life you've told me that there was nothing out there for me.' I could feel Rory's sweaty little arm wrap around my leg, clinging on to me under my skirt. 'And maybe you're right, but how would any of us know if we never leave here?' The angrier I felt, the more I whispered. 'And the worse thing is we've become so cut off from everything we don't even know when the whole thing's going to come tumbling down.' I was trembling all over. Rory squeezed in tighter against my thigh. 'We can't just cut off some part of the world and control it. The outside is always going to come bursting in.'

'Mema, is this about Hamish?' Sophie asked. ''Cause that's not the end of the world.'

'It's not the flood guy,' Mum said, shaking her head ever so slightly.

'It's not a guy,' I said, louder. 'It's much bigger.' I looked out past their heads, out towards the green. 'It's the trees.' My throat was tightening, but I was keeping the tears at bay.

Rory bit me then, right on the soft part of my thigh. I screeched, kicking out at him, 'cause I wasn't expecting it, but he only bit down harder. There was a scramble, all of us trying to get him out from under my skirt. When he appeared he was red-faced and wild. Mad as a cut snake, floundering around so much Sophie had to pin his arms down. Mum handed Lila over to me. My sister couldn't manhandle Rory on her own, so the two of them dragged him off to the bedroom to give him a talking to. Holding Lila in one arm, I lifted my skirt. Rory hadn't broken the skin, but his teeth marks were already turning a bright scarlet. My thigh was swelling under my eyes, red and bruised. I dropped my skirt again so I didn't have to look at it and Lila started up her squalling. I tucked her in against my shoulder and—stranded there beside the kitchen sink—we cried.

Later, after the smoke had cleared and everyone had cooled down—babies bathed and dressed in pyjamas—Mum and Sophie approached me in my room.

'Mema,' Sophie asked gently, peering around the doorway, 'will you tell us what's happening with the trees?'

She stepped inside, Mum behind her, and they looked at me carefully, as though I had become somehow unfamiliar—as if I had gone into the fire and come out changed.

'They're going to start felling the camphors in the paddocks and burning the woodchips to create power at the sugar mill.' I thought of how Anja and I had collected flowers and rocks and leaves and made little fairy gardens between the camphor roots. Child-altars, where we counted our blessings. It struck me that we'd always worshipped the camphors in our own strange way, laying out offerings at their feet.

'It just feels so wrong. I love those trees. The way their roots seem to hold the ground. It's like they're holding everything together.' I felt myself sigh. 'Remember how Anja had names for them all?'

'But who?' Sophie stuttered out. 'Who will fell the trees?'

I told them what I knew, what Hamish had told me.

'But how can they do that?' Sophie was just as perplexed as I was.

'Money,' was all Mum said, as though things were always as simple as that.

'Ask Frank about it,' Sophie said to Mum. 'He always knows exactly what's going on.'

Mum didn't protest, and I knew then he'd be around again soon.

'Hamish gave me the frog guy's details.' I pulled the pages from my pocket, unfolding them. 'He thinks I should call him.'

They glanced down at the paper in my hands but neither of them tried to read it.

'What do you think, Mema?' Mum asked softly.

I wondered then if being grown up was as simple as seeing when something needed to be done and doing it.

I shrugged. 'It's a start.'

Mum looked so tentative, standing there beside Sophie, as though the perimeters of her world had suddenly shifted.

'Little bird,' she said softly, and I could see she was trying to decide whether to take me under her wing, 'I never meant for you to get burned.'

'I'm okay.' I could feel my lips tremble. Mum hadn't called me that since I was small. I thought she might step towards me but she didn't.

'I'll put them on the fridge.' She reached out and took the pages from me. 'This time they won't get lost.'

We stood there, the three of us, not knowing how to be. Like all the paths we normally walked were gone. Somewhere off in the house Lila started to cry. Softly at first, but then more insistent.

'Mum,' Sophie murmured, 'can you—'

'I'll get her,' Mum said, and she walked back out, leaving my sister behind.

I looked at Sophie, delicate and pale in the evening light, carrying all that weight on her shoulders, and I wondered what she saw when she looked at me.

'Mema,' Sophie's voice was soft. 'I didn't realise you didn't like it.' I knew she was talking about my nickname. 'It was … just … habit,' she kept on, 'but I should have stopped calling you that once you got big.'

'I always liked it. Before.'

She nodded, looking me over one more time.

'You're all smudgy,' she murmured, stepping up and rubbing her fingers against my cheek. 'You must have gotten real close.'

'Yeah.'

She held up her hand to show me the blackness on her fingertips, but I all saw was Anja's battered face. None of that would rub off.

'I better go make dinner,' Sophie said. 'The bath's full if you want to hop in. Kids were in and out, it'd still be warm.'

She headed back out to the kitchen and I limped to the bathroom to wash myself off. I lay in the tub, body aching, thinking of the way the shack had burned, collapsing in on itself with a giant swoosh. Something that had stood for so long suddenly gone. Around me the house was quiet, subdued. I guessed Lila was asleep, and even Rory was keeping to himself somewhere.

After a little while, Mum called me out to eat, and when we all sat down I kept catching the two of them staring distractedly out the windows, as though checking that the world they knew was still there. The pages Hamish gave me were pinned on the fridge with a magnet, like a signal from the outside world.

Rory wouldn't look at me after the bite. I wasn't quite sure how to help him work it out. How could I tell him it wasn't alright to bite me but that I loved him nonetheless? My thigh still throbbed and I guess I was a little wounded. We sat around the table, eating, all thinking our separate thoughts, when there were footsteps on the veranda and Billy appeared in the doorway. Just like that. He glanced around the table, but mostly he looked at me. Sophie and Mum kept chewing, peering from him to me. I could feel a kind of comprehension dawn.

'Billy McKechnie,' Mum said. 'What a surprise.'

He nodded at her and then at Sophie.

'Why don't you come in?' Mum added.

'Want some food?' Sophie put down her fork. 'There's some left over.'

'I'm right, thanks,' Billy said, stepping inside the kitchen. There wasn't a spare chair so he just leaned against the kitchen sink.

So far, I hadn't managed to say a word.

'You alright?' he asked me, motioning his head towards the shack. 'You were all sooty. You get burned?'

One side of me felt a little singed from being so close to the fire and my eyes stung from all the smoke, but neither of those hurt as much as the bite on my thigh—or the weight of all the leaving on my chest—so I shook my head.

'I'm okay,' I muttered, looking down at my bowl. There was no way I could eat any more with Billy standing there staring. I pushed the bowl away from me. Rory always likes to pick through leftovers, so he climbed off his chair and sidled up beside me.

I put my hand on his head, sliding it down to his shoulders. I loved his nape, that vulnerable place at the base of his hair. He didn't slither out from under my touch.

'You want the rest?' I asked him.

He nodded, peeking up finally to check my eyes. I smiled at him and he smiled back, putting his little hand on my knee. I held the bowl up to him so he could find the bits he liked.

'He's an eater,' Billy said.

'Yeah,' Sophie replied. 'You sure you don't want some?'

Billy shook his head. 'I ate.'

Mum stood up and began stacking the dishes. Billy moved aside for her to put them in the sink.

Then the baby started to cry, away in Mum's room, and Sophie stood up to get her.

'Maybe I'll lie down with her in there,' she said, glancing from me to Billy to Rory. 'You want to come to bed with

Mummy too?' she asked him, holding out a hand. Rory took a second, tossing up between a cuddle and the food, but he chose Sophie in the end.

'Good to see you, Billy,' Sophie said as she and Rory slipped away. 'It's been a while.'

Billy lifted his hand in a wave, and I caught sight of the curve of his fingers. Even there in the dim kitchen light they were beautiful to me.

When Mum finished stacking the dishes and wiping the table she headed straight out to the shed. It was an unusual hour for her to throw pots, so I knew she was just trying to leave us alone.

I wasn't quite sure how to proceed. Billy and I hadn't done much talking.

'I've never been inside your house,' Billy said, after a few moments. 'Even when I used to hang with Sunny we never came in.'

'Too busy smoking ciggies at the shack.'

He smiled at that. 'I guess so.'

'It's all gone now.'

I thought of all those secrets I'd stored in there, all my desires. They'd spilled out. Uncontainable.

'You want to see my room?' I asked, knowing that he would.

When I opened the door I remembered my unmade bed, strewn with leaves and sticks, the rumpled towel laid out in the centre. I hesitated, but Billy was right behind me, and in the end I switched on the light and stepped in. There wasn't really anywhere to sit, just the big old bed, the desk covered with all my things, and my clothes hanging there along the wall.

Billy looked around slowly.

'I forgot to put my sheets back on,' I said, by way of explanation.

Billy nodded, but he didn't comment. I wandered over and perched on the end of the bed and he moved towards my desk. Reaching out, he touched one of my nests.

'I see heaps of these things when I'm working,' he said. 'I didn't know you collected them.'

I wasn't sure how to explain what I loved about nests.

'Sometimes you see those ones with all the moss in the centre.' Billy's voice was steady, and I had to admit he was making a valiant attempt at conversation. 'They're the ones I like.' He picked a nest up and held it gingerly in his hand. 'You know, where the bird has chosen the softest stuff for the inside.' He pointed to the middle as though I mightn't know what he meant.

I nodded, watching his fingers as they traced the centre of the nest.

'Did she say anything when you dropped her off?'

'Nah.' He put down the nest and patted his pockets. 'But she gave me this to give ya.'

He pulled a stone from the pocket of his pants and stretching out his arm, he dropped it into my palm. 'I guess it means something to you,' he said, turning back to look at my collection.

It was a sucking rock. Anja and I had rocks for all different purposes, but there were some we liked to suck like lollies. They were smooth and flat and felt just right on the tongue. I slipped it into my mouth, knowing it had been in hers. That was as good a way as any to remember her.

'You haven't got much stuff,' Billy said, turning back around to face me. 'Some girls, their rooms are full of shit.'

I tried to imagine Billy in the rooms of other girls. It was hard to picture. I slid the stone from my mouth back into my fingers.

'You alright, Mema?' His voice was soft, his head cocked to the side. I wasn't sure how to answer that. My thigh was tender from where Rory bit me. Thinking about it made me want to cry again.

'Rory bit me real bad.'

'The little blighter.'

'Yeah,' I touched the inside of my thigh through my skirt. 'He got me good.'

'He bit you up there?' Billy went still, staring at the spot.

'He was hiding under my skirt.'

Bending down, Billy grasped the hem hanging at my ankle. 'Give us a look, then.'

He didn't pull the fabric up, but peered at my face, waiting.

I nodded, wanting him to see.

It was odd watching my legs appear under the slide of the fabric. They were so familiar to me, but under Billy's gaze they looked somehow new. The higher up my legs he pulled the skirt the more I wanted him to see. I thought I'd only desire Billy in the darkness—out in the paddocks, the stars overhead and the grass beneath—but I didn't. I could feel the throb of it building in me there, right under the light, in the middle of my room, with everybody home. The skirt came up high, the bruise appearing, a sudden scarlet.

Billy stood there looking at it and then he crouched down, right there between my legs.

'It's a beauty.' He glanced up at my face. 'He must have been real mad.'

More than anything I wanted Billy to touch me the way I touched myself.

'You got your rags yet?'

I shook my head, but something about the way he said it made me close my legs. I'd had spots of blood that morning, so I knew it was near. Probably by tomorrow I'd be bleeding. I shifted myself a little away and he dropped the hem of my skirt, the fabric flopping down again around my ankles. Standing up, he stepped back from me.

'When do ya think you'll get them?'

I shrugged. 'Anytime now, I guess.'

'You gotta tell me,' Billy said, 'so I can stop thinking about it.'

It surprised me that he'd worry about that. That he'd even think it was his problem.

'It'd be my baby too.' His face was stubborn, like he was getting ready to hold his ground.

I nodded, 'cause that was true enough. But there wasn't going to be a baby.

'I'll tell you. It'll be soon.'

We were silent then. Billy turned, like he wasn't sure where to be.

'Billy?' I asked, thinking of the trees.

'Yeah.'

'Did you know they're going to burn all the camphors at the sugar mill?'

'Everyone knows that. They're going to pay for the chips by the tonne.'

'I didn't know.' How blinkered I'd been. Happy in this little bubble. Because it was easy and knowing these things was hard. I kept thinking of my tree, the one I'd pressed against in the night, the feel of it against my breasts.

'I'll probably get some work out of it,' he said. 'It's the type of thing I do.'

'Work for one of the contractors?'

He nodded, shifting his weight from foot to foot.

'Will all the farmers do it?'

'Depends how good it pays. It's a lot of mess to make if they're not paying much a tonne.'

'There's frogs in the camphors. Endangered frogs.' In the brightness of my room it sounded like a feeble defence.

'They're noxious weeds, Mema.' He said that like there was no possible response. It was irrefutable. 'You know what's funny?' he added. 'I reckon it'd cost more to run the machinery and truck the chips from the paddocks than the mill would be making from burning the stuff.'

I didn't get what he meant.

'The whole scheme will be running at a loss.'

'What?'

'Well, if it costs more to chip up the camphors than they are making from burning them, that means someone is probably subsidising the whole deal. Government or someone.'

'Because it's green?'

'So they say.'

I thought about that for a minute.

'But everyone keeps saying it's about the money.'

'Well, it is, but not in the way you'd think.'

None of it made any sense.

'Billy, you know it's not okay, right?'

He just shrugged. Turned half away from me, I could only see the side of his face.

'Mema,' he said my name like it hurt, 'sometimes I just want ...' He lingered there, out of reach, searching for words. 'Just ... be with me awhile,' he started again. 'It's all over and in a flash you're gone.'

It was true. When I was with him there was a part of me that kept an eye out for the exit. It made me jittery even thinking about it.

'I don't want to feel stuck.' I didn't know that until I'd actually said it. 'Any more than I already do.'

'But I won't hold you to nothing,' Billy said, finally. 'Sometimes I just want to be near ya.'

I smiled then, but I knew I must have looked sad. All the mismatched desires, sitting heavy on my chest.

'Guess I should let you rest.'

He was right that I was tired, so I didn't try to change his mind. I kept thinking of the frog man and how I was going to have to call him. Step outside my comfort zone, swim against the current. Billy was peering at my face, trying to read it.

'I'm sorry I told Johnno, Mema.' I could see he was ashamed. 'It was all just so weird I had tell someone.'

I guess I knew what it was like to hold a secret.

'I didn't like seeing you so torn up out there,' he whispered. 'You two looked like bushrangers on your last legs.'

Tentatively, he stepped up towards me, leaning down to give me a kiss on the cheek. Careful, like I was made of glass.

'The last stand.' I sighed, closing my eyes, breathing him in.

I liked the feel of his face up close to mine but he shifted away, walking across the floor. I heard him grasp the door handle, but he didn't turn it. I opened my eyes. His face was full of things he'd never say, as though he was the poet and I was the muse, but we didn't share the same language. Turning the handle, he opened the door and stepped across the threshold.

'Well, see ya tomorrow,' he said from the other side. And I suppose that's what we had—the possibility of tomorrow.

I closed my eyes. Listening intently, I heard the faint slapping of his feet on the front steps, slipping out into the night.

28.

The morning after the fire, I woke at dawn and trekked straight up the hill to find what was left. It was strange seeing all the burned tree trunks scorched black and leafless where usually it was so green. I tried to focus on the bright shoots that would soon sprout, on the regeneration, but it was hard standing there amongst the wreckage. The door house was mostly gone, just bits and pieces littered about. Jim was nowhere to be seen and I was glad. They'd usually keep him in the lockup till he dried out. I hoped he'd come up and see there was nowhere left to be.

I walked past the rubble, looking for Anja's hut. Further up the hill there were still patches of green. The fire had hopped from spot to spot, not burning the whole place through. It took me a while, but in the end I found it. Still standing, even though the flames had come close. I stepped through the door and the weight of Anja's absence hit me in the belly. Even with everything that had happened, the force of the feeling took me by surprise. There were traces of her scattered about. The odd stray lipstick, a few dirty clothes. I gathered them up for safekeeping. Her mother's old piano seemed to fill the space, and I thought of all the ants living inside. How invisible they were unless you banged the keys. And that got me thinking of all the other things I didn't see.

I shook my head, trying to clear it and then stepped back out the door to find Anja's hollow. After some searching I saw it, the space that had always been her safe port. Not burned out, but scorched in places. It was a big old eucalypt, turned a soft grey colour, completely hollowed out on the inside. One side of it was split and if you were small enough you could squeeze through, right into the middle. I peered through the split but it was hard to see inside. In the end I pushed myself through. I didn't much like small spaces, though I'd been in there with her from time to time. It smelled like the forest floor—of soil and damp. There wasn't much room to move, but I crouched down low, thinking of how Anja used to sleep in the hollow when she was real little, curled up like a frightened animal. Then I saw it. Her special box, pressed up against the side of the trunk. I pushed it through the split and squeezed myself out.

It was a little smaller than your average shoe box, and worn with love. I knew what was inside, all her treasures, much the same as mine—special sticks and rocks and seeds, a few polished-up gemstones from her dad, the odd piece of jewellery. And the note her mother left behind. Sitting on one of the roots I opened the lid to check. It was all there, just as I'd pictured it, but right on top was a snippet of paper with my name.

Mema, it said, *look after this for me.*

And I smiled, knowing she'd expected me to find it. I hugged the box to my chest, holding all those pieces of her close. Putting the lid back on, I tucked the box under my arm, picked up her other things and headed back down the hill. My heart was lighter after that. Anja had left her treasures in my keeping. She didn't feel so gone from me.

In the afternoon the SES came to fish out Hamish's hire car. I could hear the sound of workmen on the bridge and I wandered down towards the creek to see what all the ruckus was. Frank was there too, his truck parked off to the side, surveying the procedure.

'Mema,' he said, touching the brim of his hat.

I smiled hello. Didn't much feel like talking. A couple of the men nodded in my direction.

'It took them a while to locate the vehicle,' Frank said. 'That silvery brown colour, it blended right in.' He looked across at me, unhurried. 'Wedged down deep it was.'

I guess Frank was thinking it was a near miss. That it could have been Hamish they were fishing out and not just some big chunk of steel.

'One of them swam right down and attached the winch.' He pointed to the line of cable coming out of the water. 'Job's almost done now.'

The SES blokes had parked their truck on the other side of the bank so they could hoist the car straight out of the water. Someone turned the winch on and the slow whir of it filled the air. At first nothing happened, as though the cable was endless, but eventually it got tight, and even though the car was underwater I swear I heard the grating of metal against the rocks. Suddenly it slid into view, a monster from the deep. The cable strained, the hum grew louder, and in a few seconds the boot of the car broke the creek's shimmery surface. Then it was halfway up the bank, scraping backwards along the grass, water streaming from around all the doors and windows.

Out of the creek it didn't seem so ominous.

'Big fish,' Frank said. 'Quite a catch.'

But it was about as far from a living thing as I could envisage. I wondered about Hamish's laptop and his phone, whether they'd be trapped inside, waterlogged and useless, but I didn't cross the bridge for a closer look.

'Frank?' My voice came out quiet, his name my first word of the day. He turned to face me in that slow way of his. 'Do you think you could teach me to drive?'

When Frank smiled the lines on his face spread upwards in waves.

'Mema, it'd be my pleasure.'

The car was right up on the bank by then. It seemed oddly untouched and new. Frank and I stared across at it, waiting to see how they'd haul it away. It took a while, but eventually the men got it up onto a trailer.

Then it was gone as though it had never been.

* * *

At dusk the creek takes on a certain colour. Velvety brown. Without the dappled sunshine, its depths are muted and mysterious and all the creatures seem to come closer to the surface. The catfish linger on their nests and the eels float by like black ribbons. The turtles perch on the flats of exposed rocks and the kingfishers fly past like the brightest of talismans. Sometimes you can fool yourself into believing that the water is not alive with other beings, that when you step in, the world is all your own. But at dusk you can't forget. As the creek envelops your body and you slide into its depths, you know that you are sharing—that the world has many eyes, but not all of them are on you. Small leaves and berries fall from the trees, and even their tiny weight creates a stir in the water, a multitude of small circles spreading across the surface until their edges meet and meld.

By that shadowy time the terrain has altered. Infinitesimally, the rocks have shifted and the current ebbs around them in different-shaped swirls. Stepping in, you must tread carefully, for by evening the creek is new.

They say every hero has to leave home, but I haven't gotten there yet.

I think of the world, big as those expanding rings stretching out into the unknown. In my mind I see them widening and widening, but then I remember the world is a sphere and eventually the rings are going to blend together somewhere on the other side. Maybe I could start thinking of the whole universe, all the stars extending out forever, infinite. But that seems a bit much to swallow.

I'm just taking things one step at a time.

Acknowledgements

I would like to acknowledge the assistance of the Australia Council for the Arts who awarded me a Book2 grant in order to complete this manuscript.

Big thanks also to Varuna, The Writers House, where I spent two weeks on a fellowship program, early in the process.

To my writers' group—Siboney Saavedra-Duff, Lisa Walker, Jane Camens, Helen Burns and Michelle Taylor. I feel so lucky to have landed in your company.

Thanks always to Jan Smith, Varda Shepherd, Louise Nicholls, Michael Elliot, Iris Winter Elliot, Danika Cottrell, Jaali Da Silva, Jacob Cole, Billie Cole, Brett Adamson, Bradley McCann, Luke Wright, Christina Bandini, Nadia Bandini-Peterson, Romy Ash and Anna Krien for friendship, inspiration and support.

To Moya Costello for opening my eyes to so many different texts, my agent Jenny Darling for her straight-shooting, tenacious support, and the wonderful Peter Bishop—always such a wise voice in my ear.

For the beautiful cover photograph, big thanks to Lilli Waters.

Many thanks also to Catherine Milne and the whole team at HarperCollins, who showed such commitment and enthusiasm for this book right from the start. Special thanks to Jo Butler, who brought *Deeper Water* through acquisitions, and to my editor, Mary Rennie, who consistently offers such thoughtful, tender guidance.

And, as always, a very special thanks to my family.

Q & A with Jessie Cole

What do you think *Deeper Water* is about?

On the surface, I think *Deeper Water* is a story about awakening. Mema's awakening to the world outside, but also her sexual awakening—her belated initiation into womanhood and all that it entails.

As a novelist, I'm very interested in infatuation and desire—how easily these feelings can spring up within us, and how often they leave us perplexed and disorientated—as well as how sexual freedom can sometimes play out quite differently for men and women. I'm also curious about what a blossoming sexuality might be like one step removed from popular culture.

But on a deeper level, I see the book as an examination of modern life, of all the ways we've invented to disconnect ourselves from nature. Living the way I do, encased in forest on the periphery of modern existence, raises a number of questions. Primarily—how is it that we humans have come to see ourselves as so separate from the natural world? What do we gain by this? And what is the cost?

Tell us a little about Mema. Is she based on anyone you know?

Mema is a combination of influences. Having been home-schooled and living out in the bush, she's very unworldly, but at the same time she has an innocent knowingness. She grew up in the aftermath of a time and place where there was a lot of social experimentation—'free love' and the like—and so, in a sense, she's seen quite a bit on an emotional level, even though she hasn't strayed far from home.

She's not based on anyone I know, but the idea of her came from a teenage girl I used to see about town who had a limp. She was very appealing, in a Peruvian princess kind of way, and had a gentle-seeming self-assurance. I was fascinated by her. I think 'familiar strangers' can be really rich sources for the literary imagination. Even though I'd never spoken to this girl, and certainly didn't know her, I began to wonder about her life. How did she feel about her misshapen foot? Did it change how she moved through the world? I got to wondering if all the boys in town found her as alluring as me—or if her limp made her somehow off limits or damaged-seeming. And once I began pondering all these things, Mema's voice just seemed to come to me. Clear and unhindered. It's been a good few years since I've seen this girl. She must have moved away, but I still look for her and wonder how she is.

The landscape is beautifully detailed. Is it a depiction of your childhood home?

It is an imagined landscape, but is loosely based on a property I know well—the childhood home of a close friend. It's not very far from my place, geographically speaking, and there are aspects of the landscape in *Deeper Water*—like the creek system—that certainly occur in my home too, but overall the world of the book really only exists in my mind. I wanted to give the reader an experience of immersion in the natural world. I didn't want the book to be overtly descriptive—to tell the reader what the landscape was like—I wanted the reader to be in it. To create this experience, I definitely called on how it feels to be inside my own personal landscape, my childhood home and homeland. That said, the towns that are closest to where I live are actually quite culturally vibrant places, which isn't really reflected in my novels at all. I suppose I use some aspects of these towns and leave out others, and in the end the towns in my novels become utterly fictional places.

What fascinates you about the concept of women living without men?

I don't really think I'm fascinated by the concept of women living without men. I think it's more that it's quite reflective of the world I inhabit. On a day-to-day basis—apart from my sons—I don't come in contact with too many men. This might be symptomatic of my rural area, which has very high rates of single-parent households, or it might just be my particular circumstances, cloistered away in the forest.

In contrast, as a child in my community I always felt like the only girl among a horde of wild boys. Largely, this was circumstantial—most of my parent's friends had male children— and I have really strong memories of feeling a deep affinity with these boys, but as I've gotten older that sense of closeness and understanding has dissipated. It's partly that the boys all just moved away, but somehow in that process, masculinity has begun to seem more and more foreign to me. Unfamiliar and exotic. So, I think it's more that I am fascinated by gender—and masculinity, in particular—and, of course, I have a real stake in understanding it because I'm trying to raise two boys.

Mema discovers throughout the course of the novel that she does not know herself as well as she thought. What are you using Mema to say about how we understand ourselves and our motivations?

One of the big things I was grappling with in this novel is that we don't always know very much about ourselves. That often we think we are being honest with those around us, but there are things rolling around in the depths of us that we can't acknowledge. They are like secrets about ourselves that we don't even know. In a sense, I'm talking about the primal emotions that drive us—instincts and urges that we are often completely unconscious of. I find this stuff confusing, on a personal level. It's been my experience, in the last few years particularly, that all these things I thought about myself—or ways I defined who I was—were simply not quite right.

So, in Mema's case, she thinks she's relatively emotionally self-sufficient, not prone to passion or being in love, not especially sexually alert, but all of a sudden she realises that in many ways she is exactly the opposite. And she wasn't lying to those around her, or hiding things, she just wasn't aware of them herself. I think we unconsciously shield ourselves from the parts of ourselves we find hard to manage or accept. And so, in some ways, Mema is ambushed by this incredible surge of feeling-

eroticism–passion that she wasn't aware she was even capable of.

In a wider sense, I'm interested in how sometimes that unacknowledged underbelly of feeling can propel us in directions completely in opposition to our own moral code. I think as humans we tend to overestimate our rational selves. We believe we've overcome our animalness, but I suspect that's less than true.

Was the writing process for *Deeper Water* influenced by the success of your first novel, *Darkness on the Edge of Town*?

Darkness on the Edge of Town was written at a time when I believed publication was an impossibility. This belief was partly fuelled by my geographic isolation—I knew no writers, I had no contact with that part of the world. But it was also informed by the prominent myth that 'aspiring writers never get published'. I'd been hearing that phrase so long I had absolutely accepted it. Because of these two things, I wrote with a sense of absolute privacy. I believed no one would ever read it. I made no attempt to censor myself, and didn't judge the writing either. I just experienced it. It was an incredibly invigorating way to write. Joyful, even though the text itself was quite dark.

But when it came to starting the next book, I was in a predicament. My whole way of writing was built on the premise of privacy—how could I write knowing others would read it? I pottered and procrastinated. Finally, I spoke about it to a friend, who offered some very simple advice: 'Write, and you can choose later if you want to share it. The process of writing is still private.' And that is absolutely true. I knew it was up to me to decide if and when I wanted a story to be read, and once I understood that, I was off and running.

Which authors were you reading while writing *Deeper Water*?

I live in my childhood home in amongst my parents' book collection. They were both avid readers, but over the years the influx of new novels into the house has considerably slowed. As a result, the bookshelves are something of a living time capsule. It's an eclectic mix of things, but lots of Herman Hesse and Franz Kafka. Since having *Darkness on the Edge of Town* published, I really wanted to catch up with the fiction of my contemporaries, so I read Carrie Tiffany, Romy Ash, Tony Birch, and many others. What a rich writing culture Australia has! In terms of inspiration, I read a lot of non-fiction when I'm writing. Early on in the process I found a book called *The Secret World of Doing Nothing* by Billy Ehn and Orvar Löfgren an oddly rejuvenating read. Just recently I read Jay Griffiths' *Kith: The Riddle of the Childscape*, which was completely mesmerising.

What is next for you?

I often have a bit of a spell from writing fiction after completing a novel, but I have been tinkering with the first manuscript I completed. It is a much more autobiographical tale, and though it hasn't been published yet, it's still very close to my heart. But I'm still trying to work out how it should be. Apart from that, I'm really not sure!

Reading Group Questions

1. *Deeper Water* is not only a story of sexual awakening, but of discovering secret unknowns. What does Mema learn about herself and her family?

2. Mema is named by her mother for Artemis, the goddess of wild animals, the moon and fertility. How does this naming foreshadow her character and journey?

3. The creek is an important character in *Deeper Water*. How does nature, in its cycles of destruction and creation, reflect or impact Mema's life?

4. Mema is emotionally and physically connected with the land. Do you feel similar connections? Can you identify with Mema's relationship?

5. When Hamish is confined to Mema's place during the flood, he loses almost all contact with the modern world. How would you cope without the internet or a mobile phone in a stranger's house for days?

6. When we look at our lives through the eyes of others, we see ourselves in a new light. What does Mema learn from this experience? What do you think Hamish sees?

7. Anja is wild, provocative and impulsive, the opposite of Mema at the beginning of the novel. Does Mema show any of Anja's characteristics over the course of the novel?

8. What did you make of Mema and Anja's intimate relationship? Have you had relationships yourself that defy normal classification?

9. What is your opinion of the quality of loyalty in the context of the novel?

10. Hamish's behaviour towards Mema is ambiguous. Do you think he plays with her? How responsible are we for the feelings of others?

11. Mema's mother is a dichotomy of hard and soft, nurturing and yet cold. Is her dual nature recognisable? Did you understand her frustrations?

12. How did you feel about Mema not yet being ready to leave home at the end of the novel?